I0817805

THE GOODBYE BOYFRIEND

CHRISTINA
BENJAMIN

Published in the United States by Crown Atlantic Publishing

ISBN 978-1-7326123-4-1

Text set in Adobe Garamond

Version 1.1
Printed in the United States of America
First edition hardcover printed, December 2018

To those who put one foot in front of the other,
even when it seems impossible.

PROLOGUE

Camille's Plan for Dying
#1: Cross all items off bucket list.
#2: Graduate high school.
#3: Say Goodbye.

CAMILLE LARUE HAD her senior year perfectly planned.

And plans are great. They really are. But mostly only when they work out.

Too bad they almost never do. And it was definitely too bad that Nathan Hawthorne didn't know about Camille's plans, because he was about to throw a giant wrench into the heart of them.

1

Cami

Camille LaRue glanced up at the clock in her last period class. She exhaled with relief. *Five minutes left.* She drew a dramatic X through the date in her day planner. Three more months of school remained. *Or sixty-six actual school days if you wanted to be technical. And Camille did.* She was a habitual planner. Ticking boxes and keeping track of her self-inflicted countdown was soothing to her. She liked to know the exact amount of time she had left, so she could make the most of it.

Camille had a lot to accomplish and not a whole lot of time. She flipped to the back of her planner and glanced at her bucket list with determination—only a few items remained unchecked. That was a good thing since there were only a few months of high school left to pull them off.

She closed her eyes, fighting exhaustion. Today was *not* a good day. *You've got this, Cami. One foot in front of the other.* She mentally repeated her mantra while drumming her fingers impatiently on her desk, waiting for the bell to ring. School was the last place she wanted to be. It was a complete waste of her time—*literally*.

Only sixty-six days of her senior year of high school remained. And that miniscule number was her driving force.

Nate

SKATEBOARD TUCKED UNDER HIS ARM, Nathan Hawthorne meandered through the bright hallways of his new high school trying to keep his awe contained. But it was nearly impossible not to gawk at the rich accommodations. The posh New Orleans prep school was a stark difference from his old California public school. He couldn't believe he'd actually convinced his mom to let him come to New Orleans Academy. It had to be costing her a fortune in tuition.

Nate let out a low whistle while admiring the expansive view of campus from the floor-to-ceiling gothic windows in the student lounge. *A student lounge for God's sake!* His old school in Cali didn't even have a real gym, only a glorified rec room that doubled as the cafeteria. Therefore the makeshift gym always smelled like tater tots and the cafeteria smelled like sweat. Neither combination was something Nate particularly cared to remember about his old school, but it sort of stuck with him anyway.

But this place . . . well, Nate was pretty sure he was gonna like it here. *There was a freaking Starbucks on campus! What was not to like*?

It was unreal to Nate that people lived like this. It's not that he was poor by any means—*his mom was a doctor*. But she had a thing about living large, always telling Nate that honesty and modesty would serve him better than anything else in life. And he'd agreed with her. But he was starting to wonder if maybe his mom hadn't ever seen NOLA Academy.

The elite prep school looked more like a castle than a school. Nate's mom must've been feeling pretty guilty about ditching him his senior year to send him to a place like this. He didn't blame her for uprooting their life. She'd gotten an incredible job offer with a medical program in London. Nate was happy for her. He knew the past few years hadn't been easy on her. It was time for her to take her life back. *It was time Nate did, too.*

He pulled out the class schedule he'd just picked up from the Dean's Office. Technically, Nate didn't start classes until tomorrow, but he wanted to get the lay of the land. This was the first school he'd ever attended where a map was necessary for getting around. And he didn't want to look like the idiot, new guy showing up late for class because he'd gotten lost.

Nate studied the map, figuring he'd pick up his uniform and do a dry run of his schedule while he was on campus. He still couldn't quite believe he was in New Orleans. He'd begged his mom to let him come visit ever since his dad had moved back, but her answer was always the same. "Your dad doesn't understand adult supervision. He only speaks booze, music and women."

To Nate, it didn't seem like such a bad language to speak. But then again, he was a hormone-crazed eighteen-year-old boy who played the violin and hadn't been known to turn down a beer when it was offered. He could see his mom's point though. Nate's dad hadn't been the best role model lately. Then again, Nate's mom had a pretty jaded opinion of his dad after their divorce.

Nate tried to remain neutral during the whole thing. He loved both his parents, and didn't see the point in picking sides. Now that he was technically an adult, he really just needed a place to crash while he finished up his last semester of high school. He could've stayed in Cali. He had plenty of great friends out there who offered to let him stay. But Nate planned to go to Tulane in the fall, and was eager to get a jump on his future. *God knew he was ready for it.*

Nate was ready for a change of scenery. He'd only been to New Orleans a few times. But the city stayed with him. The brief time Nate had spent in the resilient city always left him hopeful. And now that he was back, he clung to the notion that New Orleans would help him move on. And NOLA Academy seemed like a pretty great place to start.

Nate stepped into the pool of sunlight bathing the student lounge. He let the warmth seep in, recharging him. He sighed with relief. It was already easier to breathe without being surrounded by the suffocating sadness of his past. Nate exhaled and repeated his mantra to himself—*life is good.*

He was in a beautiful city, at a great school, with his whole life ahead of him. He was good at focusing on the positive, and as he looked around at the sea of faces spilling out of the classrooms as the bell rang, he saw a lot to be optimistic about. But maybe nothing as much as the girl with the purple hair and studded combat boots who caught his eye.

She poured out of classroom 214 like a rainbow. She wore a scowl on her pretty porcelain face and a shiny black backpack. Time slowed when she walked past Nate through a sliver of sunlight. The light illuminated her features, making her eyes glow pale gray. They were the exact color of the Pacific Ocean at dawn, and Nate felt homesick when he looked into them. His heart filled like helium, spreading heat through his body. And all he knew, was that he had to know her.

2

Cami

CAMILLE WAS RUMMAGING through her locker when someone tapped her on the shoulder. She turned to see a boy with caramel eyes and floppy brown hair smiling at her like a serial killer. She didn't recognize him. But that didn't mean anything. Her high school was large, and she purposely avoided her classmates like the plague.

Camille enjoyed anonymity when she could get it. Her mother was always saying, it wasn't very *N'awlins* of her, but Camille didn't care. Being diagnosed with lymphoma as a nine year old didn't give her the warm and fuzzies when it came to being gawked at by strangers.

Ever since her diagnosis, Camille's childhood had consisted of pity friendships and sorrow-filled stares. She hated being the cancer-girl. It made her different. And that's the last thing any adolescent girl wanted to be.

No one was ever real with Camille. Adults handled her with kid gloves and peers made her feel like an outcast. It made her distrustful, and rightfully so. Her faith in her fellow classmates ended at a fifth grade sleepover when Ashley Dupree pulled Camille's wig off while she slept, dubbing her, *Sleeping Baldy.*

That stupid nickname stuck until eighth grade, when her classmates finally developed a conscience and started to understand what cancer truly meant. The pity was almost worse than the name-calling. All of it forced Camille to build an impenetrable layer of unfuckwithability around her pale skin. Camille was Teflon. Everything the world threw at her just slid off —*well, everything except the fucking cancer.*

Camille had been silently staring at the boy near her locker for almost a minute now. She was giving him her best resting bitch face. She'd perfected it over the years and was used to it scaring people off. But the strange boy just stood there, grinning like a fool. Camille tilted her head, taking in his alarming smile. He was cute. Really cute, actually. But he didn't have the usual hot guy smile she was used to—the one that was sly and crooked. The one that said, 'I want something from you.' That was the smile Camille was used to seeing in the halls at NOAH. But this boy's smile was full on dazzling. It was like he was trying to show you all his teeth at once. It was kind of offensive, but also kind of beautiful.

"What?" she finally muttered. Anxiety flooded her as she wondered if maybe he was staring because her wig was askew or one of her fake eyelashes was stuck somewhere it shouldn't be. *It wouldn't be the first time.*

"Hello," the boy greeted, his obnoxious smile growing impossibly wider.

Camille cut her eyes. *Was this guy for real?* "Who says hello anymore?"

"I do," he replied, his pearly whites glowing. "Hello."

She looked around suspecting she was being pranked, but

no phones were pointed in her direction to stream this strange encounter. She lowered her voice to a hissing whisper. "Why are you saying hello to me?"

He shrugged. "I want to."

"But you don't even know me."

"I want to."

"Are those the only words you know?" she grumbled.

He laughed. "No. What's your name?"

"Are you stupid or something?"

He stuffed his hands into his pockets and shrugged. "I've been told it's sorta my thing."

Camille snorted. "*Stupid* is your thing?"

"Yeah, why not?"

"I'm not sure if you're aware, but that's not something to be proud of. You might want to pick a new *thing*. And while you're at it, stop smiling like that and speak like a normal human."

"You're funny."

"Not trying to be," Camille said turning back to her locker to finish grabbing her things. He was still grinning when she slammed it shut.

"Do normal humans exchange names in New Orleans? I'm Nathan, by the way."

"Camille. Now put that thing away."

"Put what away?"

"That blinding smile."

"Do you need a permission slip to smile here?" Nathan asked. "I'm new to New Orleans Academy High School."

Camille snorted "Ya think? And we call it NOAH. New Orleans Academy High is a mouthful."

"Great tip!" he replied. "Got any others for me?"

"Look, I'm sorta running late. I don't have time for NOAH 101 today."

"Okay. Maybe tomorrow?"

Camille was already stomping down the hall, but Nate

seemed to take that as an invitation to follow. Unfortunately for him, *Make a New Friend,* wasn't on her bucket list. *Camille had erased that goal a long time ago, along with fall in love, and live happily ever after.*

She stopped short, turning to tell the weirdo to take a hike, but he plowed into her. Luckily, he was quick on his feet and his arms flew around her, keeping her from falling down the stairs. Unfortunately his skateboard wasn't so lucky. Camille stood stone still for the deafening seconds it took for the wood and wheels to come to its final resting place at the bottom of the staircase.

Camille stared at the mangled skateboard, panic blossoming in her chest. *That could have been her.* Death was something she thought about often. Having cancer made it impossible not to. But something about an accidental death stealing her life unsettled her. Perhaps that was why she didn't notice that Nathan's arms were still tightly coiled around her.

"Your eyes are beautiful," he said, softly.

She looked up at him. He was so close she could make out the gold flecks in his caramel brown eyes and the smattering of freckles that dusted the bridge of his nose. He was tall, with sun-kissed skin that smelled like soap and sunshine. He wasn't unattractive, that was for sure. Camille flushed when she realized it wasn't so bad being in his arms. But then he ruined it by dipping his head to her hair and inhaling deeply.

"What the hell?" Camille pushed him away. "Did you just smell my hair?"

"I've always wanted to smell purple hair."

Camille was pretty sure her resting bitch face had morphed into angry anime mode. "Where the hell are you from?"

"California."

It'd been a rhetorical question, but Nathan's answer threw her off. Camille would've expected Iowa or somewhere sheltered, but not California. Although, it did help explain his uber-sunny disposition. *Maybe that much perfect weather warped a person's brain after a while?*

"Do you always go around sniffing hair?" she asked.

Nathan laughed. It was a pleasant sound, warm and easy. "No. But your hair is exceptional and it was right there for the sniffing." He shrugged. "I just wanted to do it."

"Do you always do whatever you want?"

"Absolutely! Life's too short not to."

Camille stared at Nathan. She agreed completely. She was pretty much the poster child for *life's short*. There was something refreshing about the California weirdo that almost made her want to smile.

"Well, word of advice, Nate. Don't go around sniffing hair in the halls at NOAH unless you want to be known as a freak. Anyway, that's sorta my title around here."

"Alright, direct me to the asses that need kicking!" His eyes gleamed playfully. "No one gets away with calling a girl with hair that smells like lavender a freak."

This time she did smile. "Easy, California. There are worse things to be called."

"Amen to that."

They walked down the stairs together and Nathan stopped to pick up his beat up skateboard. It looked rough, but was still in one piece. Only one wheel had come off in the tumble.

"Sorry about your board."

Nate shrugged, his glowing smile still affixed to his face. "No biggie. I can fix it."

"Do you need a ride home or something?"

"Nah. I like walking. Gives me a chance to explore the city. Wanna join me?"

"Um, no. I've got somewhere to be."

Nate arched an inquisitive eyebrow. "Boyfriend?"

"No."

"Work?"

"No."

"Then what could be more fun than exploring the city with me?"

"One, I don't know you. Two, I'm not a tour guide. Three, you're kinda weird."

Nathan barked a laugh. "We've established we're not strangers, I've smelled your hair. And don't even try to pretend you're not qualified to show me around. You practically drip that magnetic N'awlins vibe. *And*, I think what you meant to say is that I'm charming as hell."

Camille huffed a laugh. "Oh really?"

Nathan smirked. "You can tell a lot by sniffing someone's hair."

She crossed her arms. "What else do you think you know about me?"

He tapped his fingers on his chin like he was racking his brain. "I could tell you, but I think it'd be more fun if we went on a date."

"Ha!" Camille couldn't contain her laughter. "Are all Californian's this full of themselves?"

"Go out with me and see?"

"Goodbye, Nathan. I'll see you tomorrow," she said heading toward the door.

He jogged to catch up. "Oh come on. You're the first cool person I've met here. And I'm intrigued. What's your story, Camille?"

She laughed. Somehow she was pretty sure the truth would kill the flirtatious conversation they were having. *'Oh, ya know, the usual. Just a seventeen-year-old girl with incurable cancer and a badass wig collection.'*

It didn't really roll off the tongue. And for once, it was nice to talk to someone who didn't look at her like she was tragic. So instead she said, "I don't have a story."

"Everyone has a story. Don't worry, Camille. I'll figure yours out."

"Goodbye." She laughed to herself, waving over her shoulder as she walked away. She heard Nathan laughing behind her.

"I get it," he called. "Goodbye is *your* thing, huh?"

She waved again without turning around. *He had no idea.*

"It's okay. I like a challenge." He was yelling now. "Besides, some things are worth waiting for."

"Good luck," she called pushing through the double doors exiting the school. But as she walked away from Nathan, she sort of hoped he actually would take the time to figure her out.

Nate

"MOM, I promise, Dad's place is fine!"

Nathan had told his mother that about a dozen times already, but every time she called, she asked again. *Your dad's feeding you, right? The house is safe, right? You have everything you need, right?* Nate's answer was always yes. Anything less would've put her back on a plane faster than he could spell 'helicopter parent'.

His dad's place was a bit run down. It was a shotgun shack in the Bywater and it honestly looked like it could be blown over by a strong breeze. It had to be at least a hundred years old. Nate didn't know how the hell it survived the hurricanes.

"So how's London?" Nate asked trying to deflect his mom's worry.

"Oh no you don't. I'm the parent, Nathan. Tell me about your school."

"It's great, Mom. Honestly. It's like the nicest school I've ever seen. There's a Starbucks on campus, if that tells you anything."

She laughed. "And what about your classes?"

"I got my schedule today. The dean said everything checked out with my transfer and I'll graduate on time."

His mom gave a sigh of relief on the other end of the phone. "Oh thank God."

"Mom, stop worrying. Everything's fine."

"Honey, I'm your mother. It's my job to worry about you."

"I know. But guess what? I met a girl today."

"You did?"

"Yep, her name's Camille *and* she loves me. She just doesn't know it yet."

Nate could practically picture his mom smiling and shaking her head. "Honey, that's great. I haven't heard you this excited since . . ." Her voice trailed off. She still couldn't say Tyler's name.

It's been nearly three years since Nate's older brother died and still, neither of his parents talked about him. Probably because any time they did, it turned into a screaming match that ended it tears and ultimately, divorce. But Nate still needed to say his brother's name. It hurt like hell to talk about Tyler sometimes. But the alternative—*forgetting him, or worse, pretending he didn't exist*—that hurt even more.

"Ty would've liked it here, Mom."

He heard her breath hitch. "I love you, Nathan."

"I love you, too, Mom. This place is gonna be good for me. I promise."

3

Cami

CAMILLE LET her backpack thud to the floor. "Dad, I'm home."

The pitter-patter of feet came trotting around the corner to greet her. "Poo!" Camille squealed picking up her Yorkie and squishing him to her face so the tiny dog could shower her with kisses.

Camille had gotten Poo for Christmas when she was eight —*hence the childish name.* But eight-year-old Camille thought, Poo LaRue, was the best name in the whole world. And it might be. It still made her giggle when she heard her father say it. Especially when scolding the devious pooch.

As lame as it was, Poo was Camille's best friend. The dog had been through everything with her. Chemotherapy, immunotherapy, radiation, stem cell transplants, biopsies, surgeries and countless clinical trials. Camille confided all her secrets and fears in the pint-sized pup, knowing Poo was a vault that could never betray her.

"Hey, baby girl," her father called from his office. "It's just you and me for dinner tonight. Whatcha feel like having?"

Camille perked up. Whenever her mother worked late it meant Camille and her father could eat all the delicious rich foods they loved. Her mother never let them indulge, keeping the whole family on a strict cancer-friendly diet.

With Poo cradled in the crook of her arm, Camille wandered into her father's office. Music room was a better word for it. She stepped carefully over stacks of sheet music and piles of records until she reached the red antique sofa. She sat down, listening while he pounded out a song on the piano. Camille's father was a music teacher at a local high school by day, music producer and sound mixing extraordinaire by night. He had a personal office in the house where he gave music lessons and a small recording studio across the courtyard in the converted carriage house. There was always all manner of musicians stopping by to *'lay down tracks'* with her dad. It was an entertaining way to grow up.

Camille loved that her father was so passionate about his job. Unlike her mother, the high-powered real estate attorney, Camille and her father could bond over music. But it was Camille's mother who kept them afloat. Her job afforded them their sprawling French Quarter home and covered Camille's never ending medical expenses.

Her father finished up his song and faced her. "Are you in the mood for crawdads?"

She laughed. "Always."

"How 'bout I make my famous crawfish crepes smothered in goat cheese?"

"Oh my God, Dad that sounds awesome, but I have an appointment tonight."

He frowned. "That's right. The oncologist?"

She nodded, fighting against the prickling guilt she felt lying to her father. She'd stopped going to her appointments three weeks ago.

"You feeling okay, sweetie?"

"Fine."

"Good. Well, I can make you something to go if you want?"

"That's okay, Dad. I wanna swing by the café and pick up my paycheck. I'll grab something there."

"Are you sure?"

Her father looked disappointed and if she stayed in his office one more minute she'd cave. "I'm sure," she said kissing him on the cheek. "I'm gonna get changed and then I'm off."

Camille practically ran to her room. She hated lying, especially to her father. She loved the time they spent together, and knowing they had so little of it left made things even harder. But as she stared at the unchecked boxes on her wall, she knew she didn't have a choice.

When Camille was first diagnosed with cancer, her father helped her paint one entire wall of her bedroom with black chalk paint and told her to make a wish list of all the things she wanted to do. At first it was great—a distraction from the cancer. Every time she had a bad day or had to go in for a treatment she didn't want, he'd tell her to pick something off her list and they'd do it as soon as she was well enough.

But as she got older, Camille began to realize it wasn't really a wish list at all, it was a Goodbye List—a morbid bucket list of things she'd get to experience once in her lifetime, if she was lucky, which she wasn't—hence the cancer.

That realization turned the wall from a list of dreams to a countdown of tasks she had to carry out before she died. And that date was ticking closer every day. Camille had already outlived her disease's life expectancy, but only because her mother signed her up for every clinical trial under the sun. Last year, her oncologist told Camille and her parents that they'd hit the end. There was little else the medical world could do for Camille. Her lymphoma had reached stage four. The growth was accelerating and even with extensive treatment, they could only buy her another year or so at best.

But Camille knew what that borrowed time would be like. She'd spend it in pain and bedridden, too sick and weak from the medication to even enjoy the time she had left. It prompted her to take matters into her own hands.

She made a plan. *Yes, it was a plan for dying, but what other option did she have?* Cancer had ruled her whole life. And Camille was determined not to let it rule her death, too. It was the last thing she had control over and she wasn't about to let that go. That's why she created her plan. '*Camille's Plan for Dying*.'

She knew it was morbid. But ignoring the fact that she was dying wouldn't change her fate. Camille was going to complete her bucket list and then end her life, on her terms—*not cancer's.*

She estimated she could make it to graduation if she cut back her treatments and medications on a regimented schedule. And currently things were going according to plan. She was now off all medications and had stopped treatment completely three weeks ago. Strangely, she never felt better. She knew it was false hope. It was just her body's natural reaction to not being pumped full of poison. But Camille needed to feel her best if she was going to accomplish her goals.

She stared at the empty checkboxes on her Goodbye List. They mocked her indecently. She had 66 days left to say goodbye to everything and everyone. And she was gonna be damn sure she spent every minute she had left living to the fullest.

Nate

. . .

Lightness filled Nate's heart as he rode the streetcar to Jackson Square. The sun was starting to set and the muggy air clung to him, ruffling his brown hair. It was just long enough that it was starting to curl at his neck. He knew he needed a trim, but he liked the way his hair looked when it was shaggy. It made him think of Ty. His brother had always worn his hair longer. Tyler had a devil-may-care attitude that Nathan had been so envious of. Nothing ever scared Tyler. He was only eleven months older than Nate, but sometimes he'd seemed a lifetime wiser.

Nate missed his brother every day. They'd been best friends. They did everything together—chased girls, played music, skated, surfed, and got into all kinds of trouble. Every moment spent with Tyler was a vibrant one. He'd been more full of life than anyone Nate had ever met. Ty used to say, "One day I'm gonna show you the world, little brother."

They were supposed to have a lifetime to explore the world together. And now, Nate felt that weight heavy on his shoulders. It was Nate's duty to live well, for the both of them. He was still alive and though Tyler wasn't, Nate could feel his brother with him. And he owed it to Tyler to blaze a path through the world. Because if Tyler were still here, that's what he'd be doing.

With that thought driving him, Nate planned to seize every opportunity that came his way in the hopes that Ty could experience everything through him. Nate could still feel Ty in his heart. So maybe it wasn't crazy that wherever Ty was, he could feel Nate, too. So many little things reminded Nathan of his brother. It could be a song, a bird, a laugh. Certain things conjured Tyler so realistically that Nate couldn't catch his breath. Sometimes, when he was feeling hesitant about something, he could almost hear Ty saying, "I'm right here, bro. Go for it. Grab life by the balls."

Nathan had definitely heard that today when he

approached Camille. Three years ago, Nate never would've dreamed of talking to a beautiful girl like Camille. But losing Tyler had taught him a lot of things. Mainly that life was short, and sometimes you didn't get a second shot at it.

That sentiment had changed Nate's life. Already, he was glad he'd moved to New Orleans, and now talked to Camille. She was enchanting and Nate hadn't been able to stop thinking about her. Even now, as he exited the streetcar and walked along the Mississippi, he couldn't help but see her in the fading light that shimmered purple across the muddy water. He wished he could tell Tyler about her and thank him for making him courageous.

4

Cami

CAMILLE STOOD at the service door to the tower stairs of St. Louis Cathedral. Her father played the organ for the gospel services occasionally, so she'd nicked his set of keys before she left the house. She clutched her mint green Polaroid camera in her sweaty hands. She didn't know whether it was nerves or exhaustion getting the better of her. She'd been saving this task from her Goodbye List for a while due to her insane fear of heights.

You've got this, Cami. One foot in front of the other.

She took a deep breath and unlocked the door. She turned the knob and quickly slipped through after making sure no one was looking. It was stifling in the stairwell, but Camille climbed the cramped spiral staircase before she could change her mind. When she got to the top she closed her eyes and tried to count to ten. She'd have to walk across a narrow service catwalk to get to the shutters facing Jackson Square.

She moved one foot off the platform and started shaking. All she could picture was that damn skateboard bouncing down the stone stairs at school. If she fell, that's exactly what would happen to her. But she had a feeling she wouldn't hold up as well as the skateboard. She'd probably snap like a toothpick.

"This was a dumb idea, Cami," she muttered to herself.

She took another step, her heart thundering in her chest. She'd written this stupid wish on her wall when she was eleven. She'd been having a good day and her parents took her to have a picnic in the park on Jackson Square. They sat in the shadow of St. Louis Cathedral and Camille had noticed a bird land atop the cross adorning the highest tower.

"I wonder what the world looks like from up there?" she'd mused.

"You'll have to ask the angels," her father replied.

"I'll be an angel one day soon, won't I, Daddy?" she'd asked.

Her father had looked at her sadly. "That's right, baby girl."

That night Camille had gone home and written *St. Louis Cathedral* on her wall. It was a vague enough wish. And she'd been to the cathedral hundreds of times over the years. But she couldn't put a check in the box until she conquered her fears and saw the view from the tower.

It was one of the things Camille loved most about her Goodbye List. It held her accountable. She was often vague about what she wrote on it. It was usually just a single word or two. *St. Louis Cathedral. Mississippi River. Beach.* But she knew the true meaning of each wish. And once it was on the wall, it became law.

She took one more shaking step toward the shutters. If she took another she'd have to let go of the railing. *You can do this, Cami.* It wasn't just about checking a box on her stupid list, it was proving to herself that there were still things in her life that she could control.

Having cancer had stolen so much from her and maybe it was denial, but she was desperate to cling to the things she could still conquer. Her fear of heights was one of them.

Camille closed her eyes again and took a deep breath. With each step closer to the shutters, she could hear the sounds of Jackson Square wafting up to her—tourists, palm readers, musicians, artists, panhandlers. The square was always alive with sound.

The melody of violin music lured her forward. It was a haunting tune that made her chest swell. Good music always affected Camille that way. Her father said music was in her blood, but she didn't have a lick of talent for instruments. The only musical gift she had was her voice. Camille could sing. In fact, it used to be her favorite thing to do. But cancer had stolen that, too.

Now she got winded just walking upstairs. It sort of made it difficult to carry a tune. Rather than feel depressed about losing one more battle to her disease, Camille had given up singing. But when she heard music like this, it made her want to sing from the rooftops. The thought made her smile. *She would quite literally be singing from the rooftops if she sang along right now.*

She listened closer to the song. There was something familiar about it, but she couldn't name the tune. The tempo of the music increased. Before, it had been as if the song was climbing a hill, but now it spilled down in rapid progression. The violin strings cried so soulfully it made Camille want to weep. It gave her courage. If someone could pour their heart out like that, she could certainly conquer her fear of heights. She let go of the railing and lunged for the other side.

Camille shrieked with relief when she made contact with the heavy shutters. She wrapped her fingers around the ancient iron louvers, sucking in air as the warm breeze carried the vibrant sounds of the square to her. She gazed out the slatted shutter opening to the lush lawn below where she and her family had picnicked when she'd dreamt up this crazy goal. Tourists milled about the square, reading plaques, smiling, posing and snapping photos.

Camille closed her eyes and imagined she was still sitting on the blanket with her parents as an eleven-year-old. She wished she could go back. She wished she had more time. She wished for so many things. But all she could really do, was what she'd come for. Camille held her camera up to the slats and took a photo as she whispered, "Goodbye St. Louis Cathedral."

Even with her feet planted on solid ground, Camille still felt dizzy with exhilaration. The high of accomplishing another goal on her list was starting to fade. It was always this way—exciting at first and then depressing.

The view from the cathedral tower had been spectacular. She'd watched the sun paint the Mississippi varying shades of pastel until it looked like a stretch of rainbow taffy. She glanced at the photo she'd taken. Melancholy overtook her, and suddenly she wished she could show someone—*anyone.*

Camille didn't know what was sadder, the fact that she didn't have anyone to share this with, or that she'd never get to do it again. She didn't usually let herself think that way and was grateful when she heard the violinist pick up a tune again. It was the perfect distraction.

She decided to follow the sound. She wanted a glimpse of the musician who'd helped her accomplish her goal. From the way the haunting notes carried across Jackson Square, she knew the source had to be close by.

. . .

Nate

NATE LET the music slip around him like a cocoon. He listened to the sound of his strings echo across the streets, mixing with the percussion of feet parading over the slate sidewalks. He smiled, sliding into a song he and Tyler had written together. Nate ran his bow faster across the strings as the memories flooded in. Sometimes there were things he could only say through music. And when he needed to talk to Ty, there was no better way than this.

Applause startled Nate when he finished playing. He opened his eyes, surprised to find he had an audience. He grinned and took a dramatic bow, thinking how much Tyler would've loved showing off to a crowd. But as Nate's admirers slowly melted back into the throng of pedestrian traffic, one remained—and she wore an unmistakable purple wig.

Camille stood before him, eyes blown wide, mouth gaping. Nate's face quirked into an easy smile. "So, you decided to see the city with me after all."

It was a statement, not a question, and before Camille could say anything, he slid his bow across his strings until she was trapped in the rapture of another song. This time he played just for her. It wasn't so much a song, as it was the feeling she evoked from him, put to music.

He closed his eyes, picturing her purple hair, until the image was clear enough that he could paint it. She'd traded her school uniform for yellow tights and a gray dress with the pattern of pale pink tulips on it. She still wore her studded black combat boots, which made him smile. She was like a jagged rainbow. Despite her attempts to repel him, everything about Camille drew Nate in. She was a breath of fresh air and she made him want to breathe deeply.

When he was finished playing, Camille slayed him with a look of admiration.

"Where did you learn to play like that?" she asked with awe.

"My dad."

She cocked her delicate eyebrows like she didn't believe him.

"Why do you seem so surprised? They *do* have violins in California, ya know?"

"I know. But it just doesn't go together. I mean you have the whole skateboard punk thing going for ya. But the rest . . ."

"What?"

"You and the violin. It doesn't mesh."

Nate scoffed. "And purple hair and yellow tights do?"

"Hey, I'm intriguing, remember?" Camille smirked a shy smile and Nate's heart squeezed in his chest. *Shit, this girl made his knees weak!*

"You definitely are," he replied. "So how 'bout it?"

"What?"

"Let's go have some fun! It's a beautiful night. I have my violin, you have some leprechaun-looking camera. I think we can make magic happen."

Camille laughed. "You can play Bach but you've never seen a Polaroid camera?"

"That's what that is? It looks like it's made of candy."

"Play something," she said lifting the camera to her eye.

Nate grinned and dragged his bow across the strings making his violin sing. He closed his eyes and played '*Stay With Me*' while Camille snapped photos. When he was done, she handed him one. She'd written, *Witnessing Magic,* on the wide white section that framed the bottom of the photo.

"Wow, this *is* magical," he said, admiring the photo. Camille had captured the wrought-iron balconies of the salmon-colored building behind him. They dripped with hanging ferns and bright cascading flower boxes. And the glow of gas lanterns gave Nate's image an otherworldly glow. He seemed small in the frame, but the look on his face said it all. Camille had encapsulated the magic of his music on film. He looked at her, handing the photo back. "You should be a photographer."

She smiled at him, handing it back. "Keep it."

But Nate noticed the tightness of her mouth. He reached a hand out just as she swayed on her feet. "Whoa. You alright?" His hand wrapped firmly around her frail elbow to steady her. She felt too cool for the humid weather and her pale features were nearly transparent.

"Yeah." She tried to laugh it off. "I think I just need some sugar. I forgot to eat dinner."

Nate didn't let go. "Okay. Where can we get you a sugar fix?"

"Um," Camille looked around flustered. "I-I work at the café around the corner. I guess we could go there. They have donuts."

"Donuts it is."

Cami

CAMILLE WAS MORTIFIED that she'd nearly fainted in front of Nathan. *What the hell was wrong with her?* She was used to the crash after her adrenalin wore off, but the climb to the cathedral tower must have exhausted her more than she thought. She was trembling by the time Sweet Thang's Café came into view.

If Nathan noticed her unsteadiness—and she was sure he did—at least he didn't mention it. He just kept his hand steady at her lower back, steering her to a hot pink chair once they entered the café. Nate pulled up a chair and joined her at the little bistro table.

"So you work here?"

She nodded.

"What's good?"

"Everythang, sugar."

Camille looked up as Ronnie walked around the counter. He owned Sweet Thang's Café, where Camille had worked forever. He was one of her favorite people in the world, and probably the closest thing she had to a real friend. Despite him being a forty-something gay black man with a touch of clairvoyance, they had a lot in common—namely a fabulous wardrobe and great taste in men. *Well, at least Ronnie did. Cami never saw the point in dating.*

"Hey, Ronnie," she greeted.

"Hey, baby cakes. Whatcha doin' here? You're not working tonight."

"We're on a date," Nathan replied happily.

Camille wanted to crawl into a hole. "No we're not."

Nathan winked at Ronnie. "Yes we are." He dropped his voice to a whisper. "Camille likes to play hard to get."

Ronnie's perfectly drawn on eyebrows looked like the golden arches as they climbed up his forehead. His eyes practically devoured Nathan. *This was not something Ronnie would let go.*

"Well, it's a pleasure," Ronnie purred, his southern accent deepening. He always laid on the charm when he was feeling flirty.

Ronnie turned toward Camille giving her a ridiculously unsubtle wink.

"I'm Nathan. But everyone calls me Nate." He stuck out his hand.

Ronnie shook it. "Jeronathan, but everyone calls me Ronnie. Although you can call me anything you want, bebe."

Nate laughed. "Nice to meet you, Ronnie."

"Enchanté," Ronnie crooned. He turned to Camille letting

his mouth drop open into his token *'How cute is he'* face. "So, me amours, what can I get ya?"

"Well, my date is in need of some sugar," Nate replied.

Ronnie cocked his head seeming to notice Camille's pallid complexion. Her expression begged him not to say anything to Nate about her cancer. That was the great thing about working with someone for years. Especially in food service, where you had to wear a smile no matter what you were thinking. Camille and Ronnie could read each other's looks. And Ronnie understood her current plea perfectly. He turned back to Nate. "Well, you came to the right place, bebe. Go on up to the case and pick out what ya like."

Nate stood up and walked the short distance to the case filled with sugary goodness, while Ronnie quickly whispered in Camille's ear. "You okay, baby cakes?"

"Yeah. Just over did it a bit today. But please don't say anything to him, about . . . ya know."

Ronnie pretended to zip his lips and toss away a key. "He's delicious."

Camille's face flushed, but she couldn't disagree. Nate was growing on her. She glanced over at him. He was practically drooling over the donut case.

"Holy hell," Nate yelled. "You make donuts with Cap'n Crunch and bacon on them?"

Ronnie flounced over to the counter to help Nate pick out one of the fantastical creations Sweet Thang's was known for.

"Camille, what kind do you want?" Nate called.

"She always has the sugar bomb," Ronnie replied.

"What's that?" Nate asked, but Ronnie was already putting the colorful confectionary on a plate.

The sugared donut was filled with buttercream frosting and had pink icing on top, smothered in Fruitloops, Fruity Pebbles, Lucky Charm marshmallows and rainbow sprinkles.

Nate's eyes lit up like Christmas. "Holy diabetes, Batman! Is that much sugar even legal?"

Ronnie chuckled. "What doesn't kill ya, makes ya stronger. You want one, bebe?"

"Absolutely."

Ronnie grinned, shaking his head. "It's our specialty, but I don't know how you kids eat these things."

"You only live once," Nate replied.

Ronnie threw Camille a knowing look. "Ain't that the truth?"

Nate tried to pay, but Ronnie wouldn't hear of it. Instead he brought out three bowls of gumbo, pulled up a chair and joined them. "Ya'll can't live on sugar alone," he said, passing a bowl to each of them, but it was clear to Camille that he brought it for her. She gave him a grateful nod. Somehow, Ronnie always knew what she needed.

"So," Ronnie said turning to Nate. "Tell me everything, Nathaniel."

Nate laughed good-natured. "It's just Nathan, and please, call me Nate."

"I'm sorry, bebe. You're just too delicious to be a Nate. I'm gonna keep Nathaniel. So anyway, what are your intensions for my Camille?"

"Oh, that's easy. I'm madly in love with her, so I plan to woo her until she's mine."

"Hells bells, sugar. If she won't date you, I sure as stars will." Ronnie cocked an eyebrow at Camille. "This boy is charming as hell."

Nate grinned his toothy smile at Camille with pride. "Told ya."

"Don't encourage him," she said rolling her eyes. She ate her gumbo, trying to pretend she wasn't mortified that Ronnie was playing matchmaker.

"Honestly, Nathaniel. Where'd a tall drink a water like you blow in from? You clearly ain't from 'round here."

Nate playfully looked around. "Is my California showing again?"

Ronnie clicked his tongue. "Cal-i-forn-ia." He dragged out the word into too many syllables the way only Ronnie could. "That explains it."

"He's going to NOAH," Camille added.

"Ooo-wee!" Ronnie swooned. "Cute *and* rich."

Nate laughed. "Nah, my mom just feels bad that I had to switch schools my senior year."

"Yeah, why is that?" Ronnie asked.

"My mom's a doctor and she got offered her dream job in London." Nate shrugged. "I didn't want her to give up such a great opportunity, so I decided to come here and move in with my dad."

"He's selfless, Camille. That's an important quality in a man." Ronnie turned back to Nate continuing with the barrage of questions. "Alright, Nathaniel. This is the rapid-fire round. Who's your daddy? Got any siblings? Crazy ex-girlfriends? Ever been arrested? Gotten anyone pregnant? Are you gay, straight, other or all of the above? Any weird quirks we should know about? And what's your biggest fear?"

"Ronnie . . ." Camille shot him a warning glare. At first she'd been into Ronnie's playful questions. It was nice to have someone asking everything she wanted to know, but in true Ronnie fashion, he'd gone too far. "You don't have to answer, Nate. This isn't an interrogation."

"I don't mind." Nate's easy smile said he was speaking the truth.

He tapped his fingers on his chin. Camille was starting to notice it was something he did when trying to be clever. "Let's see, my father is Charles Hawthorne, but he goes by Charlie, and he plays a mean guitar. I had the world's best older brother, Tyler Hawthorne, but he was killed three years ago in a car accident, therefore I don't drive. You can put that in the quirks column. No crazy ex's, no kids, I'm straight, and my biggest fear is not living enough."

It was silent enough to hear a pin drop in the café. Ronnie was speechless. Camille didn't think that had ever happened before. He always had a witty comeback or some kind of remark. But he was currently staring at Nate like he was a ghost.

"Did I pass?" Nate asked eagerly.

Ronnie snapped out of it, taking Nate's hand. "I'm sorry about your brother, bebe."

"Me too."

"Well, those are all good answers, son." Ronnie patted Nate's hand. "You have my permission to date Miss Camille LaRue."

Ronnie gave Camille a pointed stare and stood up, pushing back from the table. "Be nice to this one, baby cakes. I got a feelin' 'bout him." Then he sashayed to the kitchen leaving Camille and Nate to themselves.

5

Nate

Nate couldn't remember the last time he'd been so excited to go to school. He'd pretty much figured he'd be on autopilot at NOAH since he'd already gotten accepted to the Tulane music program pending graduation. Half the appeal of going to NOAH was its Tulane affiliate status. Which basically meant, NOAH students funneled enough tuition money to make acceptance at any college in the state a guarantee. *And for what Nate's mom was paying, NOAH should guarantee a freaking parade along with graduation!*

But that was beside the point. Nate's main reason for transferring to NOAH was so he could start over. He wanted to stop living in the past and restart his life again. He was also excited about getting to spend some time with his dad while exploring the New Orleans music scene. *Or those had been the things he was excited about.* Meeting Camille had sort of changed his priorities. Just a few hours together and he couldn't get her out of his mind.

Last night he'd walked her home from the Sweet Thang's. She'd offered him a ride back to his house when she found out he lived all the way in the Bywater, but he said he preferred the Streetcar. It wasn't a total lie. The streetcars were awesome, and a great way to see the city, but truthfully Nate didn't want to let Camille see where he lived after walking up to her place.

Camille lived in one of those massive two-story French Quarter homes that took up both corners of a block. It was the color of beach sand with two levels of wrap-around balconies adorned with scrawling pastel green ironwork. Wealth oozed from the place, just like the overflowing flower baskets. Nate only got a glimpse through the street door that led to the interior courtyard, but it was enough to make him second-guess his chances with Camille.

Wealth and status were never things Nate really focused on. But growing up in the average suburbs of California underprepared him for the social differences he was discovering in New Orleans. A walk through the French Quarter was an exercise in social economics. There were million dollar homes, nestled next to old rundown bodegas, homeless people begged outside restaurants that required jackets for dinner, and talented street artists and musicians peddled their wears for pennies next to galleries and jazz joints that were overflowing with tourist dollars.

Having just met Camille, Nate wasn't sure how she'd react to his father's shabby shotgun home. He didn't want to kill his chances with her just yet. And to be honest, Nate was also worried about what version of his dad he'd come home to.

Most nights his dad wasn't home at all. He tended bar at Vaughan's and picked up gigs when he could. But two nights ago, Nate arrived home to find his dad passed out drunk on the front porch. He was so tanked he couldn't figure out how to unlock the door, choosing to vomit and pass out in front of it. Nate spent the rest of the night getting him into bed and cleaning up.

Nate couldn't even be mad. He'd seen the way his father stared at him sometimes. Nathan and Tyler were only eleven months apart. They looked so much alike they were often mistaken as twins. It had to be difficult for his dad to suddenly have Nate around, haunting him like the ghost of his lost son. He knew it was hard on his mom. Nate had overheard her talking on the phone to her sister not too long after Ty's death. She'd said looking at Nate broke her heart, because sometimes she could only see Tyler.

Nate couldn't imagine what that was like for her. She must've felt like she'd lost both her sons—only seeing the son who died, while trying to see the living son.

It was different for Nate. He liked that he looked like his brother. It was like always having a piece of Ty with him. It brought Nate comfort and he sought it out at every opportunity. Like now, staring into his locker mirror, Nate examined his reflection seeking out Ty's resemblance. His eyes were browner than Ty's. Where Nate's leaned toward gold, Tyler's had held a hint of green. And Tyler had a natural crooked smile that always made it look like he was up to something. Nate grinned. His smile was wide, or trustworthy, as Ty always pointed out.

Nate gave his reflection a wink, channeling the strength he got from seeing even the tiniest hint of Tyler in himself. Nate needed all the bravery he could get, because his goal for today was to spend more time with Camille. He closed his locker to go in search of her. But halfway down the hall, three blondes corralled him.

Cami

. . .

Camille was about to slam her locker closed when she heard Ashley Dupree's high-pitched laughter float down the hall. Camille had trained her ears to pick up on Ashley's specific brand of evil so it could be avoided at all costs. Hiding behind her locker door, Camille watched as Ashley and her clones caged Nathan in. *Poor guy.* She should've warned him about the *Ashleys*—Ashley Banks, Ashley Calhoune and their ringleader, Ashley Dupree. They were NOAH's crème de la crème when it came to high school hierarchy. And they could smell hot new boys like blood in the water.

Camille couldn't help feeling a bit disappointed that she hadn't seen Nate all day. She'd secretly been hoping she'd have at least one class with him. As much as she didn't want to admit it, there was something charming about his forward flirtation and endless smile.

She watched him introduce himself to the perfect Ashleys as unreasonable jealously flared in her chest. Camille hated that she was wasting her time straining to listen to what the popular blonde girls were saying. But years of childhood teasing couldn't be erased, even if the Ashleys weren't mean to her anymore. *Well, at least by their standards they weren't.*

They didn't pick on Camille for wearing a wig like they had in fifth grade. But now they ignored her completely, which somehow felt worse. Camille already felt like she didn't belong, but the Ashleys made sure she knew it. And it wasn't just them. Camille was never invited to hang with the in crowd. She was never invited to hang with any crowd. *But then again, 'cancer friend' wasn't exactly a demographic most cliques were looking to fill.*

Camille knew she shouldn't take it personally. There were plenty other perfectly healthy kids that the Ashleys and the Antes ignored. The *Antes* was what the cool clique at NOAH called themselves. It was short for Antebellum, because they all lived in the old Antebellum homes of the wealthy garden district, and pretty much preserved the elitist ways of their pre-civil war ancestors.

The name was appropriate on many levels. It sounded like *anti* and the Ashleys and their wannabes were pretty much anti-anyone who wasn't them or threatened them. And normally, Camille would say it was impossible to infiltrate the Antes. No amount of money or kiss-assery could get you in. You had to be born into it. *And we're talkin like fifth generation born into it.* But as Camille watched the Ashleys bat their eyelashes and giggle at Nathan, she felt her stomach drop. *Maybe you only had to be the right amount of hot?*

"So, have you met anyone yet?" Ashley Banks was asking.

"Yeah. I hung out with Camille, yesterday. She's cool." Nate said, his token smile glowing.

All three of the Ashleys let their pretty pink faces sour. "Camille LaRue?" Ashley Calhoune asked.

Nate nodded. "Yeah. She makes a badass donut."

"Listen, Nathan," Ashley Dupree purred. "You're new here, so I'm gonna do you a favor. Camille's not really . . . I don't even know how to put it. She's . . ."

Camille squeezed her eyes shut. *Don't say it. Don't say I'm the cancer girl.*

"She's different," Ashley Banks interjected.

Nate shrugged. "I'm different, too."

Ashley Dupree's smile dripped saccharine. "No silly, not good-different. She's weird-different."

"Well, whatever she is, sign me up for the fan club, because that girl is awesome."

Camille couldn't help the flush of pride that washed over her. *Take that Ashleys! New guy thinks I'm awesome!* She was practically glowing. *Maybe she should give Nate a chance after all?*

The Ashleys passed a knowing look between each other, trying to suppress their giggles. "Bless your heart," Ashley

Dupree crooned. "Nathan, sweetie. Take our word for it. You can do better."

He flashed his giant toothy grin. "I plan to. I'm hoping to get another date with her tonight." He gave the stunned blondes a double thumps up and turned, making a beeline toward Camille's locker.

Shit! Did Nathan really just tell the Ashleys he and Camille went on a date? And there was going to be another one?

Camille didn't know whether to cheer or hide. The shock on the Ashleys faces was priceless, but Camille also didn't need any Ante drama in her life. She was perfectly happy with her invisible status at NOAH. It meant she was safe and could stick to her plan—*sixty-five days until graduation. Sixty-five days until freedom.*

Unfortunately for Camille, Nathan didn't know she preferred to stay invisible. He sidled up to her locker, his grin near blinding. She turned her back, pretending not to see him, but watched his reflection approaching in her locker mirror. She examined the white slice of his smile as it ate up the space between them.

Suddenly, his warmth surrounded Camille.

"Hello," he greeted as he dipped his head into her hair, inhaling deeply.

"Hey!" she whirled around, scanning the hall to see if anyone was watching them. They weren't. "No more hair smelling!" she hissed.

Nate grinned with only half his mouth. "But it's silver today."

"So?"

"So, I haven't smelled silver hair."

Camille sighed, making a mental note to wear only purple or silver wigs for the next few days until she could shake Nathan and his strange hair-sniffing habits.

"Can we go get more donuts?" he asked.

"What?"

"From that place you work at. That chocolate bacon Cap'n Crunch one was seriously like the best thing I've ever had in my life! I *must* have another one."

Camille glowed at the praise since that specific donut was on of her own creations. She tamed her pride long enough to give him a tired look. "They're just donuts, Nate."

He looked appalled. "How dare you speak ill of my new favorite dessert."

She rolled her eyes. "Do they not have donuts in California, or are you just this ridiculous about all normal things?"

He smirked. "The latter."

Nate was keeping pace with Camille as she walked down the hall trying to escape him. This time she waited until she was outside the building and far away from any stairs when she came to an abrupt stop. "Look, Nate, we're not friends. You should really listen to the Ashleys and find someone like them to flatter."

He wrinkled his nose. "The Barbie clones? No thanks. By the way, are they really *all* named Ashley, or did they have to change their names as part of initiation or something?"

Camille snorted a laugh. "No, they're actually all Ashleys. I think their parents must've read *Gone With the Wind* one too many times."

It was Nate's turn to laugh. Camille liked the sound of it. It was deep and rumbled through her. "You were just kidding about the friend thing, right?" he asked.

She gave her best *'sorry'* face and shrugged, but it just made Nate smile more. *What the hell was wrong with this guy?*

"I see what's going on here," he retorted.

"You do?" *Cami certainly didn't.*

He gave her a crooked boy smile. "You're trying to tell me we're *more* than friends."

"What? No! I—"

"Shhhh . . ." Nate put a finger to her lips, silencing Camille immediately. *A boy had never touched her lips before.* "I mean I knew you'd fall for me. But I have to say this is much faster than I'd even hoped for."

"I'm *not* falling for you," she grumbled.

"It's okay. We can play the game. So how 'bout those donuts?"

Camille made a growling sound in the back of her throat. It was all starting to make sense. *Nathan Hawthorne was insane. Cute, but insane. Why else would he be hitting on her?* She didn't have the energy to waste arguing with him, and decided there wasn't much else she could do but wait for the next shiny object to catch his eye.

"Sorry, Nate. No donuts today."

"What? Why not?"

"I'm not working."

"Even better! So whatcha wanna do?"

"I want to go home."

"Camille! Are you inviting me over? I like you, but this is so sudden," he teased.

She rolled her eyes at his mocking tone, honestly wondering where he got his energy from. *Maybe all he ate was sugar? It would explain the donut obsession, which he was still droning on about.*

"Maybe we could stop and get some donuts on the way to your house?"

"Nate! Enough with the donuts."

"But they were legitimately the best donuts I've ever had! Is New Orleans famous for them? Because if not, they absolutely should be."

Camille cocked her head at him. "You really thought they were that good?"

"My mom's a health freak. I don't get a lot of sweets. Or at least I didn't. I'm sorta on my own now at my dad's. It's overwhelming. There's so many choices when it comes to what to eat."

But Nate looked more excited than overwhelmed. Camille's heart softened a bit. She knew what it was like living on a strict health food diet. Sometimes she craved sugar like it was a drug. For that reason she kept a secret stash of PEZ in her backpack at all times.

"Are you sure I can't convince you to stop for one teeny, tiny donut? I don't want you getting the sugar shakes again," he teased.

Camille grinned. "I think I know a place you'll like even better than Sweet Thang's."

6

Nate

Nate followed Camille to a small café on Royal Street. It had a green and white striped awning and the words Café Beignet spelled out in tiny black and white tiles on the checkered floor.

"What is this place?" Nate asked as they walked inside.

"Only my favorite place in the French Quarter."

Nate could see why. It was like he'd walked into a dreamscape. The low ceiling was curved and narrow like the inside of a school bus. Someone had painted it to resemble a blue sky, complete with fluffy white clouds and tropical palm fronds. The white bistro dining sets and sparkling chandeliers made him think of Paris. *At least, how he imagined Paris.*

He followed Camille to the counter, listening carefully to the hint of French accent flavoring her voice as she ordered beignets and two café au laits. They snagged a table in the outdoor courtyard, listening to a charm of finches sing in the trees overhead.

"So this is your place, huh?" Nate asked.

"Kinda. I like to come here and just escape. Especially when I need a sugar fix," she said, dumping six packets of sugar into her coffee and stirring.

"I knew you were a sugar fiend like me."

She laughed. "You have no idea. But my mom won't even let it in the house."

"I bet I do. My mom's a PNS."

"Yikes! That *is* rough. Were you allowed to eat anything she didn't grow herself?"

Nate's brows knitted together. "You're the first person I've ever met who I didn't have to explain PNS to."

Camille flushed. "I was kinda interested in it for a while."

"I don't think you can be a sugar freak *and* a doctor who specializes in diets that prevent illness," Nate added.

"Yeah, I sorta figured that out. But my mother still makes my father and I eat like we're training for a triathlon."

Nate took a sip of his coffee. It was strong and had a bit of tree bark bite. He tried not to make a face, but Camille's smirk told him he didn't succeed.

"It's the chicory. It takes a bit to get used to," she added. "But once you do, you'll never go back to regular old coffee."

Truthfully, Nate wasn't much of a coffee guy. He had enough energy as it was. Plus, with his addiction to all things sugary, he didn't need the extra high. But he *did* enjoy wrapping his long fingers around the foam cup. There was a chill in the swampy air even though it was almost April. He wasn't used to the humidity, yet. It made everything feel clingy and heavy. He was about to ask Camille if she was cold when a waiter arrived carrying two plates of powered pastries.

"What are these?" Nate asked, examining the pillow-shaped

dough. There had to be half a pound of powdered sugar coating them.

"*These*, are the best donuts in town," she said. "But we call them beignets in N'awlins," she added with a playful grin.

Christ her grin was adorable. It made the apples of her cheeks curve into perfect circles that he literally wanted to bite.

"This is the best way to eat them," she remarked dumping the excess sugar from one of the beignets into her coffee before taking a bite.

Nate was mesmerized for a moment as he watched the powered sugar float down in a shimmering cloud from Camille's lips. Specks clung to her porcelain face and he wanted to lick them off. So he did.

Nate licked his thumb and reached across the table to press it to the sugar near the corner of Camille's mouth. She gasped, but he'd already sucked the sugar from his thumb, swearing it was sweeter having touched her skin.

"Um, okay, that goes into the same category as hair sniffing."

"Not approved?" Nate asked.

"Definitely not approved."

"Noted," Nate said, though if he was honest, he wasn't one bit sorry. He was trying to rein in his attraction to Camille, but Nate wasn't used to denying himself the things he wanted. It was sort of his new life motto. *No Regrets.*

But it was a bit different now that he found himself wanting a person. He knew he should restrain himself. Camille wasn't giving him the come hither stare that invited such advances. But he couldn't help himself. With her silver hair, shimmering pale skin, and gray-blue eyes, Camille had an otherworldly glow that drew him in. She was a flame and Nate was just another hopeless moth.

To distract himself, Nate bit into his beignet and moaned. "Shit!"

Camille almost gave him a full smile. "I know. Good, right?"

"Good doesn't even begin to describe these." He took another bite, savoring the warm fluffy pastry. It was buttery and soft, and combined with the powdered sugar it tasted like love in food form. "These are like heavenly pillows!"

He shoved the rest of the beignet into his mouth and started on the second one. Before he knew it he was holding up his third and final pastry. "Damn!" Nate exclaimed, staring down the delicious dessert. "Where have you been all my life?"

Cami

Camille was looking at Nate, wondering the same thing. *Where had this incredibly adorable, quirky boy been all her life? And why did she have to meet him now? When she was so close to the end?*

She couldn't help but wonder what her life might have been like if she'd met Nathan Hawthorne sooner. Like maybe in sixth grade so she would've had someone to sit with at lunch every day when students were still calling her *Sleeping Baldy*. Or maybe in ninth grade when she'd finally gotten boobs and felt like a girl, even though no boys seemed to notice. Or tenth grade when she'd wanted to go to the school dance but no one had asked her. *Why now? When everything was over.*

Camille knew it was stupid to feel loss for someone she'd just met. Sure, Nate was interested in her now, but it was just for the moment. Once he found out she had cancer it would all be over.

But as he smiled at her, a tiny seed of doubt bubbled in her chest. She felt a real connection when it was just the two of them together. Nate was easy to talk to, and his damn smile made something inside her sizzle to the point that it was hard to think. Each time he grinned or laughed it was like live wire struck her heart. The feeling was unexpected and strange, but in a refreshing way she enjoyed it.

She also liked how odd Nate was. He dressed like a skater, played the violin like Mozart, and smiled like a child who didn't know better. It was safe to say Camille hadn't ever met anyone like Nate before. He had a quality about him—like he truly didn't care what anyone thought about him. He was who he was, unapologetically. It made Camille feel like she was the normal one for a change. *And that was something she'd given up on.*

It was stupid, but now more than ever, Camille wanted to keep her cancer a secret. It was nice to talk to Nate about normal teenage things. At least, that's what she thought they were doing. She wouldn't really know. Her usual conversations were about how she was feeling, test results and treatment plans. She couldn't believe she'd almost screwed it up by failing to realize most teenagers didn't know what a PNS was. But Camille had her own Physician Nutrition Specialist since she was diagnosed—which was the reason she'd developed a love for all things non-health food related.

"So," Nate said, eyeing her plate of half eaten beignets. "You gonna eat those?"

"Knock yourself out," she said sliding her plate toward him. They came three to an order and she could never eat more than one. Plus, she didn't want to push it. She'd felt like crap after the donut at Sweet Thang's yesterday and didn't want to risk the wrath of a blood sugar roller coaster.

Nate polished off the beignets in record time, stretching his long limbs when he was done. "Not bad for a second date," he said weaving his fingers behind his head.

"It's not a date."

"If you say so, Cami."

She raised her eyebrows. "Cami?"

"I'm trying it out."

She hid her smile as she sipped her coffee. Very few people called her Cami. Mostly just her parents and Ronnie. It was a privilege she allowed only those who had a place in her heart. She should've stopped Nate right there—should've corrected him and told him to call her Camille. But the sudden feverish feeling in her pounding heart told her it was already too late.

"So, it's my turn for twenty questions," Nate announced. His brown eyes sparkled like liquid amber as he tapped his chin thinking. "Let's go with the same questions Ronnie asked. Parents? Siblings? Crazy exes? Arrested? Knocked up? Gay, straight, other? Weird quirks and talents? And, what's your biggest fear?"

Camille let out sigh. "Remind me to kill Ronnie tomorrow."

"Come on, it's fun. We're getting to know each other. That's what friends do."

She rolled her eyes. "I thought we were *more* than friends," she teased.

Nate winked. "Oh, we will be. But first I must learn the wiles of your feminine ways so I may know best how to woo you."

"Oh my God. If I play along will you promise to stop talking like that?"

He smirked. "I'll take it into consideration."

"Fine." Camille exhaled loudly. "My parents are Raymond and Josephine LaRue. Music teacher and lawyer-slash-health food fanatic. No siblings, unless you count my dog, Poo. No crazy exes. No exes, *period.* So, definitely never been knocked up. Straight. I like colorful tights and wigs. That's quirky, I guess. And . . ." she paused, struggling to find the right words to answer his last question.

Nate's eyes sparkled, like she was about to spill the secrets of the universe. She wanted to tell him the truth. He had a strange way of pulling it out of her. But Camille wasn't sure if *she* even knew her biggest fear. She had a lot of them. *Running out of time. Dying with regret. Losing control. Letting the cancer win.* But she was afraid to say any of those things out loud. She took a deep breath. "My biggest fear, is fear itself."

Nate leaned closer. "I have so many questions. But first . . . do you mean to tell me your dog's name is Poo LaRue?"

She laughed, stunned *that* was the answer Nate chose to focus on. "Yeah."

"That's brilliant!"

"I think so. Especially when accomplished adults like my parents scold him for biting people."

"Poo LaRue is vicious? Even better. Please tell me he's a Doberman or Rottweiler."

"No, he's a Yorkie who hates everyone but me."

Nate grinned. "I must meet him!"

"I just told you he hates everyone."

"Pfft. No one can hate me."

She shook her head at Nate's optimism. But she was starting to think he might actually be right. His charm *was* hard to resist.

"So what else?" Nate asked resting his chin in his large hand.

"What else do you want to know?"

"Only your deepest darkest secrets."

Camille laughed, but she couldn't stop the nervous butterflies from rioting in her stomach. She knew Nate was joking, but it was nice to have someone want to know her. She shrugged. "There's not much to tell."

"Somehow I doubt that." Nate's brown eyes sparkled with mischief. He cleared his throat and spoke in a news reporter voice. "Miss LaRue, inquiring minds want to know what are your plans for life after graduation?" Nate asked, pointing the coffee cup at her like a microphone.

Camille swallowed hard. *Killing myself . . .* But she couldn't bring herself to say that either. It was too real, and she was having fun in this fantasy world where she got to be normal and flirt with a cute boy. So, instead she said, "Does anyone really know what they want to do with their life?"

"I do," Nate replied dropping the reporter voice.

"And what's that?"

"I'm doing it."

"What? Eating sugary desserts until you get diabetes?"

He laughed. "No. Well, not the diabetes part. I mean living. That's all I really want. To not let any moment pass me by. To take nothing for granted. To grab life by the balls and make the most of it."

Camille was silent as Nate's words resonated. Those were all the things she wanted too. All the things her cancer made her want, but denied her.

"You okay?" Nate asked, his warm hand suddenly taking hers. "You look pale, or I should say paler, which I didn't think was possible because I can practically see your veins through your skin."

A shiver ripped through her, but it wasn't from the chill in the spring air. "I'm fine. Just cold," Cami replied, hoping the lie would cover the depression that suddenly gripped her.

Nate shrugged out of his NOAH blazer and stood to drape it over Camille's shoulders. It was still warm and smelled like him —*soap and sunshine and possibilities.* She snuggled into it.

"Better?" he asked, smiling down at her, his caramel eyes full of hope.

Suddenly Camille didn't feel like playing this game anymore. Even flirting was useless. "Yeah. Thanks. But I should really get home."

"I'll walk you."

Nate refilled their coffees for the walk and chatted animatedly the whole way. He was easy to be around, even when she was feeling drained and depressed. Nate's warmth and excitement was like a giant bubble surrounding him. It was impossible to be near him without some of it seeping in—*even if she didn't want it to.*

"This is me," Camille said when they arrived outside her house.

"I know," Nate replied, grinning. "I was here yesterday, remember?"

"Right."

"Do I get to come in today?"

Camille gestured to the razor sharp clusters of spikes adorning the pillars and gates around her home. "I don't think we'd have so many Romeo spikes if I was allowed to invite boys like you inside."

Nate cocked his head, taking the spikes in with an appreciative eye. "Those are positively medieval, but they wouldn't keep me out."

"You might be surprised how effective they are."

"Oh yeah?" A devilish smile slipped into place. "Are you inviting me to try?"

"No. I'm just saying they've been protecting the virtue of daughters from heartbreakers like you for centuries."

Nate played hurt. "You think I'm a heartbreaker?"

She ignored him and unlocked the gate to her courtyard.

"You're really not going to invite me in?"

"No," she replied, even though a tiny part of her wasn't ready to quit their flirty banter.

Nate brazenly looked her up and down. "Are you a vampire or something?" he asked, his voice low and whispery.

The question caught her off guard and she sputtered a laugh. "Are you serious?"

"You're quiet and pale and you won't invite me into your home . . ."

"And that makes me a vampire?"

Nate shrugged. "I've seen a lot of teen movies. And this *is* New Orleans."

"You're crazy. Besides, everyone knows it's the humans that have to invite the vampires in."

"Spoken like someone who knows an awful lot about vampires."

She rolled her eyes. "Maybe I am a vampire."

"Or maybe you should think about getting some sun," Nate said catching her hand and stroking a finger down the blue vein on the back of her pale palm.

His touch sparked heat in her core. "I'll take it under consideration," she replied, quoting him. Camille started to shrug out of his blazer.

Nate put his hand on her shoulder to stop her. "Keep it."

"It's your school blazer."

"I'll get it from you tomorrow."

"We don't even have any classes together," she argued.

"I'll wait for you at your locker."

Camille was out of excuses, and the way Nate was looking at her, all dimples and sunshine made her forget why she was arguing. He was still holding her hand, and with his other, he slowly reached up, tucking a delicate strand of silver hair behind her ear. The warmth of his touch sparked electricity under her skin. His voice was a low whisper, his breath stirring her hair. "You're a mystery, Miss LaRue."

She huffed a nervous laugh. "I'm actually pretty boring."

Nate shook his head. "That's what you want people to think, isn't it?"

Camille swallowed hard.

"Tell me something real, Cami."

She could barely hear herself think over the thundering of

her heartbeat. She'd never believed in things like soul mates or love at first sight, but Nate was rearranging everything. He made her want things—*things she couldn't have.*

She wanted to reply. To tell him *he* was the mystery. And he was screwing everything up. She had a plan, and he wasn't part of it. But she couldn't find her voice. Not when she was standing a breath away from him. Nate leaned impossibly closer and her mind went blank.

"You know what I think?" he whispered.

Camille stared at the cupid's bow of his lips and shook her head.

"I think you're in love with me, Camille LaRue. You just don't know it yet." His face curved into his giant smile. "Don't worry. Some things are worth waiting for." Then, he kissed the back of her hand and jogged away, leaving Camille standing at her door, completely stunned.

Nate

NATE MADE himself wait before looking back. Tyler used to say if you could count to ten and a girl was still looking after you, then you knew you had her. But time felt like it was standing still as Nate's long legs ate up the ground, carrying him further down the street from Camille's Romeo spiked estate.

10 . . . 9 . . . 8 . . .

Wait ten seconds, Nate. If she's not still looking, you have to leave her alone.

7 . . . 6 . . . 5 . . .

People do not fall into the 'take what you want' philosophy of your new life.

4 . . . 3 . . . 2 . . .

But if she's still looking when you get to . . .

I . . .

Nate turned his head, briefly, and a giant smile slide into place. He was sure the joy in his heart could power the world at that very moment, because Cami was standing right where he'd left her, staring directly at him.

Game on . . .

7

Cami

Over the next few weeks, walking to Café Beignet after school became Camille and Nate's routine. And much to the Ashleys' dismay, so did Camille wearing his blazer. The only way she knew this bothered the Ashleys was because Ashley Dupree asked her about it in first period today.

"So, are you guys, like together?" Ashley asked.

Camille had to look around to make sure Ashley was really talking to her. "What?"

"You and the new boy, Nathan Hawthorne? Are you dating?"

Camille's face flushed. "No!"

"Then why do you wear his blazer to school every morning?"

Camille wondered what Ashley would say if she knew Camille also slept with it because she loved the way it smelled like Nate. She shook the pathetic thought from her mind. "We walk home together after school sometimes, and I get cold so I borrow it."

Ashley's pretty face wrinkled into a scowl. "Does he live near you or something?"

"Sorta."

Camille didn't know why she said that. Nate lived in the Bywater, which was nowhere near her house in the French Quarter. But from the envious glare Ashley was giving her, Camille had a feeling that for the first time in Ashley's privileged life, she was wishing she didn't live in the rich Garden District she called home.

Camille should've been a big enough person not to care that she had something the Ashleys were jealous of, but she wasn't. It made her giddy to watch them watching her with Nate. And even though nothing romantic had happened between them since the day he kissed her hand, Camille couldn't stop thinking about Nate—*and wanting more.*

She knew it wasn't fair. It was too late for her to fall in love. She knew it in her bones. But when Nate leaned close to her or smiled at her, Camille lost sight of everything—*even the cancer.*

AT LUNCH, Nate joined Camille in the student lounge. This too had become part of their routine. It seemed strange to her that she'd eaten nearly every meal at NOAH alone until Nate showed up. She could barely remember her lonely lunches lost in a book or a soundtrack. In just a few short weeks, Nate had changed everything.

Now, she couldn't imagine not sharing headphones with him, listening to music while he talked animatedly about what kind of songs he wanted to play on his violin, or some new movie or book he was in to. Nate did most of the talking, but

Camille thought it was nice to have someone else's voice rattling around in her head for a change.

Nate's other favorite thing to talk about was his brother. Camille couldn't help thinking his stories were so unbelievable they had to be true. And she loved the way Nate's face lit up when he talked about Tyler. Yesterday, Nate told her about the time he and Ty had streaked across their football field during a game. Their principal made them clean his bathroom as punishment. So Nate and Ty drew spiders on the toilet paper rolls and then put Pop-Its under the toilet seat. Nate said the principal's screams were heard throughout the entire school the next day.

Today, Nate was showing her a picture on his phone from when Tyler stained Nate's teeth blue for school pictures in ninth grade by mixing food coloring in his toothpaste. Camille snorted her herbal tea down her shirt when she looked at Nate's blue Cheshire grin. And of course that was the exact moment the Ashleys flounced into the student lounge.

They were hazing a group of young Antes by making them set up a folding table and drape it with a glittering silver and white tablecloth. By the time they were done decorating, it looked like Harry Winston spilled a diamond wonderland all over the lounge. And of course, the Ashleys decided to make their way over to where Camille and Nate were sitting.

Ashley Dupree ignored Camille completely, batting her eyes at Nate. "Well hello, handsome. Fancy meetin' you here."

There was nothing fancy about it. If the Ashleys noticed Camille was wearing Nate's blazer to school, then they certainly knew where he ate lunch every day. *Something was up, and it was most certainly of the variety that Camille wasn't going to like—as were all things that involved the Ashleys.*

"Hey . . . Ashleys," Nate said greeting them all at once. "What's up with all the glitz?"

"I'm so glad you asked, sweetie." Ashley's voice was so

syrupy it made Camille's teeth hurt. *Who did she think she was fooling?* Camille had seen Ashley Dupree make grown men cry with her cutting insults. There was nothing sweet about the girl.

Ashley invited herself to sit down and continued laying on the charm. "I'm on the prom committee, naturally, and the theme was just announced today, so it's time to start selling tickets."

"Cool. What's the theme?" Nate asked.

Ashley looked insulted that he couldn't tell from the glittery décor, but she smiled anyway. "Why it's *Just Say Yes*."

Nate's eyes lit up. "Like the Snow Patrol song?"

Ashley looked perplexed. "No. More like the philosophy."

Nate clapped his hands. "Even better. I'm in."

"Fantastic! How many tickets will you be purchasing?" she asked coyly.

"Two."

"Oh. Do you have a date already?" Ashley asked.

"I will as soon as Cami agrees to go with me," Nate said turning his radiant smile in Camille's direction.

For the first time, Camille felt Ashley Dupree's eyes shift to her. Pure hatred rippled off her, but her fake smile remained in place. She laughed playfully. "You mustn't be talking about Camille LaRue?"

"Why not?" Nate asked.

"Because I've known her since kindergarten. And she doesn't go to dances. Isn't that right, Camille?"

It was exactly right. Camille had never been to a dance. But then again, she'd never been asked. But even the idea of going to prom with Nate wasn't enough to make her overcome her fear of being judged by her peers on the dance floor. She'd made it nearly eighteen years listening to them whisper about how she didn't fit in. She didn't need to go to a dance and have them ruin that for her, too. At least if she never experienced the humiliation of a high school dance, it could still remain sacred in her dreams—*where it belonged.*

Camille realized Nate was staring at her.

His eyes sparkled in that excited way of his when he was cooking up an idea. “Oh, I get it. You’re waiting for one of those epic prom-posals.”

“No really,” she sputtered. “I—”

But Nate was already on his feet. “Say no more! I have much to do!” He kissed Camille on the cheek and loped off down the hall, leaving her alone with Ashley Dupree. She was glaring at Camille.

Ashley lowered her voice so no one else in the lounge could hear her. “You can’t possibly think he actually wants to be your boyfriend.”

“Why do you care? Don’t you have a boyfriend in college?”

“And don’t you have cancer?”

The words hit Camille like a slap to the face. She stood, grabbed the rest of her lunch and stormed off campus.

CAMILLE NEVER CUT CLASS. She always felt guilty about all the school she missed when she wasn’t well enough to attend. The truth was, she was a good student and enjoyed academics. When she was little, she told her father that she wanted to learn everything. She knew now how stupid that was. No one could learn everything—*especially someone who wasn’t expected to make it to her eighteenth birthday.*

Usually Camille didn’t let that get to her. But today, her desire to soak up the world’s knowledge wasn’t enough. What she really wanted was to get the hell off campus before someone saw her crying. That, and the fact that she was scheduled to work at Sweet Thang’s. She knew Nate would insist on walking her and she didn’t think she could handle his enthusiasm right now. Camille's boots pounded pavement, jarring her bones as she thought about how much she wanted to prove Ashley Dupree wrong.

CAMILLE WAS STILL FUMING when she blew through the open storefront at Sweet Thang's.

"Hey, baby cakes!" Ronnie called from the kitchen.

"Hey," she grumbled.

"Ooo. Somebody's in a mood. What's got your britches in a bunch, sugar?"

"Nothing."

"It wouldn't happen to be the certain tall, dark and handsome boy I see following you all 'round the Quarter like a lost puppy, would it?"

"I don't want to talk about Nate."

"Oh come on, Camille! I'm livin' through you. I've been with Hector so long I don't even remember what the thrill of the chase is like. Don't get me wrong, I love him to death. He's the gold at the end of my rainbow, but honey, sixteen years of lovin' the same man is hard work anyway you slice it. I need some young love in my life and if you ain't gonna give it up, you'll be the one explaining to Hector why I had to go off and get me a piece on my own."

"Oh my God! Fine. But only if you promise to never talk about your sex life again!"

Ronnie gave her a look that said he promised no such thing, but he also knew she was only teasing. Boy talk was what bonded them. And Ronnie always gave the best advice.

Camille sighed deeply. "I don't know where to start."

"How 'bout with what's got you so cantankerous today?"

"Nate asked me to prom."

Ronnie mock fainted. "The nerve of some people."

"But I don't do proms or dances, Ronnie."

"Why not?"

"You know why."

"Just 'cause you're sick, bebe, don't mean you can't have fun."

"I know . . . I just think it means more to Nate. And it wouldn't be fair."

"You still haven't told him?"

"No."

"Why not?"

Camille shrugged. "It's nice not having to talk about cancer all the time. You're the only other person in my life who treats me like a human rather than a lab rat."

"Listen to me, sugar. Do you like this boy?"

"Yes. I don't want to, but I can't help myself."

"Well, take my advice and get outta your own way for once."

"But he makes me want everything I can't have, Ronnie."

"Who says ya can't have love, bebe? That's what we're talkin' 'bout, right?"

She nodded. "But this is hard enough as it is. If I let him in . . . I don't think . . . I don't think I can say goodbye to someone like him."

"Camille, look at me. He's the one. I knew it the moment that boy followed you into this shop. He's the one you've been waiting for. I see it clear as day. And I know he's been through some hardships to get to you, so you better be brave enough to embrace destiny when it knocks on your door, child."

"Ronnie—"

"Don't you 'Ronnie' me. You know I'm not wrong about these things."

Camille let him wipe the tears from her eyes. When he was done, he handed her a hot pink apron, but didn't let go.

"None of us know how long we have, baby cakes. Love's a

gift and every ounce of it is meant to be cherished for how ever long we can hang onto it."

"I know."

"Good. 'Cause, sugar, that boy is the one. He's gonna give you the sky and all the stars in it. All you gotta do is let him."

Camille went to work refilling the salt and pepper shakers while she thought about what Ronnie said. She'd never really believed in all the clairvoyant voodoo nonsense Ronnie spouted . . . but then again, he was strangely right about a lot of things. Especially when it came to matters of the heart.

Women came from all over Louisiana to have Ronnie do psychic readings. He always said he knew his way around the heart better than the kitchen. Of course that didn't stop his love sick customers from buying out the place after a good fortune.

Ronnie had been telling Camille she'd meet a tall, dark and handsome stranger since she was a little girl. But he said that sorta thing to everyone. Although, a few years ago, he'd said something very specific, that had stuck with Camille. She hadn't given it much thought, until now.

Camille remembered the conversation perfectly. She'd been arguing with Ronnie, about finding true love, and how she wouldn't know it even if it bit her on the ass. But Ronnie said, "Don't worry, baby cakes. You won't have to look for it. He'll find you. And once he does, he's not gonna let go. It's gonna scare you, but don't fret, he'll know some things are worth waiting for."

Nate had said those exact words to her the day they met. In fact, he'd said it twice now.

Stop it, Cami. You're reading way too much into this. Just stop thinking about Nate.

Her phone buzzed and she pulled it out to see a text from Nate.

Nate: where r u?

Camille thought about ignoring him, but a flurry of messages lit up her phone.

Nate: did u go get donuts without me?
Nate: :-(
Nate: u ok?
Nate: do u have the sugar shakes?
Nate: walking alone is lonely.

Camille could see the text bubble blinking on her phone as Nate typed his next message. She knew he would just keep texting until she replied.

Cami: I'm at work.
Nate: sweet!!!! C u soon <3

So much for the ignoring Nate idea.

8

Nate

NATE GRINNED as he walked up Conti Street toward Sweet Thang's. The night air was cool and full of possibility. After school, he'd rushed home on the streetcar to fetch his violin, travel amp and supplies. He'd even changed into his lucky shirt. Tyler had given it to Nate to wear at the only skate competition he ever won, giving the shirt legendary powers. It was a bit small on him now, but Nate didn't care. It was the shirt's magic he needed. He paired it with his faded jeans, striped socks, black Converse and winning smile. *Who could resist saying yes to prom with this version of Nate? Hopefully not Cami.*

Nate ducked into a hardware shop two doors down from Sweet Thang's, sharing his plan with the shop owner. Once that was squared away, he went to work setting everything up. By the time he dragged his bow across the strings of his violin, the sun had sunk behind the old buildings, casting a golden glow over the French Quarter. It was times like these that made the city's magic tangible.

Closing his eyes, Nate let himself fall into his song. It was one he'd been working on for a while. It'd been incomplete until he met Camille. She was the missing ingredient the song needed. That was one of the many things Nate loved about his violin. He could pour his hopes and fears into it, and poetry came out—*and poetry was meant to be shared.*

Nate played louder and harder, until the city itself seemed to join in the song bleeding from his violin. The wind blew the chimes of the nearby palm readers. The *clip-clop* of the mule-drawn carriages provided the beat. And the steady buzzing of cicadas brought the bass. Nate loved that music could involve everyone, making individuals a part of something bigger for one perfect moment.

As the final note echoed down the narrow streets, Nate kept his eyes closed, cherishing the moment a bit longer while he steadied his breathing. When he opened his eyes, the view made his throat bob. Camille stood still as a statue in the street, her willowy silhouette illuminated by the streetlights. She was wearing a hot pink apron over her white t-shirt and black leathery leggings. Her long silver hair was braided over one shoulder. She looked like a bakery goddess and suddenly Nate wanted to lick powdered sugar off her for the rest of his life. *Focus, Nate!*

"What do ya say, Cami?" Nate asked pointing to the flickering tea lights he'd lit before starting to play. They were on the sidewalk in front of him and spelled out PROM with a question mark at the end.

She was either speechless or frozen, because she didn't reply, or move for that matter. She just stood there, staring at Nate like he was a lunatic. Which, he might be. *Because who threw together a prom-posal like this in a day for a girl he'd only known a few weeks?* But Nate didn't care. Especially not when it came to Camille. She made him feel alive. More alive than any of the other crazy things he'd done in pursuit of living since Tyler died. And somehow, Nate knew, taking Cami to prom was something he had to do.

"Sugar, if she won't say yes, I will," Ronnie called, poking his head out of Sweet Thang's.

At that Camille moved, swatting Ronnie away while hissing something at him that Nate couldn't hear. Ronnie retreated back into his bakery, but there wasn't much point. The storefront was made up of a massive garage door that was always open since the shop dished out sweets 24/7.

Now that Cami had reanimated, Nate asked his question again. "Will you go to prom with me, Camille LaRue?"

"Nate . . . I-I can't."

"Why not?"

"I don't really do that kinda stuff."

Nate raised an eyebrow. "Were you raised by a reverend that believes rock n roll should be banned?" he asked quoting *Footloose*, which was secretly one of his favorite movies.

Camille smiled. *She must've caught the reference, which made Nate like her even more.* "No. I'm just not into that kind of stuff."

"Are you into me?"

She bit her lip, but didn't respond.

Better than a no, at least. Nate sighed. "Okay, okay. I get it. I need to do better."

"No, Nate that's not it. This . . . I don't even have words for this," she said watching the blazing candles melt puddles of wax onto the sidewalk. She'd stepped close enough that the light danced over her features like moonlight on water. "It's not the way you asked, or you, it's just . . . I don't know if you've noticed, but I'm not really part of the popular crowd at NOAH."

"I know. That's part of the reason I like you so much."

Surprise flickered in her gray-blue eyes. "It is?"

"That and you know all the best donut places in town."

She laughed. "Seriously, Nate. Thank you. This was beautiful," she said, reaching out to run a finger over his violin. They were standing toe to toe now. "I think prom would be a letdown after this."

"Believe me, this is just the tip of the iceberg for us, Cami." His fingers met hers, sizzling with attraction on contact. Her eyes lingered on his for a moment and Nate felt electrified. Staring into Camille's eyes was like dangling off the edge of the world.

As if on cue thunder rumbled in the not so distance, making Nate jump. The gentle breeze from earlier picked up.

"You better come inside," Camille said looking skyward. "Storms roll in quickly around here."

Nate glanced at the threatening clouds, calculating how long it would take him to get home. Large drops were already starting to fall. He'd never make it to the Canal Street line without getting his gear soaked. And it wasn't like he needed to be asked twice to hang out at Sweet Thang's. The bakery had two things essential to Nate's life—*donuts and Cami.*

THANKS TO THE RAIN, Nate, Camille and Ronnie had the bakery to themselves. Ronnie let Nate pick the toppings for a new donut he was concocting and Nate had nearly keeled over when he saw the rows upon rows of candies, cereals and other delicious toppings stored in the kitchen. It was a sugar freak's dream come true.

Camille caught Nate drooling and smiled. "Impressive, huh?"

Nate grinned. "Not as impressive as your smile."

"Oh my God. It's sweet enough in here without your sappy one liners."

"Ignore her, sugar," Ronnie crooned. "I think it's darling. You can flatter me with sweet nothings anytime."

"Thanks, Ronnie," Nate replied. "Glad to see *someone* appreciates my sense of humor."

Camille stuck her tongue out and Nate's heart melted a little bit more. She was beyond cute. She was kitten-in-a-basket-of-yarn adorable. And the more time Nate spent around her, the harder it was for him to not wrap her up in his arms and never let go. His attraction to her was borderline smothering, and Nate found himself looking for something to distract him from the suffocating feeling in his chest. Luckily, he didn't have to look any further than Ronnie.

"So, Ronnie, I got to play twenty questions with Cami yesterday," Nate said.

"Did ya now?" Ronnie's cat-like green eyes darted to Camille. She glared back, communicating something unspoken. "Learn anything interesting?" Ronnie asked.

"Tons. But I was wondering if you wanted to play?"

"Oh, sugar, there ain't nothing ya can't tell from lookin' at me. I'm gayer than a chorus line and can cook my way to any man's heart."

Nate laughed. "Yeah, I was pretty much picking up on that."

"How 'bout we play a different game?" Ronnie asked, eyes sparkling.

"What'd ya have in mind?"

Ronnie pulled out a hot pink chair and sat down. "Ever had your fortune read?"

Nate stuffed his hands in his pockets. "Can't say I have."

"Well, then it would be my pleasure to pop your mystical cherry."

"Ronnie!" Camille scolded, coming out from behind the counter, her arms folded in disapproval.

"What? I'm not gonna make him do it. Besides," Ronnie dropped his voice. "I already know how all this works out," he said gesturing between Camille and Nate with a knowing grin. "In case you're wondering."

"I do, too," Nate said, with confidence. "She's crazy about me."

"You're both crazy," Camille muttered going back to polishing the spotless glass counter.

"Actually," Nate said, furrowing his brow. "I do have some other questions I'd like to ask."

"Ya see, Camille. The boy's practically begging me. Whatcha interested in knowing, bebe?"

"It's about my brother," Nate said, trying to keep the pain from his voice. For some reason it was easier to say Ty or Tyler. When he said the word brother, it held more power over him. Like that one single word summed up all of their relationship, making it seem that much more impossible that Tyler had been erased from the world.

Ronnie patted the chair, inviting Nate to join him. When he did, Camille cleared her throat. "I'll just give you two some privacy."

"You don't have to," Nate replied.

"No, I do. This is the routine," she said, like having fortunes read in the middle of the café was second nature.

Ronnie smiled. "The picture's always clearer when no one else's aura is around to distort it."

"Oh." Nate sort of wanted to ask Camille to stay. Not many things scared him. But whatever Ronnie might reveal about Tyler would be easier with Camille by Nate's side. *Everything felt easier when she was around.*

"So how does this work?" Nate asked once Camille disappeared into the kitchen.

Ronnie held out his hands, palms up, and Nate obediently placed his own hands in them. "Just think the questions you have in your heart and I'll do my best to see the answers," Ronnie instructed, giving Nate's fingers a little squeeze.

Nate closed his eyes and took a deep breath. He didn't really know exactly what he wanted to ask. At night when Nate was alone with his thoughts, all kinds of questions crept into his mind. *Like why did Tyler have to die? Why didn't they have more time? Would it every stop hurting so bad?*

Nate wasn't sure he'd asked anything, but the way Ronnie squeezed his hands told him otherwise. When Nate opened his eyes, Ronnie was smiling knowingly at him.

"Nathaniel, I know you already know this, but your brother is still with ya, bebe. The ones we love never truly leave."

"I know," Nate said, fighting the tightness in his throat. "But sometimes I-I don't know what I'm supposed to do without him. His life was cut so short. It's like I want to make him proud by living enough for the both of us, but I don't always know how to do that. And sometimes . . . sometimes it feels like I'm chasing something. I don't know if it's him or something I'm supposed to do. But I can never catch up. I can never catch my breath."

Ronnie's big hands squeezed Nate's. "Sugar, the only life you're meant to live is your own. And you're livin' it. Nuthin could make your brother prouder."

Nate nodded, but he couldn't help feeling let down. It was stupid to think Ronnie would actually give him some kind of wisdom from Tyler. Nate didn't really believe in that kind of thing anyway. And he knew Ronnie meant well, but his words felt generic, like something one of Nate's many grief counselors would say.

"Thanks," Nate murmured, his voice tight.

"By the way," Ronnie said, "Nice shirt."

Nate's heart leapt to his throat. "What?" *There was no way Ronnie could know Nate was wearing Tyler's old shirt.*

Ronnie gave Nate a familiar crooked smile and winked. It was so very Tyler-like that goose bumps raced up Nate's spine.

He squeezed Ronnie's hand and for the first time in a really long time, Nate felt a little less alone.

Ronnie let go of Nate's hands and fanned himself, returning to his natural charisma. "My, there are some good genes in your family tree, sugar."

"You saw him?"

"I see a lot of things," Ronnie replied. "But here's what you need to know. Your brother is okay. And you're gonna be okay too, bebe. But you gotta stop feeling guilty. You're here for your own reason."

"And I don't suppose you know what that is?"

"Some things are better learned than told."

Nate nodded. It may have seemed like a vague answer, but that was enough for him. He didn't want to know the particulars of his future. He always thought knowing something like that would shape the way he lived too much.

Nate started to stand, but Ronnie grabbed his hand.

"One more thing, Nathaniel. It's about Camille."

He sat back down.

"Camille is very special to me. She's not as tough as she wants everyone to think. She doesn't let many people in. But when she does . . . the girl's got a lot of love in that heart a hers. But I've never met anyone more afraid of it. Be careful with her, okay?"

"I won't hurt her," Nate said, meeting Ronnie's stern gaze.

"I know you won't. I think you could be good for her, but she won't make it easy on ya."

"I'm up for the challenge. Besides, the best things in life are worth fighting for, right?"

A sullen look crossed Ronnie's green eyes. He looked like he was going to say something else but instead he nodded before standing and walking toward the kitchen door. "Camille, it's time you take this boy a yours home."

She poked her pretty silver head out from the back. “Has he worn out his welcome already?”

“Never, but I can feel this storm gettin’ stronger. You better head out now while ya still can.”

“But I’ve got another two hours left,” Cami argued.

“Ain’t nobody coming out for sweets in weather like this. I’ll call Hector down to keep me company.”

“But my car’s at home. I didn’t drive today.”

“I know that, baby cakes,” Ronnie said giving Camille a knowing look. “But the rain’s gonna let up just about . . .”

The pounding of the rain stopped as if someone had simply switched off the faucet. It made Nate’s skin prickle. *Was Ronnie really that psychic?* But before he could ask the question, Ronnie held up his phone, smirking at the weather app showing the storm radar. “You’ve got about fifteen minutes ‘til it starts back up again. I’d run on home now if I were you.”

9

Cami

"So," Camille asked as she put her Range Rover Sport in drive. "How'd your reading go with Ronnie?"

"Actually, much better than I expected," Nate replied. "I don't usually believe in that sorta stuff."

Camille was still winded from running home from Sweet Thangs, but she managed a smirk. "Me either. But why'd you agree to do it?"

"I didn't want to be rude."

She couldn't contain her laughter. "That's *so* not a reason to let someone read your fortune."

"Yeah, you're probably right."

"I'm definitely right. What if he told you something you didn't want to hear?"

Nate shrugged. "Luckily, he didn't."

"Just be careful. Ronnie's one thing, but there are a lot of people in this town who will take advantage of you. You're way too trusting, California."

"And you're way too skeptical, Na'wlins."

"I'm not skeptical."

"Oh really? Have *you* ever let Ronnie give you a psychic reading?"

"No." *Not really much point in looking into my future when I know I'm terminally ill.*

"Well you should," Nate taunted.

"And why's that?"

"Because then he could confirm that I'm the man of your dreams."

Camille snorted. "Oh my God. Do you practice these lines in the mirror or something?"

Nate laughed, too. "No, actually that's one of Ty's. He was always way better with the ladies than I am."

"Oh." Cami was silent for a moment. "I'm sorry."

"Don't be. I like talking about Ty. It makes it feel like he's still part of my life, ya know? My parents never talk about him. They act like his name is a bad word. It drives me crazy."

"Sorry," Cami said again.

"You don't have to apologize."

"Right. Sorry. I mean . . ." she sighed. "Apparently I'm not good at this."

Nate grinned. "You're better than you think."

"So what did Ronnie tell you that made you a believer?" Camille asked after a while. "I mean, if you wanna share."

"At first, he just said a lot of generic stuff that I've heard before, like you're gonna be okay, you're allowed to live your life, blah, blah, blah. But then, he said 'nice shirt' and winked."

"And that changed your mind?"

"Ty gave me this shirt. I know it's stupid, but when Ronnie winked at me with that crooked smile, I swear it felt like Ty was right there in the café with me."

Camille watched Nate's wistful smile twist his features while she drove through the pounding rain. She'd never really believed in psychic powers or mediums, but she knew many others did. And the idea that people took comfort in signs from those they'd lost gave her a sliver of peace. "It's not stupid," she said quietly.

Nate took her hand and squeezed. "Thanks."

She drove like that for a while, in the silence, with Nate's hand wrapped warmly around hers. His thumb traced blazing circles on the back of her palm, and Camille was grateful the rain forced her to focus on the road.

She followed the GPS and pulled up in front of a narrow purple shotgun house in the Bywater. It had definitely seen better days. The porch roof sagged and the pillars looked weary under the weight. Even the stairs leading up the house looked unstable. There was a ratty couch on the porch and the front door was open, only protected by a torn screen door.

This couldn't be where Nate lived. The place looked abandoned. Camille was about to double-check her GPS when Nate interrupted.

"There's nothing wrong with Google maps. This is the right place."

She looked at him, trying to mask the shock from her face. "This is your dad's house?"

"Yeah. It's a 'fixer upper,'" Nate said using air quotes. "It's not as bad as it looks. I've been helping him renovate it. We've mostly been focusing on the inside, as you can probably tell," he said lightly.

Camille schooled her features. *Apparently she wasn't doing a very good job hiding her worry.* "Right."

"I'd invite you in," Nate said, "but it looks like the AC went out again. Thank God for the rain or I'd probably be sleeping on the porch again."

Camille's eyes widened with alarm. "Nate—"

"Kidding. I know it's not Casa LaRue, but it's nice enough inside. You don't need to look so worried."

"I'm not worried."

"Right," Nate said tucking a strand of hair behind her ear. "If your eyes got any wider I'd be able to see your brain, which come to think of it, might not be such a bad thing."

"Why's that?"

"Cause I think you only say about ten percent of what's going on in that pretty head of yours." Nate leaned closer. "Tell me what you're thinking, Camille LaRue."

"I'm thinking, if your house is so great, why are you still in my car?"

Nate grinned. "That's easy. I just want to enjoy our date for a little bit longer."

"This isn't a date."

"In my head it is, and this is the part when I kiss you."

"Okay, even if this was a date, I would *not* be kissing you right now."

Nate leaned back against the headrest and closed his eyes. "Shhh. You're ruining it."

"Ruining what?"

"Our first kiss."

Camille swatted him.

"Wow," he crooned.

"What?"

"You're a *really* good kisser."

She blushed but couldn't help laughing. "Oh yeah?"

Nate grinned and leaned over the center console until his face was mere inches from hers. For a brief second, Camille thought Nate was actually going to kiss her. And for an even briefer second, she kind of wanted him to.

Instead, Nate whispered, "Yeah," in her ear, sending a heat wave over her skin. He leaned back and unbuckled his seatbelt.

"Thanks for the ride, Cami. And thanks for letting me talk about Ty. He would've liked you."

"You're welcome. And I'm pretty sure I would've liked him, too."

"Good night," he said, giving her hand a quick kiss before grabbing his things and dashing up the rickety stairs to his house.

He gave her a giant smile and waved before disappearing inside. Camille waited a few minute before pulling away, just in case he'd been lying and the house really was inhabitable. But when he didn't come back out she backed out of his driveway, her heart heavy with the feeling that for once she'd have to change her plans. Because it seemed Nate needed her to let him in, more than Camille needed to lock him out.

Nate

NATE LAY on his back staring up at the cracked ceiling. The fan creaked noisily, circulating the humid air. He'd been right about the AC being out. But that was the least of his worries. His dad was having another bad night. Nate found him passed out on the couch with an empty bottle of bourbon in his hand. After getting him to bed and opening all the windows to get some air into the stifling house, Nate retreated to his room.

He couldn't stop picturing Camille's face when she'd pulled up to his rundown house. The place wasn't really that bad. It'd just been neglected for a while. With some rehab and attention it could easily be fixed up. The thought made Nate smirk, because it was basically an analogy for his dad. He hadn't always been such a mess. But after Tyler died, he just sort of fell apart. And instead of leaning on each other, his parents tore each other apart with blame over the accident. But it wasn't anyone's fault. Tyler was killed in a car accident. It sucked, but it wasn't anyone's fault. He lost control of his car. He wasn't drinking or on drugs. It was just an accident.

Nate studied the jagged crack that ran the length of the ceiling. It split off into dozens of tiny fissures that ran off in different directions. It was hard not to think of them as different paths his life might have taken if Tyler were still alive. *Would he be in New Orleans? Would his parents still be married? Would his mom have taken the job in London?*

She would absolutely freak out if she knew how bad Nate's living situation was. The house looked exactly the same as it did when Nate's dad bought it. His dad grew up in New Orleans, but moved to California for college, where he met Nate's mom. After Hurricane Katrina, his dad came back to NOLA to help the first responders. He'd stayed for a while, helping rebuild homes in his old neighborhood and apparently bought this house in the process. He'd supposedly been working on it on and off for a few years whenever he visited New Orleans while touring with his band. But from the looks of it, his father must've done more partying than fixing. *Half his dad's problem, according to Nate's mom.*

Nate thought back to what he and Ronnie had talked about. *All good things are worth fighting for.* Nate studied the cracks in the ceiling again. He would never have chosen this path for his life, but this was where he was now. His only choice was to make the most of it. And although he didn't normally put a lot of stock into Ronnie's type of fortune telling, Nate *did* believe things happened for a reason. He still wasn't sure why Tyler was taken from him, but this new path Nate was on had brought him to Camille, and from the moment he met her, he knew that he was meant to know her. *Now if only he could convince her of that.*

10

ami

Saturday morning Camille laid in bed with Poo, reading—*or trying to read.* It was sort of impossible to focus with the flurry of texts from Nate. She'd been doing her best to ignore them, but her stupid eyes kept wandering to the blinking notifications on her cell phone.

Nate: Good morning sunshine.
Nate: What do u wanna do today?
Nate: Wanna get donuts?
Nate: Come on, I know you do!
Nate: Are u at work?

She decided if she texted back she'd just be feeding his obsession, or whatever this was. When she'd dropped Nate off last night, she'd had a moment of weakness, thinking maybe she and Nate could be good for each other. But by the light of day, she'd come to her senses. Camille couldn't offer Nate anything. The sooner he knew that, the better.

She looked at her phone, contemplating the proper etiquette for confessing she had cancer via text. Sighing, she put her phone down and gave up. She'd just have to wait until she saw him. It would be harder to break the news in person, but he deserved that much.

For a moment, Camille thought maybe Nate got the hint, because the texts had stopped. But after a half hour of radio silence, the messages continued.

Nate: Not at work, huh?
Nate: Ronnie says hi.
Nate: He thinks you're being shy because we kissed.

Camille's cheeks flushed scarlet. She slammed her book shut and caved, finally texting a response.

Cami: We did NOT kiss!!!
Nate: In my head we did.
Nate: And it was . . . wow!
Nate: Come hang out with me.
Nate: Ronnie says u should take me to Café du Monde.
Nate: If you don't come out I'll just come over.
Cami: I won't let you in.
Nate: So you *are* home?

Crap. Camille didn't reply.

Nate: I'm coming over.
Cami: Don't come over.
Nate: Why?
Cami: I'm busy.
Nate: Busy thinking about me?

Of course she was busy thinking about him. Nate made it impossible to focus on anything else with his incessant texting. But even worse than that, he was right. Last night Camille's dreams had been filled with Nate. Laughing with him, touching him, kissing him. But she couldn't have those things. And the more she thought about it, the more upset it made her. She'd always known she wasn't going to get to fall in love and she'd made peace with that. But then this tall, sexy boy with his goofy California smile showed up and screwed everything up.

It wasn't fair—*to either of them*. Maybe Camille should just text Nate about the cancer already. If he knew she was sick it would scare him away. And it would be better for both of them if Nate gave up before getting more attached.

Camille was lost in thought when she heard the doorbell ring. Poo sprang off her bed, a barking blur of ferocity as he raced downstairs to the front door. Cami walked into the hall and peered over the railing. She saw her father walk out of his office toward the front door. Poo was already there, scratching, jumping and barking his little brains out.

"Poo! Bad Poo! That's enough," her father yelled, trying to

shoo the tiny dog away from the door with his foot. "I said no more, Poo!"

Cami was shaking with laughter at her father's word choices. And it only got worse when Poo latched onto her father's bare foot.

He roared, trying to shake the dog off. "Camille! Can you please call off your hound?"

But Camille only ducked her head back from the railing so her father wouldn't see her. She listened to him grumble as he scolded Poo before scooping up the crazed fur ball and opening the door.

She held her breath as she listened.

"Can I help you?" her father asked.

Please don't be Nate. Please don't be Nate.

"Hi, Mr. LaRue. I'm Nathan Hawthorne. I go to school with your daughter, Camille. Is she home?"

Shit!

Camille's heart was in her throat. She was wearing polka dot pajama pants and her Cedric Diggory quidditch jersey. And that wasn't even the worst of it. She had no wig or makeup on! Camille scurried back to her bedroom, trying to catch her breath. This had never happened before. No one ever showed up to surprise her. At least no one who thought she was a completely normal, healthy seventeen-year-old.

A few minutes later, her father knocked softly on her door. "Cami, you have a visitor."

"Tell him to go away."

"Honey? What's wrong?"

She cracked the door with tears in her eyes, revealing herself in her hideous true cancer patient form. "Dad, I can't let him see me like this."

Her father gave her a tight smile. "Honey, it's not a big deal—"

"Dad, he doesn't know!"

"Know what?"

Camille's eyes pleaded with her father for understanding. She loved him to death, but he was never good with understanding the workings of his teenaged daughter's mind. "About the cancer," she whispered.

"Oh! Okay. Um . . ." Cami could see the confusion wash over him. "Well, I'll stall him while you get ready."

Camille knew it was stupid. She'd already decided she was going to tell Nate she had cancer to spare them both the heartache of whatever this was. *What did it matter how he found out?* She could have her father tell him, or just walk downstairs without her wig or makeup on. That would certainly send Nate running. But deep down, a tiny part of her didn't want to give up the way that Nate looked at her—*like she was beautiful and worthy and normal.*

So she nodded to her father, watching him walk to the stairs. He paused to look back at her. "Honey, you know you're beautiful just the way you are, right?"

"Dad . . ."

"I know, I know, it's a *dad* thing to say, but it doesn't hurt to remind you every once in a while."

"Thanks, Dad. But please go distract Nate while I get ready."

He gave her a thumbs up. "I'm on it."

Camille closed the door and locked it, just in case Nate slipped by her father. She grabbed a pale lavender wig with shoulder-length waves from her hair tree, which was actually an old hat tree she'd painted canary yellow and used to house her array of colorful wigs. She secured her hairpiece and ran to her vanity to paint on her face. Her fingers were trembling as she drew on her eyebrows. *Breathe, Cami. None of this matters. It's all just an illusion. No matter how perfect you make it, he'll see who you really are soon enough.*

. . .

Nate

"So this is the famous Poo LaRue?" Nate asked when Mr. LaRue came back downstairs.

Camille's dad looked stunned for a moment as his eyes settled on Nate, scratching the tummy of the belly-up dog on his lap. "Looks like he likes you." Mr. LaRue said.

"The feeling's mutual," Nate replied in his dog whisperer voice, which pretty much sounded like baby talk.

Mr. LaRue chuckled. "Well you're gonna have to tell me your secret, because that shaggy mongrel doesn't like anyone but my daughter. I've got the scars to prove it."

Nate smiled. "No secret. Animals just like me."

"So, Nathan, is it?" Mr. LaRue asked.

"Yes," Nate placed Poo on the floor and stood to shake Mr. LaRue's hand. "You can call me Nate."

"Well Nate, it's nice to meet you. You can call me Ray. Cami's getting dressed. She'll be down in a minute. Can I get you a drink?"

"Sure."

Nate followed Ray into the massive kitchen where he poured them each a glass of iced tea. The LaRue's home was like something out of a magazine. Everything was larger than life and perfectly decorated. No wonder Camille had balked at Nate's house. From the street the LaRue's house looked like a historic New Orleans villa, but on the inside it was like a *Home & Garden* show room.

The kitchen ceiling vaulted up two stories, with gas lanterns hanging past the second story balcony. They hovered just above the white marble island, where fruit and flowers and cookbooks were perfectly arranged on the counter tops, like a cooking show was about to start filming at any moment. And the giant stainless steel refrigerator with the LCD touchscreen built in actually spoke, prompting Ray to enter the iced tea into his food diary.

"Nice house," Nate remarked as he sipped the unsweetened tea.

"Oh, I can't take credit. It's my wife's doing. She really has the touch for this sorta thing."

"I'll say."

"I'll pass on the compliment," Ray said, his dark eyes sparkling.

Camille looked nothing like her father. Where Ray was tall, with bronze skin, dark eyes, black hair and features that leaned toward Creole decent. Camille was small, fair-skinned and pale eyed. She seemed more likely to be the daughter of a fairy prince than the strong southern man standing in front of Nate. He wondered if Camille took after her mother as he followed Ray from the kitchen through a hallway of photographs. There were hundreds of pictures of Camille. Baby Cami, childhood Cami, preteen Cami, and the current brooding model that Nate adored.

He paused to study the photos. Young Cami had wavy brown hair, but her heart-shaped face, porcelain complexion and clear gray-blue eyes were still the same. In the preteen photos, her hair was a short pixie cut, then long and blonde, then pale pink, then black, and in the most current picture it was a silvery-gray that faded to lavendar.

"She smiled more back then," Ray said at Nate's side. He seemed lost in thought, a wistful look in his eyes. "I wish she smiled like that now."

"She smiles," Nate replied. "She just makes ya work for it."

Ray laughed. "Ain't that the truth?" His eyes cleared and he clapped a hand on Nate's shoulder. "Do you like music, son?"

"Love it."

Nate followed Ray into a massive room with exposed brick walls and hardwood floors covered in layers of expensive looking rugs in rich gold and red hues. A drum kit sat gleaming in one corner, a baby grand in the other. An impressive display of guitars hung on one of the walls, while the other housed a massive vinyl collection and numerous platinum records.

Nate felt like he'd walked into a musician's dream world. "It's like the Hard Rock Hall of Fame in here."

"Well that's about the best compliment you could've given me," Ray replied beaming as he sat down on the piano stool. "Do you play?"

"Yeah, a little." Nate definitely played more than a little. His dad taught him how to play guitar, piano and the violin, but Nate felt intimidated surrounded by so much greatness.

"Well give one of them a test drive," Ray said, noticing how Nate was staring at the wall of guitars.

"Really?"

"That's what they're there for."

"They look expensive," Nate said.

Ray waved him off. "Nah, I've been collecting them for years. I give music lessons, so most of them have too many hours on them to be worth anything. But that's what they're meant for, am I right?"

Nate grinned, plucking a powder blue Gibson Les Paul off the wall. "So do you play in town?"

"Nah. Gave that up when Cami was born. I teach at a local high school, do private lessons sometimes, but I mostly just fool around in here in my free time."

"Not a bad place to pass the time."

"My sentiments exactly." Ray swiveled toward the piano and started playing.

Nate instantly recognized the song and joined in on the guitar.

"You gotta plug it in if you're gonna play the Les Paul," Ray said nodding to the stack of amps. "That baby likes to wail."

Nate didn't need to be told twice. He plugged in and let the electric thrum from the Gibson reverberate through the room.

"That's it!" Ray yelled. "Crank it up."

Grinning, Nate turned up the amp and picked up the song. They got to the chorus and Ray shook his head. "Now if only we could convince Camille to join us."

"Does she play?" Nate asked.

"Better. She sings like an angel."

11

Cami

When Cami came downstairs to find her father and Nate rocking out in his office, she wanted to crawl in a hole. *I said distract him, Dad. Not make a best friend and form a rock band.*

She cleared her throat, but even that wasn't enough to break through their jam session. She decided to let Poo do what he did best, make a racket.

"Get 'em boy," she whispered and the little dog sprang into action, howling and barking like a crazed Gremlin. It worked like a charm. Both her father and Nate stopped playing and noticed Camille leaning against the French doors.

"Cami!" Nate called. "Sing with us?"

"Um, no way."

"Oh, come on. Your dad says you sing."

"Sang," she corrected. "And it looks like you two are doing just fine without me."

"You didn't tell me Nate here was a bona fide rock star," her father said.

"Yeah, well he should be. Charles Hawthorne is his father."

"No shit? You're Charlie Hawthorne's boy? He's a great musician. What's he up to these days?" Ray asked.

"Bartending at Vaughan's."

"I didn't even know he was back in town."

Nate shrugged. "Has been for almost three years."

"Where's he playing?"

"He doesn't really play anymore."

Ray's animated face went slack. "That's a damn crime! You should bring him over. Seriously, anytime. You both have a standing invitation to jam."

"Okay, Dad. Nate and I need to be going."

"We do?" Nate asked, looking surprised.

"Do you want me to take you to Café Du Monde, or not?"

Nate bowed low. "After you, Madame."

"Let me just go grab my purse," Camille said "Dad, can I talk to you for a moment?"

"Sure, honey."

Camille waited until she'd dragged her father out of hearing distance from Nate. "Dad, I said distract him! Not embarrass me."

"Since when does my music embarrass you?"

"It doesn't! That's not the point."

"What did you want me to do, Cami?"

"I don't know. Be a southern father and talk about virtue and Romeo spikes or something."

"Honey, I don't have any experience in this kind of thing. You've never brought a boy over before. You gotta tell me what you want me to do."

"Just be a dad!"

Her father smiled. "Do you like this boy?"

"Does it matter?"

"Yes."

"Well *you* obviously do," she shot back.

"Yeah, but I'm asking if *you* like him, Camille."

"I don't know. I need to go get my purse. Just don't adopt him while I'm gone."

Nate

When Ray returned to the music room, he seemed like he'd morphed into dad mode, asking where they were going and who else would be there.

"Cami's taking me to Café du Monde. I sort of have this obsession with donuts, so she's been taking me to all the best places in town. It's just us going. Although, Ronnie made me promise to bring him a bag of beignets afterwards."

"Ah, you've met Ronnie?" Ray asked.

"Yeah. He's great. Cami brought me to Sweet Thang's. I don't know how she does it. I'd eat myself stupid if I worked around all that sugar."

Ray laughed. "Yeah me too. But Josie would kill me."

"Is that Mrs. LaRue?"

"Yes." Ray smiled, his eyes crinkling in the corners.

"Cami said she's a stickler for health food."

"That's putting it mildly," Ray replied.

"Ya know, we could smuggle you a bag of beignets if ya want?"

"Nah, you kids go have fun. Just don't stay out too late." Ray's cell phone started buzzing. He glanced down. "Shoot, I gotta take this. Do me a favor, run up and tell Cami to bring a jacket. It's supposed to rain again today."

"Sure thing," Nate replied, but Ray was already briskly walking away.

Nate wasn't sure where Cami's room was or if Ray really intended for him to wander around until he found it. But, after sitting alone in the foyer with Poo staring at him unblinkingly, Nate decided to give himself a tour.

"Okay, Poo, wanna show me where Cami's room is?"

The little dog yipped and hopped around in circles at Nate's feet.

"Come on, let's go little guy. Where's Cami? Where's Cami?"

Nate followed the dog upstairs and around the iron-railed hallway to Camille's room. He knew it was hers because the door was cracked open and she was inside changing her top with her back to him. Nate's eyes zeroed in on her black lacey bra. It was such a stark contrast from her pale skin that he couldn't look away. He was mesmerized by her beauty. He knew he shouldn't be staring, but he'd never seen something so beautiful. She was like an elegant black and white photograph —*timeless and breathtaking.*

Nate was about to clear his throat to announce his presence, but Poo drew Camille's attention first. She whipped around, clutching her shirt tight to cover her chest.

"Nate! What the hell?"

"Sorry!" He immediately turned around and faced the door. "Your dad sent me up to tell you to bring a jacket 'cause it's supposed to rain."

Nate heard shuffling behind him as Camille grumbled under her breath.

"You can stop staring at the door," she muttered. "I'm dressed."

Nate turned, stuffing his hands in his pockets with mild embarrassment. "Sorry, I didn't mean to—"

Camille cut him off. "Let's just pretend it never happened, okay?"

"Okay. But I really didn't see anything, just your bra. I mean the back of your bra, really, and—Hey, sweet wall," Nate said, suddenly distracted by the colorful mural behind Cami. He moved further into the room, drawn toward the wall that was painted entirely black. It was covered in rows of neat white handwriting. Polaroids were taped next to some of the words with checkmarks next to them.

"Whoa! This is one of those *Before I Die* walls, right?" Nate asked. "I've always wanted to write on one and you have one in your room? How cool is that?"

"Uh, yeah. I guess . . ." Camille replied, still looking uncomfortable.

Nate decided to keep focusing on the wall until the awkward bra-moment passed. "Have you really done all these?"

"Only the ones with checkmarks by them."

"That's nearly all of them. Look, you only have *Graduation, Beach and Mississippi River* left. Wait, have you really never seen the Mississippi? It's practically in your backyard."

"I've seen the Mississippi. But I put it up there because I want to go swimming in it."

Nate scrunched up his face. "Isn't it kinda polluted?"

"Yeah, but it's a NOLA thing. If you're born and raised here, ya kinda have to do it."

"Right . . ." Nate let his eyes study the list, skimming over the items she'd checked off and the photographs accompanying them.

There was a family photo next to the word, *Picnic.* It was taken on grassy knoll and Camille looked like she was about ten or eleven. She smiled at the camera wide and vibrant. The word, *Origami,* was next, and a tiny butterfly made out of the page of a book was taped next to the word. *Drive in Movie* had a picture of Camille's booted feet propped on a dashboard, with a black and white flick playing on the big screen in the background.

"What movie is that?" Nate asked.

"Casablanca."

"Hmm, never seen it."

"Seriously? That's a crime."

"That good, huh?"

"It's pretty much my favorite movie."

Nate smiled, making a mental note to watch *Casablanca* immediately. He turned back to the wall. The next word was, *Hike,* and a photo of Camille's boots on a dusty trail accompanied it. Then there was, *Sprinklers,* with a photo of Cami's bare toes hidden in blades of glistening grass.

Nate stepped back, scanning the list. He wondered at what point Camille had decided to take photos of her feet rather than her face? His eyes fell back to the family picnic photo and he saw what her dad had been talking about. Camille didn't smile like that anymore. Or at least Nate hadn't seen it yet. And suddenly, he decided it would be his goal in life to do so.

He sat back on the bed next to Camille, smirking at the list. *Bicycle, Bird Watch, Bowling, Bubbles, Build Fort, Dancing in the Rain, Finger Paint, Fireworks, Fishing, Fly Kites, Handprint Art, Jump Rope, Magic Show, Mini Golf, Pillow Fight...*

"Your *Before I Die* wall is in alphabetical order?"

"So?"

"Living on the edge, huh?"

Camille only picked at the navy blue paint on her fingernails.

"What happens when you want to add a new thing to the list?"

"I don't."

"What do you mean?"

"I mean, these are all the things I want to do. I don't need to add anymore."

"What? That's crazy talk. I can think of like a million more things to add."

"I don't need to do a million things before I die, just the ones that are important to me."

"Well, then I can think of one really important thing that's missing."

"What?"

Before Camille could stop him, Nate was at the wall scribbling his name between *Mini Golf* and *Pillow Fight*."

"Stop it!" Camille leapt to her feet and grabbed the chalk from him.

"There," Nate said. "That's what you were missing."

"Is everything a joke to you?"

"No." He could tell from her pinched expression and watery eyes he'd hit a nerve. "Cami, what's wrong?"

"It's not funny, Nate. You can't just show up and insert yourself into someone else's life. It's not okay."

"I wasn't trying to insert myself. I just like hanging out with you."

"You don't even know me!"

"But I want to."

Cami

CAMILLE SAT down on her bed. She knew this was the moment she'd been waiting for. Nate said he wanted to know her. It was the perfect opportunity to tell him about the cancer, because it was pretty much her identity. *Camille LaRue—cancer girl.*

Poo jumped up on the bed and crawled into her lap. Camille knited her fingers through his silky tan and black fur. Nate sat beside her and before she could get enough courage to get the words out, he took her hand. And surprisingly, Poo didn't bite him.

"What do you think about starting today over?" he asked.

She laughed. "Too bad it's not possible."

"Sure it is. Give me your phone."

Camille gave Nate a weary look.

"Come on, play along."

"Fine," she muttered standing up to fetch her phone from her desk.

When she came back, Poo was sprawled across Nate's lap. The sight stopped Cami in her tracks. Poo hated everyone. Especially strangers. A chill ran through her as she remembered a conversation she'd had with Ronnie ages ago.

"I'm tellin ya, Sugar. That boy's gonna roll in like a hurricane and turn your world upside down."

"So does my mystery man have a name or am I just supposed to throw myself at all tall, dark and handsome strangers?"

"Don't give me that sass, baby cakes. All I know is your boy is out there and he's gonna win your heart. Hell, even that fussy little dog of yours is gonna like him."

"Now I know you're lying. Poo hates everyone."

CAMILLE HAD LAUGHED IT OFF. But now, as she watched Poo roll over in Nate's lap, she couldn't help but wonder if maybe—*just maybe*—it was another sign that Ronnie was right.

She handed Nate her phone, still in a bit of a trance from Poo's behavior. Nate didn't seem to notice as he tapped out both sides of a text conversation on their phones.

Nate: Good morning, Camille.
May I escort you to Café du Monde today?
Cami: Hello, Nathan. Why yes. That sounds lovely.

Nate: Splendid. I'll ring your doorbell at 11:11.

NATE HANDED HER PHONE BACK, grinning from ear-to-ear. "See how easy that was?"

Camille sighed, wishing it really could be that simple. She was about to protest, but Nate was already on his feet, and out the door. She watched his head disappear down the stairs, with Poo hot on his heels. A moment later she heard the front door shut. She peered over the railing to see Poo scratching at the door woefully. *Traitor.*

Camille glanced at her phone. It was 11:10. Any second the doorbell would ring, and she'd be greeted with Nate's brilliant smile. She felt her resolve begin to crumble. She didn't want to be the one to wipe that smile from his face. But she knew telling him about her cancer surely would. Honestly, she was surprised he hadn't figured it out by now. He'd been in her room, which displayed a *Before I Die* wall, and a shrine of wigs. As far as she knew, these weren't normal fixtures in a teenager's bedroom. And if Nate had really seen her in her bra, he must have noticed her scars. She'd had dozens of surgeries over the course of her treatment. Tiny scars crisscrossed her body like a roadmap of suffering.

Maybe there was something fundamentally wrong with Nate. Poo liked him, which wasn't normal. And from his ceaseless smile, it was obvious he saw the world through some intense rose-colored glasses. Perhaps losing his brother had distorted his reality—*because who in their right mind could possible want Cami?*

Ding-Dong. The doorbell pulled Camille from her dark musings. She jammed her camera in her purse and grabbed a jacket before rushing downstairs. Her father poked his head out of his office, still on a phone call.

"It's just Nate. I'll see ya later, Dad."

Her father looked puzzled, but nodded and ducked back into his office. Camille lured her traitorous dog into the kitchen with a treat and scurried back to the front door before Poo could follow. She opened the door and found herself stunned by Nate's smile. It was brighter than the sun.

"Hello, gorgeous," he said offering her his elbow. "Shall we?"

Camille was finding it was nearly impossible to say no to Nate. And on a day as sunny and warm as this, she decided to stop trying.

12

Nate

"Oh my God! I seriously don't know how I've survived eighteen years without beignets in my life. Does the rest of the world know about these?" Nate asked stuffing the powdered pastry into his mouth.

"I'm pretty sure they do."

Nate continued to cram large sugary bites into his mouth.

"Which beignets do you like better? Café du Monde or Café Beignet?" Camille asked.

"That's like asking me which parent I like better."

She laughed. "Fair enough."

"Just to be sure, though. I think you need to take me to every place that serves beignets in New Orleans."

"That might take a while."

Nate grinned, knowing full well his face was covered in powdered sugar. "Good."

Camille had taken Nate to the famous Café du Monde as promised. But instead of sitting beneath the iconic green and white stripped awning with the tourists, she led Nate up to what she called, the best seat in the house—the Moon Walk.

The beautiful riverside promenade curved along the Mississippi River, dotted with benches to enjoy the view while the gentle breeze offered relief from the constant humidity.

"So this is the place, huh?" Nate asked from his spot beside her on the sun-bleached bench.

Camille seemed lost in thought. "Huh?"

"Where you want to go swimming?" Nate prodded.

"Oh. Yeah."

"Well," Nate licked the grease and sugar from his fingers. "There's no time like the present."

He was on his feet, pulling his shirt over his head when he felt Cami's hands on his chest. "Whoa. No way," she yelped, pushing him back toward the bench.

"I thought you said you wanted to go swimming."

"I do, but not now."

"Why not?"

Camille seemed to notice her hand was still on his chest. It hadn't slipped Nate's mind for a moment. Feeling her hand above his heart only made it beat faster. *He wondered if she noticed.*

"I have a plan," Camille huffed. "And it doesn't involve swimming today."

"Do you have a plan for everything?"

"Pretty much."

"Well that doesn't sound like much fun."

"Not all of us can just do whatever we want whenever we want to, Nate."

"Sure we can," he said kicking off his shoes and scooping Camille into his arms.

She squealed but looped her arms tightly around his neck

as he headed for the river. There was a wide set of stairs leading straight into the water, as if daring them to walk right in—*challenge accepted.*

Nate marched toward the stairs with Camille in his arm.

She started to squirm. "Nate! Nate! No! We can't do this."

Nate only grinned at her, his face inches from hers. "Cami, it's time to live a little."

Cami

CAMILLE WAS SHAKING as Nate descended the staircase to the river. She could see trash collecting in the weeds below the levee wall. *He wasn't going to do it. He was just trying to scare her. He'd probably get right to the edge and stop.*

She'd seen enough teen romance movies to know this was all part of the flirting process. Scare the girl you like so she holds you a little tighter. Camille cursed herself, realizing she was playing right into Nate's hands. Her grip on his neck was practically lethal.

3 steps to the water. 2 steps. 1 . . . He was going to stop. He had to stop!

That's what a normal guy would do. But Nate was definitely *not* normal. When he stepped onto the last submerged step Camille screamed.

"Nate! Stop."

"I've got you, Cami."

He took one more step and they were in the river! The step dropped them down to Nate's waist and Camille shrieked, practically climbing up him like he was a beanstalk. Her legs were wrapped around his waist now and her arms clamped so tightly around his neck that his face was buried in her chest.

"Cami, I'm not complaining about the view, but I sorta need to breathe here."

"Nate, this isn't funny!"

"It sorta is," he said smirking up at her.

"My phone is soaked," she yelled.

"Mine too."

"And my boots! These are my favorite boots!"

"Cami, those are just things. Things can be replaced. But this," he said letting go of her with one arm, so he could gesture to the river. "This is living!"

She gripped him tighter. "Do *not* let go!"

"I've got ya."

"You're insane!"

"I know. It's fun, right?"

"Fun?"

But before Camille could reply, Nate took another step into the river, submerging them completely. She was shivering from fear and exhilaration.

Nate's eyes were shining. "Ready?"

"For what?"

"We're gonna swim. Unless . . . you weren't lying about the knowing how to swim thing, were you?"

"No."

"Good. Then let's go."

"Where?"

"To the next set of stairs."

"But—"

Nate had already let go of the railing and they were moving. Standing still against the current was impossible. They bobbed as the water got deeper until they were floating at a steady pace.

"Cami, we gotta swim. We'll both sink if you keep holding onto me like this."

Panic ripped through her and she shook her head rapidly. "I can't. I can't."

"Yes you can. Give me your hand. I won't let go."

Camille looked into Nate's bright eyes. The sun sparked off the gold flecks, making them glow. "I won't let go," he repeated.

It was as if those four little words had awoken some unknown source of bravery within her heart. She nodded and untangled herself from Nate, letting the churning Mississippi cradle her as they drifted down the river.

"Swim," Nate yelled, grinning like a fool.

She did.

"Kick your feet."

She did that too.

"That's it! Wahoo!" he screamed. "This is livin, Cami! No plan, just livin!"

She couldn't help but laugh. Her heart was soaring. She was doing it, swimming in the Mississippi River. This wasn't at all how she'd planned it. She'd been saving this task for last. Because Nate was right, the river was terribly polluted and Camille wasn't all that sure her weak immune system could handle it. She'd planned on going for a swim closer to graduation in case she got sick from the polluted water. But as she swam, her hand tight in Nate's, Cami suddenly didn't care that he'd blown her plan to smithereens. This was much better than the way she'd planned it.

The sun sparked off the water like glitter on glass. Seagulls sang overhead, and every time Cami looked over, Nate grinned back at her. He howled like a crazed *Teen Wolf* fan.

"Come on, let me hear you!" Nate howled again, and this time Cami joined him.

"See I knew you could go off script. You can thank me later," he teased, blowing her a kiss.

Camille splashed him. "Let's keep going."

"I've created a monster!"

"There's another set of stairs under the bridge. We'll climb out there."

"You sure?" he asked.

She nodded. "Just don't let go."

"Never."

13

Cami

Camille and Nate dripped all the way back to the stairs where he'd first carried her kicking and screaming into the river. He still hadn't let go of her hand, and secretly, she hoped he wouldn't. She couldn't stop giggling. Camille couldn't believe she'd done something so wild. A few tourists even gave them hi-fives as they walked by. She couldn't remember that last time she'd felt so bright and alive.

"I'm pretty sure we're on YouTube right now," Nate said, grinning spectacularly.

Camille bumped him with her shoulder. "You're a bad influence."

"Just you wait."

When they got back to the bench, Camille let out a sigh of relief. Her camera and purse were still under it with Nate's shirt, shoes and half eaten bag of beignets. She set her sopping boots on the ground and picked up her Polaroid camera.

"Come on," she said, tugging Nate toward the stairs.

"Are we going again?"

"No, just come here."

Camille led Nate back to the partially submerged stairs. They stood in murky river water and she faced him, moving closer until their bare toes were touching. Cami aimed the camera down and clicked a shot. They waited, nearly chest to chest, for the image to appear.

"I want one," Nate said, his breath tickling her cheek.

She moved a bit closer and snapped another picture. They sat down on the stairs, stretching out in the sunshine. Both of them comfortably silent, listening to the roar of the river and the call of the sea birds.

"I miss the water," Nate said after a while.

"Yeah?"

"Yeah. It's different here. In California, the ocean is everywhere. It's like the whole state has this constant breathing sound from the push and pull of the waves."

Camille's heart squeezed at the longing in his voice. "Do you miss California?"

She watched his throat bob as he swallowed hard, nodding once.

"I've never been. Will you tell me about it?" she asked.

Nate's face lit up as he talked about growing up in California, and Camille found herself imagining him wandering the sun drenched beaches he'd grown up exploring with Tyler. She could practically see the two of them surfing waves, tearing up skate parks, eating snow cones on the pier, playing music with their garage band.

Everything he told her was like a vibrant spark, stoking an ember to life inside her. Being like this with Nate was dangerous. He was all golden skin and coiled muscles stretched over smooth, hard lines. She followed the path of his torso to where his wet jeans hung low on his hips. His stomach was smooth and flat. He was thin, but muscles rippled below his skin. They funneled into a V that led beyond the waist of his pants. And Camille couldn't keep her eyes from wandering there.

A shirtless Nate was like a summer heat wave. The kind that made the humid air hazy when it rose from the street. That kind of simmering heat was hazardous. It made you see things that weren't really there. And that's what Nate did to Cami. He made her see all the things she wanted but couldn't have.

Nate

NATE GRABBED Camille's camera while she was soaking up the sun next to him. She looked so beautiful lying on the bank with her eyes closed, her mouth quirked into a slight smirk as she listened to him talk. The sun made her pale skin glow with an almost angelic quality. He aimed the camera and captured the photo. The click startled her, and Nate clicked one more photo, catching Cami's gorgeous gray-blue eyes wide with surprise.

"Hey," she protested, sitting up and snatching the camera back. "No photos while I look like a drowned rat!"

"You look gorgeous, as always," he said tucking a piece of hair behind her ear.

Miraculously, Camille kept her head above water during their swim. *Smart, since the water was pretty gross.* Nate had been careful to make sure he didn't swallow any. But even if he caught the stomach flu it would've been worth it to see Camille smile like she had when they'd climbed out of the Mississippi, howling with laughter. Her smile was even brighter than the one he'd seen in the family portrait on her wall.

Nate grinned to himself. *Mission accomplished.*

"What are you so smiley about?" Camille asked.

"Nothing. Just wondering what else we can cross off that list of yours."

"Oh no. I draw the line at one bucket list adventure a day."

"How 'bout something that's not on the list?"

"Like what?"

Nate plucked a wildflower from the bank and tucked it behind her ear. "Come to prom with me, Cami."

He watched her eyelids flutter as color warmed her pale cheeks. "Nate . . ."

"I know, I know. Just don't say no yet, okay?"

She hesitated, but after a moment nodded, a shy smile playing at her lips. "Okay."

Nate's heart skipped a beat. He hadn't expected her to agree. *He could work with okay.* He kissed her hand and pulled her to her feet. "Come on."

"Where are we going?"

"Home. I told your dad I wouldn't keep you out late."

Camille looked down at her damp clothes. "I can't go home like this."

"I have an idea."

14

Cami

CAMILLE COULDN'T STOP LAUGHING. Nate's brilliant idea had been to buy new clothes at a souvenir shop on Decatur Street. The rule was they could each pick out an outfit for the other to wear. Thinking Nate was going to choose one of the rude or hideous novelty t-shirts for her, Camille went all out, buying him a pair of gold lamé harem pants with *Who Dat?* printed on the ass, and a t-shirt that made him look like a topless woman covered in Mardi Gras beads.

When they exchanged bags and she pulled out a tutu made up of Mardi Gras purple, gold and green, and a white tank top that read *NOLA bride,* she knew she'd won whatever little game they were playing. They both went into the dressing rooms and changed into their ridiculous outfits. Camille could hear Nate's groan from the other dressing room. She had to stifle her giggles, picturing his face as he opened his bag. She almost felt bad—*almost.* But that thought quickly disappeared when she saw him come out of the dressing room, owning his new look. He shook his screen printed boobs and yelled. "NOLA gone wild! Give me some beads!"

Camille snorted with laughter. "You look incredible."

"I feel incredible," he said grabbing his fake boobs.

"This may be your best idea yet."

"Camille LaRue! Are you having non-scripted fun?"

"Oh shut up and shake your boobs already."

THE WALK HOME TOOK FOREVER. People kept stopping Nate to hi-five him or congratulate Camille on their marriage. And the looks all the uptight tourists gave them made every penny she'd spent completely worth it. To Nate's credit, he rocked his ensemble. He even earned a few beads from a street performer on the walk home. Camille couldn't remember ever laughing so hard. *It felt good.*

"So, what are we doing tomorrow?" Nate asked when they got to her front door.

"Tomorrow's Sunday," she replied.

"So?"

"So, it's sorta family day at our house."

"Oh."

Nate's crestfallen look made Camille want to take her words back. "Besides, I'm sure you have something better to do than spend everyday with me," she said trying to make him feel better.

He stuffed his hands in his pockets. "Not really. It's pretty much why I get out of bed in the morning."

He'd said it with his usual joking tone, but it tugged at Camille's heart the way nothing ever had. Suddenly, all she could do was look at Nate's big brown eyes and the gentle line of his perfectly kissable lips.

She swallowed, reluctant for their day to be over. "Um, do you want a ride home?"

"Yeah."

THE DRIVE HOME went faster without the rain. And this time, when Camille pulled up to Nate's, she didn't make a face even though the house actually looked worse without the rain to distort the extent of dilapidation.

"I had a really great time today," she said, truly meaning it.

"Yeah, I've been told I'm fun to date."

Camille rolled her eyes. "You *had* to ruin it, didn't you?"

Nate just smirked and closed his eyes, leaning against the headrest.

"Nathan Hawthorne!" she teased. "You better not be kissing me in your head again."

"You know I am. And it's a second date kiss. Steamy!"

"You're sorta building this up in your head. I think the real thing might let you down."

Nate opened his eyes and smiled in a way that took her breath away. He moved closer, his hand cupping her cheek while his thumb traced her bottom lip. "Not possible," he whispered. Nate's warm lips grazed her cheek. "Goodnight, Camille."

In her head she said goodnight, but in reality, she'd lost the ability to speak—*she'd lost everything, but the ghost of Nate's lips on her cheek.*

Nate

. . .

Nate lay awake staring at the cracks in his ceiling again. His heart was pounding. There was no way he was going to sleep anytime soon. Today had been the best day he'd had since Tyler died. And that feeling was both encouraging and terrifying. Nate loved the fact that he'd proven he could grasp that sublime joy that used to come easily before he lost Ty. Camille had a unique way of bringing it out in him. She was enchanting to be around, and it was impossible to look at her and not get lost in the glowing joy her shy smile evoked.

But at the same time, when Nate was with Camille, he thought about Ty less. And Nate was so afraid of forgetting his brother that it physically hurt. Sometimes he would think of Ty until he felt his throat tighten and tears prick his eyes. He wanted to be certain he could still remember every detail of his brother to the point of excruciating pain. Being able to call forth that familiar ache somehow made Nate feel less alone. And he was grasping for any way to hold on to his brother.

Nate closed his eyes and visions of Camille floated before him. If he thought he'd been drawn to her before, now he was obsessed. Seeing the fear in her eyes turn into a triumphant smile after they swam in the Mississippi was addicting. It'd awoken something in him, and Nate realized he'd do just about anything to continue to make Camille smile. *And don't even get him started about the way she looked when she'd climbed out of the river—all soft curves and wet clothes.*

Thinking of Cami made Nate want to do things that he barely had the willpower to control. But now, with the feel of her so sharp in his memory . . . the way she'd clung to him, her chest heaving against his, the trust in her eyes when she took his hand . . . he couldn't stop replaying it. Camille lingered near every time he closed his eyes. Nate could almost smell her lavender fragrance if he concentrated hard enough. He wanted to steal something of hers so he could keep it with him always.

Nate had never met someone so wonderfully intoxicating.

Camille was like a snowflake—fragile and unique—and he never wanted to let her go. But he was terrified the fierceness with which he wanted to hold onto her would shatter her loveliness apart.

He rolled over and looked at the Polaroid he'd taken of Camille. Maybe if he looked at her enough he wouldn't be constantly stunned by her beauty. *Yeah right. He'd have a better chance of winning the lottery than not losing his breath every time he looked at her.*

Nate thumbed through his collection of photos from Camille. He now had four. One she'd taken of him on the day they met, one of their feet in the Mississippi, and two of her lying by the river. She'd written *Goodbye Mississippi* on the photo of their feet. Nate thought back to the photos he'd seen on her *Before I Die* wall, realizing that they had *Goodbye* written on them as well. *What a sad thing to write after such a fun experience.*

Nate grabbed a pen and crossed out *Goodbye*, writing the word *Hello,* instead.

15

Cami

IT WAS NEARLY impossible to think of anything but Nate on Sunday. Luckily—*or unluckily*—Camille's phone was destroyed in their impromptu swim in the Mississippi. Otherwise, she'd be tempted to text him. Or at least see if he texted her.

Who was she kidding? It was Nate. He'd definitely text.

Camille was actually half surprised he hadn't shown up at her house already. She was dressed just in case—wig and makeup securely in place.

She'd checked *Mississippi River* off her wall and taped the Polaroid of her and Nate's feet to her bedroom wall last night after taking a long hot shower to wash the pollution off of her. She was still checking her temperature today, worried she might have swallowed some of the water, tempting her already fragile immune system to throw in the towel. But so far, so good. She'd survived another family Sunday, lying to her parents about her treatments and plans, trying to smile as they talked about summer vacation and college courses.

It was torture lying to her family. But she couldn't exactly say, *"Mom, Dad, those plans sound great, but I'm done. I've lived a good life. Much longer than any of us expected. But enough is enough. I'm tired of fighting and I've made my peace with it. I'm ready to say goodbye. And I want to do it on my terms."* They wouldn't understand and the worst part was, she couldn't even blame them. But her mind was made up. She was tired of fighting cancer. And she didn't have the energy to fight with her parents about it.

Camille was currently lounging on her bed with Poo in her lap. She was scrolling through Pinterest, which was never a good thing. She'd typed *Bucket List* into the search bar and was torturing herself by looking at all the things she didn't have the courage to write on her wall.

Damn Nate and his smile. It conjured infinite possibilities.

And now Camille was thinking about his smile, and how sexy it was, and how much she wanted him to kiss her for real and not just in his mind. *Ugh!*

Camille typed *Boyfriend Goals* into the search bar. That kind of torture was even worse than the bucket list torture. The bucket list photos were just dreams on steroids—unattainable things for even the average non-cancer diagnosed teenager. But a boyfriend . . . Nate was right in front of her, asking her to take a chance on him, to go on a date, to go to prom. And suddenly, she wanted to. She wanted all those things like a drowning victim wanted air.

This is so stupid, Cami! Get a grip.

But she was hopeless. She might as well just admit she had feelings for Nate.

"The sooner you admitted you have a problem, the sooner you can solve it," she muttered.

Camille was sure she'd read that in one of her coping with

cancer books. But the problem was, she didn't want to get over liking Nate. He was kind and funny and adorable in his own weird, addicting way. He'd snuck up on her and now that she'd seen inside his big, beautiful heart, she couldn't get him out of her mind.

The faint sound of the doorbell rousted Poo from Camille's lap. Her door was cracked open just enough to let Poo escape. Cami climbed out of bed chasing after him to spare her parents more scars on their toes from her ferocious guard dog. But by the time Camille got to the stairs she heard Nate's voice and her heart tripled in size.

"Hi Mr. LaRue. Is Cami here?"

"Hey, Nate. She is." Her father turned to call her, but Camille was already thundering down the stairs.

She greeted Nate breathlessly. "Hey, I was just thinking about you."

"You were?"

Camille couldn't believe she'd just blurted that out! And in front of her father! Luckily her mother walked into the foyer and saved her the embarrassment of answering Nate's question.

"Hello," her mother said. "May we help you?"

"Hello. You must be Cami's mom," Nate said grinning as he glanced between the women, noting their resemblance.

"And you are?"

"Nathan Hawthorne. I go to school with Cami."

"Josephine LaRue," she said shaking Nate's hand.

"I was just stopping by to see if Cami wanted to get beignets with me?" Nate said.

"I'd love to," Camille replied.

Camille's mother gave her a stern look. "It's Sunday, honey."

"I know but—"

Camille's father interrupted. "Ah, let the kids have some fun. We were just going to watch a movie anyway."

Camille had never heard her father disagree with her

mother, who presently looked stunned. But Camille wasn't about to wait for her mother to recover. She grabbed her coat and purse from the hall tree and dragged Nate out the door.

Nate

"So, you were thinking about me, huh?"

"Oh, shut up," Camille replied nudging him with her shoulder.

He could tell she didn't really mean it by the way her cheeks blushed, so he took a chance and reached for her hand. He couldn't fight his smile when she slid her fingers through his like it was the most natural thing in the world. *Because it most certainly was not.*

Everywhere their skin touched was like getting shocked by tiny pleasant bolts of electricity. Camille's touch made Nate come alive. He wanted to run his fingers over every inch of her pale skin. It looked especially radiant in the moonlight as they strolled toward Jackson Square.

"So," Camille asked. "Where are we going?"

"I told you."

"More beignets? Really?"

"Oh, did you think I was kidding about trying them all? I looked it up. Did you know there are three Café Beignets?"

She laughed. "Yes, but everyone knows the best one's on Royal, and I already took you there."

"Well, tonight we're going to the one on Decatur."

"Decatur? Really?" Camille practically snorted a laugh. "I didn't think you'd show your face on that street again after our shopping spree."

"It takes a lot more than screen printed boobs and shiny

pants to scare me, Camille LaRue. Besides, I have a new plan to woo you."

"Oh yeah?"

Nate smiled and held out his skateboard that had been tucked under his arm.

"Oh good, you fixed the death trap?"

"Yep and I'm gonna teach you how to ride it."

"Um, no way."

"Come on. I noticed it's not on your *Before I Die* wall."

"And neither is splitting my head open or breaking bones."

Nate stopped walking. His voice turned serious. "I'd never let that happen to you."

Camille gazed up at him, her eyes widening at whatever she read in his expression. "I know, Nate. I was just teasing." She ran a hand up his arm and it gave him goose bumps. "Are you, okay?" she asked.

"Yeah. Sorry. I think . . . never mind."

"What?"

Nate shook his head. He'd hoped seeing Camille would put him in a better mood. He wanted to keep things light between them. But today was the anniversary of Tyler's death. His dad was at work and he hadn't been able to get his mom on the phone, which only increased his bad mood. Nate hadn't planned to come to see Camille, especially after she'd told him Sunday was family day. *Who was he to steal her family time just because he didn't have his own anymore?*

He'd taken the streetcar to the French Quarter and rode his skateboard aimlessly through Latrobe Park for a while before he found himself standing at Camille's door.

She was staring at him now, her eyes like glittering satellites reflecting the full moon back to him. She took his hand, squeezing life back into his fingertips. "Hey, come on. Let's go get beignets."

THEY GOT their food and coffee to go. Camille was right, the Decatur Street Café Beignet had nothing on the quaint Royal Street location. The only advantage was Decatur Street was a stone's throw from the Mississippi.

Nate followed Cami back up to the wide promenade overlooking the river.

"I see why they call it the Moon Walk," Nate said gazing at the sparkling path the moon carved on the rippling water.

"Actually, it was named after Mayor Maurice "Moon" Landrieu . . ." Camille trailed off when she caught Nate's raised eyebrows. "Sorry, I know a lot of useless facts about New Orleans."

"I love that about you."

"Really?"

"Well, among other things," he said, nudging her with his shoulder.

"Like?"

"For one, you're a really good kisser."

Camille laughed.

Nate didn't think he'd ever get enough of that sound. "And . . . I love the way you squeal when you're scared."

"Hey! That was one time. And don't get any ideas, mister. Night swimming is *not* on my bucket list."

Nate smirked. "Noted."

Cami

CAMILLE FOLLOWED Nate to their bench—*not really sure when it became 'theirs'.* But somehow, sitting there together two days in a row seemed to make her feel a strange possessiveness toward it.

They sat side-by-side, sipping café au laits and eating beignets. It was nice—just being with Nate. He didn't have that need to fill the silence with chatter like most people did.

Camille watched him as he sipped his coffee, staring out at the river, his head bent, eyes following the boats trudging upstream. She liked him like this—*distracted*. She could study him up close, absorbing the perfect planes of his face. The breeze from the Mississippi played in the soft curls of his dark hair, exposing hidden places she wanted to touch—the nape of his neck, his temples, his forehead.

Camille studied Nate until the faraway look haunting his normally bright eyes began to worry her. "Are you sure you're alright?"

Nate seemed to come back from wherever he'd been. He smiled. "Yeah."

But his smile was only half it's normal wattage. *Definitely not alright.*

"What are you thinking about?" she asked.

"My brother."

Camille slid her hand into Nate's and squeezed. "Do you miss him?"

"Everyday."

She bit her lip. "How do you do it . . . still find the strength to be happy and smile after losing someone you love?"

"I'd be lying if I said it was easy." The smooth line of Nate's mouth hardened. "I feel like I owe it to him to be happy. Like because I'm still here I need to live enough for the both of us." He rubbed the back of his neck sheepishly. "It sounds kinda stupid when I say it out loud."

"I don't think so." Camille thought it sounded like the best thing she ever heard, and she wished she had someone to live for her. Someone to do all the things she wasn't brave enough to write on her wall.

"I'm really sorry about your brother."

Nate turned to face her. His eyes were bright again. "Don't be sorry, Cami. If you remember anything I ever say let it be this. Sorry wastes time. Ty never apologized for anything and my brother knew how to live. That's what I want. To live my life full throttle. I don't want people to say I'm sorry when I'm gone. I want them to say, 'that guy knew how to live'."

Camille was quiet for a while, letting Nate's words sink in. She finished her coffee while she pondered his philosophy. It was so simple, yet so perfect. Just live and don't be sorry for any of it.

She stood up and held out her hand to Nate, pulling him from their bench. "I'm ready."

"For what?"

"Teach me how to skateboard."

A surprised smile spread across Nate's handsome features. "Really? What changed your mind?"

"Some cute guy told me to live like I'll never be sorry. And I'll definitely be sorry if I pass up free skateboarding lessons."

Nate's grin ate up his whole face, returning his smile to its fully obnoxious level. "A cute guy, huh?"

Camille rolled her eyes. "You always focus on the wrong words."

"I think I focus on the right ones."

Nate put the skateboard on the pavered Moon Walk and took Camille's hands, guiding her onto the board. He kept a tight grip on her waist as she settled her hands on his shoulders. She was almost eye level with him, and that meant she was kiss level. The thought made her dizzy and she lost her balance, forcing Nate to pull her closer as the board zoomed out from under her feet.

"I think that might be enough for your first lesson," Nate said setting her down on her feet.

Camille's body missed the feel of Nate's the instant he let go of her. "One more time," she begged.

"Yeah?"

"Yeah."

Nate retrieved the board and helped her back onto it. "Okay, widen your stance a little. That's it. And bend your knees."

"Like this?"

Nate chuckled.

"What? Am I doing it wrong?"

"No."

"Then what's so funny?"

"I've never seen a pair of leopard print ballet shoes on a skateboard before."

"They're Tory Burch."

"They're hilarious."

Camille looked down. She laughed too when she saw the mash up of her leopard flats, green tights, and pale pink skirt above the skateboard. "I sorta wish I had my camera right now."

"Here." Nate fished his phone from his pocket and handed it to her.

"Yours still works after our swim?"

"Waterproof," he said smirking.

Cami had to let go of Nate's shoulders to take the photo she wanted of their feet and the skateboard. "Don't let go," she said, trying to hold still.

"I got ya."

And she truly believed he did.

16

Nate

CAMILLE OFFERED to give Nate a ride home once he'd walked her back to her house. Not wanting their time together to end, he'd quickly agreed. He said goodnight to Camille's parents and followed her through the courtyard to the gated driveway, where her sleek white Range Rover Sport waited in its stall. There were two Mercedes SUVs parked next to it.

Nate whistled low. "Sweet cars."

Cami shrugged. "I don't know anything about cars. Are you into them?"

"Not really."

"What kind to do you have?"

"I don't."

Camille paused. "Oh . . ."

Nate scratched his head. "I used to have a sweet old pickup

truck that me and Ty fixed up in Cali. But I sold it after his accident. Haven't driven since."

Camille turned toward him. "You don't drive at all?"

"Nope."

"How do you get around?"

Nate knocked on the deck of his skateboard.

"So you really haven't driven in three years?"

"No need. I've got a board, and I've always lived in cities with great public transportation."

"Wow."

"Wow, like what a freak, or wow like that's impressive?"

"Just wow," Cami replied. "I guess I just take driving for granted. I can't really wrap my head around not doing it."

Nate sighed, running his hand through his hair as he settled in the buttery leather seat of the Range Rover. "I know, I know. I should suck it up and drive already."

Camille put a hand on his. "You'll do it when you're ready. Don't let anyone push you."

"Thanks, Cami."

She nodded. "I hate being pressured into things. It's like other people always think they know what's best. You can't be bullied into doing things you don't want."

Nate caught the slight flare of her nostrils. Camille was speaking from experience, and the desire to find out who was bullying her and beat them senseless flared in his chest.

Cami

Camille pulled into Nate's driveway, and like clockwork he closed his eyes and leaned back against the headrest.

It was time to fight fire with fire. Camille closed her eyes too waiting to see how long it took Nate to notice she was playing his game. He interrupted the silence rather quickly. He must've noticed her eyes were closed because she could hear the smile in his voice when he spoke.

"Are you imagining we're kissing too?" Nate asked.

"Maybe," she replied, trying to hide her smirk.

"Here's a wild idea, how 'bout we kiss for real?"

Camille opened her eyes and flashed Nate a smile. "Maybe next time."

He grinned like a lunatic.

"Why are you smiling like that?" she demanded. "I didn't say yes."

"You didn't say no, either." Nate leaned in. "Thanks for tonight, Cami." He gave her a quick kiss on the cheek leaving her breathless and alone with a horde of wild butterflies in her stomach and miles of regret on her lips.

The whole drive home Camille thought of nothing but kissing Nate—*definitely next time.*

17

Nate

THANKS TO HAVING his skateboard back, Nate arrived at school early for a change. He was grinning like a fool as he approached Camille's locker. He looked around to make sure the coast was clear. *So far so good.* Nate set his backpack on the floor and carefully pulled out his supplies, working swiftly to be sure he was finished before Camille arrived.

When he was done, Nate stepped back to admire his handy work. *This is gonna work.* He snapped a quick photo with his phone and started stuffing things into his backpack. He was almost done when a group of guys in his grade sauntered by. Nate glanced at the clock. Camille would be here any minute. He was in a rush to get out of the way, but one of the guys stopped him.

"Seriously, bro?"

Nate grinned. "Seriously."

The NOAH student shook his head. "You're making the rest of us look bad. You know that, right?"

"Sorry, but she's worth it." Nate replied.

The boy laughed. "Well, good luck man."

Cami

CAMILLE RUSHED DOWN the hall toward her locker. She'd gotten a late start this morning. She still hadn't replaced her cell phone and the old alarm clock she'd dug out of her closet apparently didn't work—*which she found out the hard way when Poo woke her up with sloppy kisses demanding his breakfast.*

Camille hated rushing to get ready. That was always when something went wrong, like her wig glue didn't set or her eyelashes fell off. She had a strict routine for getting ready to ensure she'd show up at school looking as crisp and pressed as any other NOAH student.

She was so late she decided to drive to school, and kept glancing at her reflection in the rearview mirror to make sure she didn't forget anything. But her feelings of anxiety only grew as she scurried down the hall. She kept catching strange glances from students. And they weren't because of her hair color—which was a soft platinum blonde with wavy pink tips today. Everyone at NOAH was used to her colorful wigs and tights by now. *So what was the issue?*

Camille stopped short when she noticed a cluster of freshman girls in front of her locker. They were giggling and taking photos. It made Camille's stomach drop. *Did someone write something cruel on her locker?*

Her first thought was, *God, please don't let Nate see it.*

She pushed through the group of girls so she could see what they were gawking at. And when her eyes settled upon her locker, her knees almost gave out. Hundreds of tiny paper butterflies had been arranged to spell the world PROM with a question mark.

Nate.

She walked forward in a trance, feeling like she was in a dream world as she examined the butterflies. On closer inspection, she realized they'd been folded from the pages of a book, just like the one she'd made when she wanted to learn origami in sixth grade.

Nate's voice suddenly broke through her daze. "I used *Gone with the Wind*," he whispered. "Figured you wouldn't mind since you said people around here read it too much anyway."

Camille turned toward him. "Nate, you did this?"

"Yeah." His giant smile dimmed a bit. "Wait, did you not know it was me?"

Of course she knew it was him. How many people did he think were asking her to be their prom date?

But Camille couldn't seem to form words. Because behind Nate, a group of students were gathering, all watching her like they were waiting for some grand gesture. But this wasn't a movie. Nate wasn't going to sweep Camille off her feet and live happily ever after. A happy ending wasn't in the cards for her, and with so many eyes on her, Camille felt it more than ever.

"So what do ya say?" Nate asked, nodding toward the butterflies.

But Camille barely heard him. She couldn't tear her eyes away from the Ashleys, who'd just joined the growing mob of students staring at her like she was a circus sideshow. Ashley Dupree was glaring at Camille, and suddenly all she wanted to do was disappear.

"I'm gonna be late for class," Camille mumbled, and then ran down the hall without looking back.

. . .

Nate

Nate paced the lounge during his lunch break waiting for Camille. His stomach had been in knots since the locker incident. He couldn't stop replaying it in his head. He thought his gesture was romantic as hell, but Cami had run from him like he had the plague. Nate loved that Camille was different from anyone he'd ever met, but it certainly threw him for a loop when it came to asking her out. He kept reminding himself that the ordinary wouldn't be good enough for Camille. She deserved better. She deserved out of this world. But Nate was having trouble figuring out what exactly that was. *Apparently not paper butterflies, moron.*

Camille walked into the lounge and Nate hurried over to her.

"Hey, about this morning . . . I thought . . . I don't know . . . Did I totally freak you out?"

"No, Nate, I'm sorry. It's not you."

Nate held up his hands. "You're not about to give me the '*it's not you, it's me*' speech, are you?"

"But it *is* me," Camille protested. "I hate being the center of attention."

Nate let out a sigh. He was a complete jackass. His promposal had pretty much guaranteed the entire school was talking about Camille right now. He should've guessed that wouldn't be her thing. She already told him she didn't like going to dances or hanging with the in-crowd. She'd basically been screaming 'I hate attention' at him, and what did he do? Shine a spotlight on her. *Smooth, Nate!*

He slumped down in a chair at their usual table, running his hands through his hair in frustration. "So, I'm an idiot."

Camille joined him. "Nate, you're not an idiot."

"Really?"

"Well maybe a little bit," she teased. "But stupid *is* your thing, right?"

"Yeah." Nate gave her a half-hearted smile. "I'm sorry, Cami. I thought it would be romantic."

"You destroyed a library book and defaced school property for me. That *is* sorta romantic in a criminal behavior kinda way."

This time Nate laughed for real. "True. But I guess I can retire Criminal Nate?"

"Yeah. I think that's a good idea. Besides, I like Regular Nate, just fine."

Nate perked up. "Did you just admit you like me?"

"Don't let it go to your head."

"Too late." Camille's words made his chest fizz and pop. It was probably the best thing she could've said to him. *Game on!* "So, what are you doing tonight?"

"Working at Sweet Thang's."

"Cool. Ask me what I'm doing tonight."

She smiled, playing along. "What are you doing tonight, Nate?"

"I have a date tonight."

Camille froze, her forkful of salad suspended in the air. "Really?"

"Yeah. I met this really cool girl. We went swimming and skateboarding and tonight we have a date at Sweet Thang's."

"I take it back," she said swatting at him. "You *are* an idiot!"

Both of them were laughing when Ashley Dupree's syrupy voice interrupted. "What are you two giggling about?"

"Oh, ya know, just our love of *Gone with the Wind,*" Nate said.

Ashley's face lit up. "Really? Did you know I was named after one of the characters? I just adore that book."

Camille nearly choked on her juice with laughter. Nate had to pat her back.

"Yep, us too," he replied sarcastically.

"Well, what a coincidence. Anyway," Ashley smiled sweetly. "I was just stopping by to remind you to purchase your prom tickets. Clearly you're going after that charming prom-posal, right Camille?"

"Actually, not yet," Nate said, hoping to spare Camille the attention. But Ashley was already glaring in her direction.

"Camille LaRue! Don't tell me you didn't say yes to that enchanting proposal?" Ashley scolded.

Nate laughed. "It's a little game we like to play. Besides, I like a girl who's hard to get."

Ashley's hands were on her hips. "Well, if she won't go with you, Nathan, I'd be flattered to."

"Thanks, Ash, but I'm only going to prom if Cami does."

Ashley huffed, tossing her glossy blonde hair over her shoulder and sashayed away.

18

Cami

NATE WALKED Camille home from school as usual. Her new cell phone was waiting when she arrived.

"Finally!" she exclaimed pulling the phone from the box as she shouldered open her front door.

Nate followed her inside. Camille didn't have the energy to push him away today. Plus, even Poo liked the guy. So it seemed kind of inevitable that he was meant to be in her life at this point.

Camille knew sooner or later she'd have to tell Nate the truth about her cancer, but secretly she was hoping he'd just figure it out on his own. She hated having that awkward conversation. And in her own twisted mind, she sort of hoped the more time they spent together before he found out, the more likely he would be to stick around after. Because as selfish as it was, Camille liked having someone to hang out with other than her parents, Ronnie or her dog.

Nate lounged on her bed with Poo, while she changed in her en suite bathroom. She could hear him babbling baby talk to Poo and it was making it impossible to keep a smile off of her face. When Camille came out of the bathroom dressed for work, Nate was studying her wall again.

"Hey," he said. "How come you write goodbye on all your photos?"

Camille shrugged. "I dunno." *Liar.*

"Well, I think you should write hello instead."

"Hello?"

"Yeah. You know, like hello world, check me out. I just swam in the Mississippi!"

Camille laughed. "You really don't seem to get the concept of *'I don't like attention'*, do you?"

"I get it, but it's not true."

"What?"

"You like my attention," he said flashing a grin.

Camille's cheeks flushed. *True! Very, very true.* "Maybe," she admitted.

"Just not at school?" Nate asked.

"Nate, no . . . I dunno. School just isn't my favorite place. The girls there can be . . ."

"What?"

"Girls."

"What's that mean?"

"It means they're two-faced. They're nice to your face and then talk behind your back and I don't want to give them anything to talk about."

"Cami who cares what people think? Especially high school girls. We're graduating in a few months. We'll never see most of these people again. Let them say whatever they want. We live without apology, remember?"

"Right. I might need you to pound that into my head."

"Want me to spell it out on your locker?" Nate teased.

Camille rolled her eyes at him.

"What? Too soon?"

"Come on Romeo, I'm gonna be late for work."

Nate

NATE HELD his skateboard in one hand and Camille's hand in the other, swinging it playfully as he walked her to Sweet Thang's. Her moodiness from school seemed to evaporate, which gave him hope for tonight.

After the disastrous butterfly locker fiasco, Nate texted Ronnie to tell him to tone down the plans for this evening. Nate hadn't been lying when he told Camille he had a date planned for tonight. And with Ronnie's help and a little luck, he might be able to pull it off.

When they breezed into Sweet Thang's, the shop was buzzing with customers. Nate gave Cami a quick kiss on the cheek and told her he'd stop by later. He rode his board around back to the narrow alley the storefronts used as a loading bay. Ronnie had outdone himself. *Good thing Nate had said tone it down. He couldn't imagine what it would've looked like otherwise.*

Currently, one of Ronnie's hot pink bistro sets from the restaurant was set up under a few cords of white lights. There were white candles and a simple gold vase of white roses on the table, which was covered with white linen. The place settings were gold and glittering, and a white faux fur rug rested beneath it all. A mirrored dressing screen stood in the corner, draped with fairy lights for ambiance. In front of it was an old-fashioned steamer trunk, holding a basket of blankets and an old wind-up record player. Nate walked over to it and saw the album he'd asked Ronnie to find was queued up and ready to play. *Perfection.* The scene was simple, elegant and hidden away —*not at all attention seeking.*

Ronnie peeked his head out the back door. "Whatcha think?"

"It's perfect, Ronnie. Thank you."

"Not at all," Ronnie said waving him off.

"I've gotta run and pick up a few more things."

"Okay, bebe. Just text me when you're ready and I'll send our girl your way."

Nate listened to the rhythm of his skateboard wheels thumping over the pavement as he made his way down the busy streets of the French Quarter. He couldn't wipe the smile from his face and he knew he had Camille to thank for it. Nate was usually a happy guy, but since losing Ty, Nate's smile took more effort than it used to. Camille had remedied that.

Nate knew it was crazy. He'd only known Camille a short time, but already he was falling for her—*and hard.* He wondered what Ty would've said about it. He'd definitely be teasing Nate for crushing so hard, especially on a girl that was pushing him away. But Nate knew if he told his brother the truth, that this was it, Cami was the one—*and Nate was convinced that she was*—Ty would pat him on the back and give him one of those rare genuine smiles, free of his usual mischief. He'd probably say something encouraging like, "Go get your girl, little brother."

The thought made Nate grin. He hopped off his board and kicked it up into his hands. He nodded up to the sky, letting happiness expand in his chest. "I'm working on it, bro. I'm working on it."

Nate walked into UAL and a sales girl greeted him. "Can I help you find anything?"

"Actually, yes." Nate pulled a Polaroid from his pocket and handed it to her. "Got anything like this?"

She smiled. "Let's see what we can do."

NATE LEFT the store with a box tucked tight under his arm. He couldn't wait to give it to Camille. He was already picturing the look in her brilliant gray-blue eyes. Every time he looked into her eyes he saw a little bit more of her. And each glimpse helped him find a piece of himself again and keep hold of it. It was like she was helping him rebuild himself—slowly collecting the pieces of Nate that had shattered apart when Tyler died.

But Nate was finding as he put the pieces back together, the picture he was building wasn't just of himself anymore. He was collecting little puzzle pieces of Cami, too. Secret gems she tried to keep hidden. But they fit with his pieces seamlessly. Camille was entwined in Nate's life now in an irreversible way, and it gave him hope.

Nate checked the time. He had one more stop to make before heading back to Sweet Thang's.

Cami

"BABY CAKES, can you take the trash out back for me?" Ronnie called from the kitchen.

"Sure." Camille took off her apron and started gathering the trash bags.

"Thanks, sugar. I'd do it myself, but I can't leave the glaze when it's at this fragile stage."

"I don't mind," Camille replied. "Besides, it's sorta what you pay me for."

"Yeah, but I don't like making you do the heavy lifting 'round here."

"Luckily, your food's so good there's never much in the trash but napkins anyway."

"Camille LaRue, are you dishin' out compliments today?" Ronnie teased.

"Yeah. I guess I am."

"Well maybe you should try some on that boy a yours."

She rolled her eyes. "He's not my boy."

"He could be. You clearly like him."

"Stay out of it, Ronnie."

Ronnie put his hands up in surrender. "What do I know? I'm just a clairvoyant genius, who's never wrong 'bout matters of the heart!"

Camille stuck her tongue out at Ronnie as she backed out the door leading to the alley. But the strange brightness and music that greeted her made her turn around. She'd spun so quickly she almost missed the satisfied smirk on Ronnie's face as the backdoor to Sweet Thang's closed with a heavy thud, then a lock.

Nate was standing next to a bistro set, under rows of glittering white lights strung across the alley. He was wearing a bowtie and royal blue blazer with black velvet lapels, and his brightest smile yet.

"Nate? What is all this?"

"It's a non-attention grabbing, non-date."

"In an alley?"

"Yes! It's the exact opposite of the center of attention."

"But like nine other businesses use this alley. We can't just—"

He waved her argument away. "Ronnie took care of it. And he helped me make your favorite dinner. Okay, he did most of it, but he let me put the bacon on the sliders."

Nate guided Camille over to the table, and pulled the chair out for her, placing a napkin in her lap before taking his own seat. He unveiled the silver domed platter before her, which revealed sliders à la Ronnie, which basically meant extra cheese and chocolate glazed bacon. It was Camille's favorite meal in the world.

"Nate . . . I can't believe you did all this."

He waved her off. "Ah, it was nothing."

"No, I mean it. This is . . . really nice. Thank you."

His face lit up, rivaling the candles on the table. Camille fought back tears as she studied the beautiful date Nate had set up for her. She still couldn't quite believe it. No one had ever done anything like this for her before. And the fact that Nate brushed it off made her want to cry, because she suddenly realized how abnormal it was that she'd never been on a real date, or had anyone make her dinner other than her parents or hospital chefs.

Camille took a bite of her dinner to try to hide her emotions.

"You look really pretty tonight," Nate said.

She stared at him as if he were from another planet. Her pink and blonde wig was in a messy braid and she had at least one pen tucked behind her ear. She was wearing stretchy black jeans with holes in the knees and a worn-soft oversized gray t-shirt. She felt anything but pretty. Yet somehow, the way Nate looked at her made Cami believe she truly was—*at least in his eyes.*

And that subtle realization turned their non-date into something real.

"Thanks, Nate. You too."

He laughed, tugging at the lapels of his jacket. "I feel pretty."

Camille rolled her eyes, but smiled, happy to be back to their casual teasing. "You know what I mean."

"I got you something," Nate said, passing her a large box tied with a bow.

"What's this?"

Nate wiggled his eyebrows excitedly. "Open it and find out."

Camille carefully undid the bow and lifted off the lid. She dug through the layers of tissue paper until her hands wrapped around soft black leather. She pulled out the most stunning pair of black combat boots she'd ever seen."

"Oh my God, Nate! These are for me?"

"I felt bad about ruining your other pair in the Mississippi."

Camille stared at the boots. They were studded with shiny black gems from ankle to shin and the inside was lined with a pretty black and pink rose pattern. Plus, they had that buttery new leather smell. She hugged them tight to her chest.

"You like?"

"I love!" she exclaimed.

"Put 'em on," Nate insisted.

Camille pulled out the stuffing, kicked off her faded gray Converse and slipped the boots on. They hugged her feet like warm slippers and she wanted to sigh.

"They're perfect, Nate. Thank you so much." Camille stood up to give him a hug.

Nate wrapped her in his arms and she drank in his smell —*sunshine and possibilities.*

"How did you know my other ones were ruined?"

Nate loosened his hug, but didn't let her go entirely. "I noticed you hadn't worn them since we went swimming and then I saw them on your windowsill the other day. They looked a little rough."

Camille laughed. "Yeah, apparently my boots aren't a big fan of the Mississippi."

Nate pulled a Polaroid from his pocket and handed it to Camille. "I sorta borrowed this from your room to show the sales girl," he said handing a photo of her booted feet back to her.

"Sneaky. But how'd you get the size?"

Nate smirked, rolling up his jacket sleeve to reveal two marks on his forearm. "Traced it on my arm. You have surprisingly large feet for such a tiny girl."

"Hey! Don't you know you're not supposed to insult your date?"

"Wait? Did you just admit this was a date? Never mind. Don't answer that," Nate said quickly tugging her onto the mock dance floor, outlined in colorful sidewalk chalk.

"What are you doing?" she asked as he twirled her into his arms, swaying to the soft music coming from an old record player she was just now noticing.

"The shoes fit, but the true test is if you can dance in them," Nate replied, smiling at her.

He spun her again, and this time when he pulled her back, his hands found her waist. She could feel his warmth everywhere through the thin material of her t-shirt. Being so close to him made her feel like she was floating. She wasn't quite sure what to do with her hands, which currently had a death grip on the lapels of his jacket.

Nate seemed to sense her nerves. He drew her hands to rest on the back of his neck, one at a time and pulled her closer. "You're a good dancer."

She laughed. "And you're a bad liar."

"Just relax. Dancing doesn't require a plan, Cami. Just follow the music."

She let Nate lead her in a slow circle, but her heart was pounding so hard she could barely hear the music. There was something familiar about the song, but being in Nate's arms was intoxicating, and Camille found it difficult to concentrate on anything but breathing.

"I think this should be our song," Nate murmured against her ear.

His voice sent shivers down her spine and Camille strained to calm her nerves enough to listen to the song. Recognition hit her with the ferocity of a freight train. Nate was playing *'As Time Goes By'*. She would know that song anywhere. It was from her favorite movie.

She gazed up at him, emotion tight in her throat. "You watched Casablanca?"

He nodded. "You were right, that movie's great."

Her heart skipped. She wanted desperately to say, *you're great.* But she was afraid she might cry or worse, kiss him. Instead she leaned her head against Nate's chest and danced until the song was over.

They danced until the record skipped. Nate stopped it and blew out the candles on the table before taking Camille's hand again and pulling her down the alley.

"Wait. Where are we going?"

Nate grinned. "Our date's not over yet."

"But I'm not done working."

"Yes you are!" Ronnie called.

Camille and Nate looked up to where Ronnie and Hector were waving from their apartment window above Sweet Thang's.

"Ronnie! Who's in the shop if you're up there?"

"Quit worryin' so much, baby cakes. I gotcha covered."

"But—"

"No buts, Camille. I've been runnin' this shop since before ya were born. Now go out and be young for once, child."

19

Nate

"JUST FOLLOW THE GPS," Nate said for the tenth time.

"I am, but this would be easier if you told me where we're going," Camille argued.

"I told you, it's a surprise."

After Camille gave up arguing with Ronnie, Nate walked her home so they could get her car for the next portion of their non-date, which was starting to feel pretty much like a real date. Nate couldn't help noticing that Camille was the one who reached for his hand on the walk home. She also wore her new boots, smiling every time she looked down at them.

Now all Nate had to do was get Camille to Burgundy Street.

"Okay, park here," he said pointing to a street side spot on Marigny Street.

Camille gave him side-eye but parked without argument. Nate was beginning to understand that surprises could be added to the list of things Cami wasn't a fan of. But he didn't care. This would be worth it. He was determined to get to know more about her. And this was the perfect opportunity.

"Now what?" Camille asked once she turned off the car.

"Follow me."

Cami

Camille rounded the corner onto Burgundy, her hand securely in Nate's warm one. And when she saw where he was taking her, she was grateful he was holding onto her, because shock nearly buckled her knees.

"What is this place?" she asked in awe.

"It's NOLA's very own *Before I Die* wall. I looked it up on Facebook after I saw the one in your room. And I figured since you didn't want to write all over the perfect one in your room, we could work on this one together."

"I had no idea this was here."

Nate winked and pulled a pack of colored chalk from his back pocket as he led Camille toward the wall. It was massive, stretching the entire length of the old concrete building. Someone had painted it black and stenciled BEFORE I DIE . . . in bold white letters. Under the heading, thousands of statements and drawings layered and overlapped each other in colorful waves of chaos.

Camille read them as she walked up. *Hike a mountain. Go back to school. Buy mom a house. Make a difference. Want to live. Go to Scotland. See the world. Have sex everywhere. Apologize. Go to the moon. Forgive myself. Save all the cats. Conquer my fears. Stop war. I want to be seen. Spread love. Find myself. Save a life.*

The words flooded in. So many of them were thoughts

Camille had herself. She looked over at Nate, he was already scribbling something on the wall.

Show Cami something new.

Camille walked over and stole his piece of red chalk, drawing a box next to what he'd written, and then adding a checkmark to it.

Nate grinned, pulling out a new piece of blue chalk. This time he wrote, *Teach Cami that she doesn't always need a plan.*

She smirked, repeating her box and checkmark.

Nate pressed his blue chalk back to the walk and scribbled, *Learn something no one knows about Camille LaRue.*

Camille scrunched up her face, thinking of something clever to write. But when she looked at Nate and his gorgeous smile, all she could think about was how much she wanted to kiss him. The night he planned had been perfect, and it made her heart ache. Somehow, while she wasn't paying attention, she'd let this boy in and he made her want everything she couldn't have—*and she'd never felt more terrified of anything in her life.*

Camille walked up to the wall, but she couldn't bring herself to write an answer to Nate's question. As usual, he sensed her apprehension and lightened the mood.

"That was a broad question. How 'bout something more specific. If you could go anywhere in the world, where would it be?"

"I dunno . . . I guess I've never really thought about it."

"Come on! Play along. We're being held at gunpoint and a magic portal appears. It can take you anywhere in the world. Where does it go?"

"Um . . . maybe—"

"We're being held at gunpoint, Cami! Five, Four, Three, Two."

"Okay, okay! Paris! My portal goes to Paris!"

Nate's smile threatened to swallow the night sky. He nodded to the wall. "Write it down."

Camille wrote Paris on the wall and liberation spread through her like warm honey. They spent the next twenty minutes laughing and writing all manner of ridiculous goals, wishes and dreams on the wall. Camille doubled over in laughter when Nate wrote he wanted to star in *Rocky Horror Picture Show*. She followed that up with wanting to be a mermaid for a day, which Nate said was hot. But at some point, their goals turned real, and Nate wrote, *Before I die . . . I want to fall in love.*

Camille approached the wall and wrote directly under Nate's statement. *Before I die . . . I want to stop being afraid.*

Nate stood so close to Camille that their elbows touched. "What are you afraid of?" he whispered.

Camille brought her hand back to the wall and added, *of my heart,* to her previous statement.

Nate moved closer, tucking a piece of hair behind her ear. "Me too." His voice sent goose bumps racing across her skin. "Tell me something you're afraid of, Cami."

She shook her head. "It's your turn."

"Okay." Nate faced the walk and scribbled furiously. When he finally backed away, Camille read what he'd written.

Before I die . . . I want to kiss the girl of my dreams. Her name is Camille LaRue.

Camille took her piece of red chalk and drew a box at the end of Nate's sentence. Then she took a deep breath and added a giant checkmark. When she turned around Nate was standing in the moonlight, his face full of hope and apprehension. Camille took a step toward him, then another. Nate filled in the space that remained. His fingers lightly dancing across her jaw, drawing her lips to his.

At first his kiss was slow and timid, but the electricity it sent through Camille made her want more. She threaded her hands around his neck until she was entirely in Nate's arms. Her feet left the ground as Nate pulled her closer, kissing her fully. Her lips parted, letting him in as her fingers finally roamed his soft brown hair. She'd longed to touch his unruly hair for so long and it didn't disappoint. His hair was soft and full and she couldn't get enough of feeling it slide between her fingers.

Camille exhaled the blinding bliss building in her chest. She'd never felt so desired. Nate kissed her like he thought she might disappear. And his desperation only made her want more. Maybe tonight was a dream. Maybe the spell would end tomorrow. Maybe this was all the happiness Camille would be promised. And if that was the case, she wanted to soak up every ounce of it. Camille threw herself into the moment and kissed Nate with abandon.

There was something thrilling and forbidden about kissing on an empty moonlit street. And for the first time, Camille wasn't thinking about anything but Nate, and the feel of his lips on hers, the way their bodies fit together, the heat pulsing through her, and the pounding of her heart against his.

It was wrong. She knew each kiss was selfish and dishonest, but she didn't care. She felt alive and she didn't want to let go.

20

Cami

"Goodnight," Camille murmured for what had to be the hundredth time, but Nate couldn't seem to find his way out of her car. And she didn't particularly mind.

They'd kissed under the moon on Burgundy Street until a light rain started to fall. They ran back to the car in a fit of laughter, which doubled when they realized both their faces were smudged with colorful chalk. Wiping it off each other had turned into more kissing—*another thing, Camille didn't mind.*

She'd barely been able to tear herself away long enough to drive Nate home. And now that they were in his driveway, he didn't seem to want to leave. He leaned in and kissed her again. Both their lips were kiss-stung and raw, but Camille still couldn't stop. *She couldn't believe this was what she'd been missing out on for seventeen years.*

She ran her fingers over Nate's perfect face, trying to memorize every line and curve. He did the same and it sent fireworks blooming throughout her chest.

The buzzing of Camille's cell phone was the only thing able to break them apart. She saw it was her mother calling and answered.

"Hey, Mom."

"Camille. Where are you?"

"Out with a friend."

"I need you to come home, right now."

"Is everything okay, Mom?"

"Yes. Just please come home. I need to discuss something with you."

"What is it?"

"Camille. This isn't a discussion for the phone. I'll see you at home." Then she hung up.

Camille was stunned. *Her mother hung up on her!* She'd never done that before. *This wasn't good. Had she spoken to one of Cami's doctors?* A million thoughts ran through her mind.

"Is everything alright?" Nate asked.

"Yeah, my mom just wants me to come home."

"I didn't get you in trouble, did I?"

"If you did, it was worth it," she teased.

Nate kissed her again. "Goodnight, beautiful."

"Goodnight."

Camille waited until Nate disappeared into the house before letting out a tiny whoop of joy. *She'd just kissed Nathan Hawthorne!* And it was all she could think about. Well, that and the tiny fact that her mom was acting really weird. But that thought took a backseat as Camille drove home reliving her and Nate's make out session like it was a romance movie trailer.

Camille's phone rang again and she hit answer on her car's touch screen. "Hello?"

Ronnie's voice boomed over the speakers. "Hey, baby cakes.

Sorry to interrupt but I thought you'd wanna know your mama came lookin' for ya tonight and she seemed perturbed."

"Yeah she got a hold of me. I'm driving home now."

"Are you in some kinda trouble, bebe?"

"No. I think she just wants to go over some medical stuff with me. We haven't been able to catch up lately. You know how she gets."

"Well, as long as it's nuthin serious, tell me how your date went."

Camille squealed. *Actually squealed!* "Omigod! Ronnie it was amazing. He kissed me!"

"You go girl!"

"Ronnie, I swear I thought I was having a heart attack. My heart was pounding so hard I couldn't think straight or breathe or anything." Camille caught her breath and sighed. "Is it always like this?"

Ronnie laughed. "Oh baby cakes, you're in trouble."

"What? Why?" For a second Camille thought maybe she *was* having a heart attack as her heart flipped over in her chest.

"Because you're in love."

"No I'm not. I've just never been kissed. Which is sad and pathetic and now it's all I can think about."

"Sugar, you think I don't know love when I see it? You two are meant for each other. And what you're feeling, that doesn't happen from just any old kiss. That feeling is rare and meant to be cherished."

Camille's heart was pounding again and it made her voice soft. "Really?"

"Oh yes. But you gotta keep it real, baby doll. No more lying to yourself or that boy. You hear me?"

"Yeah. Thanks, Ronnie. I had a really good time tonight."

"That's good to hear, bebe. You deserve it. Now say hi to your mom an' them."

"I will. Goodnight."

Camille's heart sank when she hung up. Ronnie was right, and it deflated the cloud she'd been floating on. She had to tell Nate the truth. *That is if she survived whatever she'd done to make her mother so upset.*

Dread settled in Camille's stomach. She had a pretty good idea why her mother was so mad, and it was only going to get worse.

Nate

NATE FLOPPED ONTO HIS BED. He'd taken a cold shower when he got home, but nothing could wipe the smile off his face. *He'd kissed Camille LaRue—his dream girl.* Sudden bursts of joy kept seizing him and making him want to dance around the room or cheer like he was at a soccer match. Nate's heart was near bursting. He wished there was someone he could talk to.

As usual, his house was empty when he got home. But this wasn't something he could share with his dad. They weren't close like that anymore. It was the kind of thing Nate would've told Tyler. The thought evoked a stabbing sadness within Nate. But just as quickly, the pain was carried away by his memories of Camille's face. Her shy smile, her quiet laughter, the way her lips felt against his. Nothing could steal the joy he felt kissing Cami tonight. Not even missing Tyler. And for the first time since his brother's death, Nate felt hope lodge itself in his heart and outshine his despair.

21

Cami

Camille's mother didn't even wait for her to get inside before she started yelling. Her eyes were tearstained and she waved a bottle of pills around as she shouted. "How could you do this, Camille? How could you sit there and lie to us?"

"Mom—"

"No, it's my turn to talk, Camille, and you're going to listen. I want to know what your plan was. I found your medications. They've been untouched for months."

"You went through my room?"

"Well, I had to when the oncologist called to see if you planned to reschedule, *again*. Did you think you were just going to lie to us and pretend you were going to your appointments forever?"

"Not forever . . ." Camille whispered. "Just until I turn eighteen."

The color drained from her mother's face. "Then what?"

Camille couldn't meet her mother's eyes, but it didn't stop her from catching Camille's unspoken meaning. *Not forever, Mom. Just until I'm old enough to make my own choice.*

"No . . . Camille, no. We have been over this. You are not going to just give up. I know it's hard but—"

"You don't know anything!" Camille yelled.

Tears exploded from her eyes. She rarely cried in front of her parents, but her emotions were too close to the surface tonight. She was done lying and hiding. She knew this would have to come out at some point and she didn't see any reason it shouldn't be now.

Camille moved toward her parents, pleading with them to understand. "I'm done. I don't want to do this anymore. I can't live like this. The drugs and the treatments aren't helping anymore. They just make me feel sick and weak."

"But they give you more time," her mother argued.

"For what, Mom? I'm not going to get better. We all know that. And I'm okay with it."

"Well, I'm not!" her mother screamed. "We've worked too hard to get you here. You have to keep fighting, Cami."

"I *have* been fighting! But I'm done now. This is my choice, Mom. It's my life. And I don't want to spend the time I have left going to appointments and taking drugs that make me feel half dead. And I'm so sorry I lied, but I knew you'd be like this. And I just can't do it anymore."

"Camille!"

"No, Mom. I'm done!" The words came out with such finality they echoed through the room. Camille was shaking and she hated the look of devastation on her parents' faces. She pushed past them and ran upstairs to her room.

She heard her mother try to follow, but her father must've stopped her.

Camille collapsed on her bed, letting Poo climb into her lap.

She sobbed into his silky fur. "I'm sorry." She wasn't sure who she was saying sorry to—herself, her parents, Nate, Ronnie, Poo . . . there was a long list.

Poo licked her tears like he always did, which only made her cry harder. "They had to know this was coming, right?" she asked Poo.

Camille was almost eighteen. She'd far outlived her life expectancy after diagnosis. But it hadn't been much of a life for the past few years. She was grateful for everything the doctors and her parents had done, but enough was enough. Camille didn't want six more months of a half life when she could have three of a real life. It was simple math. *Why couldn't her parents understand that?*

But no one could. Only those who'd been through a debilitating disease knew how it continued to eat away at you on the inside, stealing bits of you away each day. And Camille had fought long and hard. She'd staved off the darkness and exhaustion that made her want to give up more times then she could count. But everyone had a breaking point, and Camille was at hers.

She had a plan and she was going to stick to it. Routine was what had gotten her this far. She just had to keep going a little bit longer. She needed to tick two more boxes off her wall. *Beach* and *Graduation*. Then she could finally rest and let go of it all. She even planned how she would do it. She'd been taking medicine since childhood. By now she knew what combinations proved lethal. She didn't want her death to be tragic or obscene. She just wanted to say goodbye to everyone she loved and drift off to sleep one last time.

She knew it sounded selfish, but deep down she didn't think it was. She was a burden on her parents. There were so many things they'd given up to provide her with the stable life she needed. Her father quit working to be her full-time caregiver when she was first diagnosed. And her mother worked constantly to be able to afford Camille's endless medical bills. It was time they got a chance to live again. And when Camille was gone, they could.

Her parents were strong. They would heal from this. And so would Nate. If he could survive losing his brother, she would only be a bump in the long, wonderful road of his life. She was just a girl that he kissed a few times. She didn't really matter to him.

But even as she thought it, Camille knew it wasn't true. Nate made her heart hurt in a way not even cancer could. He made her ache with love. And every second she spent with him would never be enough. She missed him even when they were together.

Her parents' voices drifted upstairs. They were still arguing.

"It's her choice, Josie. You know how much pain she's in. She's fought long and hard. If this is what she wants . . ."

"She's my daughter, Ray!"

"I know, baby. I know. She's my daughter, too. But we have to think about what she wants."

"She can't ask us to do this," her mother sobbed.

Camille couldn't stand to listen to her parents crying. She grabbed a hoodie, kissed Poo and climbed out her window.

Despite all Camille's talk about Romeo spikes, her house wasn't much of a fortress. It had been outfitted with fire escapes long before she moved in. Anyone wanting to break in only needed minimal upper body strength, because of course her parents kept the ladders in perfect working order—*God forbid a fire kill Cami before the cancer did.*

Her parents truly thought of every precaution. Even Camille's car was virtually a tank. She slipped into the driver seat and started the near soundless engine of her Range Rover with a push of the button. She hit the remote for the gate and counted the seconds to freedom while it slowly rolled open.

The benefits of having such a large house was that it was

easy to sneak out of. Especially when the cars were kept in the old detached carriage house that had been converted into a garage. All Camille had to do was take the fire escape to the street and walk in through the courtyard entrance.

While she waited for the gate to open, she kept the headlights off. She held her breath until she was a block from her house. She didn't really know where she was going, only that she needed to get away. She couldn't stay in her house a moment longer. It was sucking the life out of her—*at least what she had left of it anyway.*

By the time Camille knew where she was going, she was already there. She parked in Nate's driveway, still wiping tears from her eyes. She shouldn't go in. It was late and she was a mess. All she'd accomplish was upsetting Nate and ruining the memory of their perfect night by telling him the truth.

"That's what I deserve," she muttered to herself.

But then Nate would never kiss her again. He'd never look at her like she was beautiful and desirable. Again she was in tears. She couldn't do it. She couldn't ruin the only good thing that ever happened to her. She knew she was only delaying the inevitable. Nate would eventually find out she had cancer. But with the rest of her world crumbling around her, Camille only wanted to hold onto Nate tighter.

A knock on the driver's side window startled her. When Camille looked up, Nate was staring at her, a look of genuine fear in his eyes.

"Cami?"

The worry in his voice made her cry harder.

Nate tried the door handle, but the car was locked. "Cami, can you let me in?"

That was a loaded question. She shook her head. Her vision blurred so badly from the tears she was having trouble seeing Nate. It made it easier to not let him in. Because she knew if she saw his face, that would be it, she'd let him into her heart fully and he would tear it to pieces.

"Please, Cami. I need to know you're alright."

His voice was ripping her apart. She was already mourning her loss of his affection, which she knew was stupid, because Nate wasn't hers. Even if he wanted to be and she let him in, they couldn't have a future together. She could never belong to someone the way she wanted to belong to Nate. Camille belonged to cancer. And her destiny was written a long time ago.

"Cami. It's killin' me to see you like this. Please. Let me in. Tell me what's wrong so I can make it better."

"I'm sorry," she whispered, knowing he couldn't hear her. "I'm so sorry."

Nate

NATE POUNDED on the window when he heard the car ignition turn on. There was a desperation in Camille's gray-blue eyes that unsettled him. He didn't know what was wrong, but he couldn't let her leave like this. Not after the way he'd lost his brother. He wouldn't lose another person he loved to a car wreck, and Camille definitely shouldn't be driving in the state she was in.

"Cami, please let me in. I want to come with you, okay?"

She just kept mouthing *I'm sorry* as she backed out of the driveway, so Nate did the only thing he could think of. He leapt onto the hood. It must've startled Camille, because she slammed on the brakes and he slid into the windshield.

Camille was out of the car in a flash, screaming his name. "Nate! Nate! Omigod! Are you okay? I'm so sorry!"

"Well that's one way to get you out of the car," he groaned climbing off the hood.

Camille was shaking, touching him all over as if checking for bruises. Tears streamed down her face and she was whispering *I'm sorrys* like it was some sort of prayer. There was definitely something wrong, and suddenly Nate couldn't get his arms around her fast enough.

"Hey, hey, I'm okay. Camille, look at me." He placed his large hands on either side of her face and forced her eyes to meet his. "I'm okay."

Her pretty features crumbled as she wrapped her arms around his neck and sobbed. "I never wanted to hurt you."

"You didn't. I'm okay. I promise you, beautiful. I'm okay."

Nate held her for a while, and when her shaking stopped he pulled back to look at her. "What happened?"

"Can we . . . can we go somewhere?" she whispered.

"Sure. Where do you wanna go?"

"Anywhere. I just-I wanna keep moving." She hiccupped between sobs. "I can't-I can't stay here,"

"Okay. Let's go."

Surprising him, Camille walked to the passenger side and got in. Nate froze. He hadn't driven since Ty's accident. But as he looked at Camille, he knew she needed him more than he needed to hold onto his fear. He took a deep breath and opened the driver's side door.

22

Nate

"Do you want to talk about it?" Nate asked after a while.

They'd been driving for about thirty minutes. In that time Camille teetered between crying and collected about half a dozen times.

"I got in a fight with my parents."

Nate was surprised she answered. "About what?"

"Stuff."

"Stuff you wanna share with me?"

"I can't," she whispered.

"That's okay. But if you do wanna share, I'm here for you, alright?"

She nodded, and Nate reached over to take her hand. They drove like that for a while—filling the silence with all sorts of heavy things left unsaid. Nate wasn't sure what was going on with Camille, but he was pretty sure it was more than just a fight with her folks. He'd met them both. They seemed like good people. And Camille wasn't a problem child. She didn't skip school or get bad grades. This was definitely something more.

He knew he was a new addition to her life and he prayed he wasn't the reason for whatever this was. *The last thing Nate wanted was to get Cami in trouble.*

He knew it was no use worrying. Camille wasn't going to tell him until she was ready and he wasn't going to push her. The best thing he could do for her, was just be there. *That was something Ty had always been good at.*

Nate pulled off the road onto a dirt path, squinting for any signs of recognition. He'd only been here once before with his dad. It was years ago and during daylight. Nate prayed his memory served him.

"Where are we going?" Camille asked when they'd bumped down the dirt road quite a ways.

"My dad took me out here once. And I remember thinking it was a really nice place to just be. And if I'm right . . . Ah ha!"

Just as they rounded the bend, the road opened up into a dirt parking lot with a fence marking the mouth of the bayou. The headlights made the water glow green, like an alien planet.

Nate parked and turned off the lights. He cracked the windows a bit to let the night sounds in. Crickets, cicadas and bullfrogs picked up their songs, and after a while even the lightning bugs returned, floating across the lagoon like stars over the ocean. The moon was bright, but the thick trees filtered the light so it dappled the forest with thousands of tiny rays of light. When the wind blew, the shafts of light danced through the trees like a disco ball made of moonlight.

Nate turned to look at Camille. Her large eyes were illuminated by a moonbeam as she stared toward the water, looking utterly beautiful. She took his breath away. He didn't know when it started, but his love for her stretched farther than he could see—*like moonlight on water.*

He wanted to reach out and touch her, but sometimes Nate felt like Camille wasn't real. Like touching her would shatter her perfection. And tonight when they'd kissed, he'd felt like the luckiest guy in the world.

Nate offered Camille his hand and she surprised him by moving closer. She perched on the large center console so she could rest her head on his shoulder. She reminded him of a tiny bird trying to get warm. She didn't look comfortable at all. Nate pushed his seat back and tucked her into his side. It felt like heaven to have her next to him. He could've stayed like that forever, just listening to Cami breathe against him.

Cami

CAMILLE SOAKED up the peace she felt being so close to Nate. He was kind and patient. She loved that he didn't push her to talk or make her feel bad for acting like a hot mess in front of him.

"Thank you for taking me here tonight, Nate."

"You're welcome. I want you to know you can always come to me. With anything, Cami. I mean it."

She nodded.

"And I don't know what your fight with your parents is about, but just give it time. Time makes most things better."

She squeezed her eyes closed. *Time was the one thing she didn't have.*

Thunder rumbled in the distance and heat lightning lit up the sky.

"Do you want to head back?" Nate asked.

"Not yet."

Rain began to splash down and Camille watched Nate roll

up the windows. When he looked back at her, a huge mischievous grin had replaced his normal smile.

"Come on," he said opening the door, pulling her behind him.

"Nate! Are you crazy, it's starting to rain."

"Exactly!"

Camille stared at him through shielded eyes. She had no idea what he was talking about and her look told him so.

"Dancing in the rain!" Nate called over the thunder as the rain picked up. "It was on your *Before I Die* wall!"

"Yes, and I've already done it."

Nate only grinned wider. "Not with me, you haven't." He pulled her toward him and dipped her so suddenly that she shrieked. Before she had time to recover, he was spinning her around the muddy forest.

They danced among the lightning bugs and rain until Camille was dizzy with laughter. Nate hollered into the storm, coaxing her to do the same.

"No, I feel silly."

"It *is* silly, but it makes you feel better. Come on, Cami. Show me what you're made of."

She yelled, but the rain gobbled up the sound.

"You can do better that that," Nate teased.

Camille screamed again. This time she filled it with her anger at her parents.

"That's it! Let it out!"

She screamed again, for the cancer she hated and all the things it stole from her. She screamed until her voice was cracked and raw and her screams turned into sobs. Nate pulled her to him again, holding her tight, while she shook. He bent closer, brushing her wet hair from her cheeks as he kissed her tears away.

Soon he was kissing her lips and she pulled him closer, never wanting to stop. Being with Nate made everything else fade away. The warmth of him seared her soul. She could see steam rising from their drenched clothes. And suddenly she couldn't get enough of him. Nate was air and her lungs were starving. She ran her hands under his shirt. He was all lean muscles and tension. Camille gave the wet fabric clinging to him the slightest tug and Nate did the rest, pulling his shirt over his head.

His body in the moonlight was dizzying. She'd never seen such perfection up close. She couldn't think, and for once, that was a blessing. She let her body take control, kissing Nate like he was her salvation. He lifted her up like she weighed nothing. Camille wrapped her legs around his waist while Nate kissed her throat. She let out a moan of pleasure and Nate whispered her name like a prayer.

"Camille . . ."

Her hands were in his hair, pulling his face to look up at her. His eyes were ablaze and she couldn't remember ever wanting anything more. "Nate," she whispered. "I want you."

It was all the encouragement he needed. Nate quickly carried her back to the car. They stripped off the rest of their soaked clothes in the back seat steaming up the windows as their passion escalated.

Camille's hands explored Nate's body like it was a map to freedom. Their bodies molded together desperately—swells and hollows, muscles and softness. Nate's mouth roamed over hers, his tongue running teasingly along the seam of her lips. He ran his hands down her chilled skin and over her hips, drawing her firmly against him. Nate made a hungry wanting sound low in his throat, and anguish washed over Camille. Her body responded to his like they'd been made for each other.

Nate crushed her against him as if they could fit into each other's emptiness. "Cami." He panted her name between kisses, letting frantic words spill from his lips. "You make me feel alive . . . for once . . . I'm living . . . and I can stop running."

Her heart swelled. She wanted to say, *you make me want to stay alive.* But she couldn't. So she drew him closer still until there was nowhere to go but beyond. Camille shivered at the sensation of Nate pressing against her.

"Is this okay?" he whispered.

"Yes. Don't stop."

"Cami, we don't have to do this."

"I want to, Nate. I want it to be you."

He stilled, his eyes like molten amber. "Is this your first time?"

She swallowed hard but nodded.

"Are you sure?"

She nodded again. "I've never been more sure of anything in my life."

Nate

NATE HELD Cami tight until they both caught their breath. His body was trembling with exertion and emotion. This wasn't his first time, but Nate had never felt anything like this before. Being with Camille was indescribable. It was as if someone had lassoed his heart and tethered it to hers. Every beat of her heart echoed in his chest. And every time she touched him, she left a ghost of sensation behind.

Camille's cheek rested on his chest, her eyelashes fluttering against him. He kissed the top of her head drinking in her lavender scent. Nate twined his fingers through hers and whispered into the darkness. "You're beautiful."

Camille propped herself up to look at him, a shy smile playing at her face.

"I have to tell you something," he whispered.

"What?"

"I think I'm falling for you."

The biggest smile he'd seen yet, traveled across her delicate features. She tried hiding by burying herself in his chest but Nate wouldn't let her. Camille squeezed her eyes shut and bit her smiling lips.

Nate groaned. "Oh no, none of that."

"What?"

"No lip biting."

"Why not?"

"Because it makes me want to bite them."

She giggled.

Nate kissed her nose. "Come on, it's getting cold. Let me take you home."

"I don't think I'm ready to go home."

"My house then?"

"Okay."

NATE MANAGED to get his boxers back on and found a blanket in the back for Camille. Once they were on the road again, he asked a question he was dreading.

"Do your parents know where you are?"

"No."

"Would you let me text your dad so he knows you're safe?"

Camille didn't reply.

"It's not good to worry them, Cami. I know from experience."

"Okay, but I'll do it."

Nate watched her tap out a message on her phone. Satisfied he dropped the subject. Their night had been too perfect to push things. He drove the rest of the way home while Camille fell asleep. She was still passed out when he pulled into his driveway. Rather than wake her, Nate carried her into his house. She rousted when he set her on his bed.

"Where are we?" she asked her voice sleepy and soft.

"My room."

"Can I stay with you?"

Nate pulled her tight, still snuggled in her blanket. "Always, Cami. Always."

23

Cami

THE NEXT MORNING Nate drove Camille home. It was a blessing that his dad wasn't around when they woke up, which according to Nate was a normal occurrence. Camille was pleased to see that the inside of Nate's house wasn't as bad as the outside. *Well, his bedroom and bathroom at least.* She hadn't seen much else.

She'd expected to feel awkward after last night, but it was just the opposite. She felt at ease with Nate. He held her hand, kissing it every few minutes as he drove her home. They hadn't talked much, but they didn't need to. Nate brought a calmness to Camille that she seldom had. And it seemed she had the same influence over him. His jerky motions and quick wit were left behind in the bayou, stripping him down to the boy beneath. And Camille loved that side of Nate—the shy, quiet side, where he smiled softly and glowed just for her.

The closer she got to her house, the more she wished she could just wrap herself up in a cocoon of Nate and pretend the real world didn't exist. Camille didn't know how much time she had left, but one thing she knew was that she wanted to spend all of it with Nate.

"Are you sure you don't want me to come in?" he asked when they parked on her street.

"Yeah. I think it'll be better if you don't. There's probably going to be a lot of yelling."

Nate pulled her close and kissed her head. "Do you regret it?"

Camille looked up at him, eyes shining. "Not a single moment."

"That's my girl." He kissed her again and she clung to him.

"I don't want to say goodbye," she whispered.

"How 'bout hello?" Nate crooned, kissing her just below her ear.

"Hello," Camille whispered, giggling at how silly it was to say hello when parting.

"Until our next hello."

"Wait!" Camille exclaimed. Nate hadn't made a move to untangle himself from her yet, but already anxiety flooded her. "Ask me again," she insisted.

"Ask you what?"

"You know!" She was bouncing on her toes.

It took Nate a minute, but a sly smile split his face as he caught her drift. "Okay, give me a second." Nate teasingly cleared his throat and smoothed his hair.

"Just ask me already," she said impatiently.

Nate gallantly got down on one knee. "Camille LaRue, will you go to prom with me."

"Yes!"

Nate stood up, wrapping his arms around her. Cami

stretched to her tippy toes and kissed him on the lips before running breathlessly toward her house.

Nate

NATE SAT on the streetcar seeing nothing of the vivid scenery that rolled by. He could think of only Camille, replaying back their night together over and over in his head until it became as familiar as a fold in a page.

He hadn't expected anything like that to happen between them. At least not all at once. It was overwhelming. He'd only hoped for a kiss, but he couldn't help thinking he'd gotten himself a whole new world. Nate found it both comforting and intoxicating.

Before he'd met Camille, he'd wanted to see the world. Now Cami *was* the world. He should find that thought terrifying. He was eighteen, with his whole life ahead of him. But somehow, his life finally felt whole. And it was because Camille was in it. After last night, he couldn't imagine it any other way.

Cami

CAMILLE CREPT UP THE STAIRS. She couldn't believe she'd snuck in without waking her parents. It was early, but still . . . After the fight they'd had and the way she'd left, she expected them to be waiting up.

As she moved through the quiet halls of her house, Camille had a sneaking suspicion Nate might have texted her father in order for the National Guard not to be staking out her front door right now. Camille's text last night certainly wouldn't have warranted this level of calm. All she'd said was, *I'm somewhere safe.*

She found Poo curled up in her bed when she tiptoed into her room. She let him shower her with sloppy kisses.

"Hi Poo! Did you miss me? I missed you, too. You'll never believe the night I had. That's right, I was with Nate. We love him, don't we?"

Poo wiggled his furry haunches in excitement and Camille laughed. She sat on the edge of her bed. She was wearing Nate's t-shirt and sweats. They smelled like him and she wanted to bury herself in that scent. It brought images of last night flooding back to her. She couldn't believe the difference a night could make.

Last night she'd been at the end of her rope. Once her parents found out that she'd made her choice to stop treatment, it made everything so real and hopeless. But now—after what she'd experienced with Nate—Camille felt the unfamiliar tingle of possibility wash over her.

She stood up and walked over to her desk. Years ago, she'd pushed it up against the corner of her *Before I Die* wall to hide the goals she was too scared to attempt and too sentimental to erase. Camille grabbed the edge of the desk and with staggering effort, slid it away from the wall. It revealed four words.

Kiss. Love. Prom. Paris.

Suddenly they didn't seem impossible.

24

Nate

NATE HADN'T SEEN Camille since they spent the night together. Her parents were royally pissed. They took her phone away and grounded her. The only way Nate knew this was because one of her parents had texted back after Nate's five hundredth message. His money was on Ray, since the message wasn't scathing. It only said, *Cami's grounded with no phone privileges. Thank you for returning her safely.*

Nate figured Ray was doing him a solid since Nate texted him after Camille fell asleep at his house. The last thing Nate wanted was for her parents to stress out thinking she was missing. He'd seen what that kind of worry did to his own parents the night Tyler didn't come home.

Thinking about everything his parents had gone through losing Ty made Nate extra attentive over the weekend. He called his mom and told her all about Camille. And Sunday, his dad surprised him by being home, and sober. They spent the day together working on the house. The inside was really starting to come together. And Nate enjoyed catching up with his dad. He actually asked what Nate was up to, so he took the opportunity to tell him about Camille, too.

"Sounds pretty serious," his dad said.

"Yeah, I really like her, Dad. It's sorta scaring me."

"Good, it should. Love's not something for the faint of heart."

It struck Nate as a strange thing to say, but then again his dad was pretty jaded when it came to relationships. "We're going to prom," Nate added. "I'm weirdly excited."

"You, excited?" his dad teased. "Shocking."

"Yeah, yeah."

"No, I get it. Believe it or not, I remember those days. All nerves and excitement."

"You do?"

His dad laughed. "I'm not dead, Nate. Just old."

Nate was quiet for a while. He'd never seen his dad date or flirt or really show much emotion at all since the divorce. The only comfort he sought was in the bottom of a bourbon bottle. So it was strange thinking of him in Nate's shoes, young and in love. And the more Nate thought about it, the more he realized that's what this was with Cami—*love*.

"She's stolen my heart, Dad. I feel sick when she's not around. I think I'm in love with her."

His father chuckled. "Yep, sounds like it to me."

"Was it like that when you met Mom?" Nate asked.

His dad had been smoothing spackle over the seams in the drywall when Nate asked the question. He stopped, looking lost in thought for a moment before responding. "Yeah. It was."

"Do you miss her?"

His dad sighed, turning to face him. "Listen to me, Nate. I've made a lot of mistakes in my life, but the one I regret the most is not letting the people I love know just how much they mean to me. I haven't been a good role model to you. And for that, I'm sorry. But it's clear your mother did a good job with you. And I'll always love her because of it."

"You did a good job, too, Dad."

His dad waved him away and started back on the spackle.

"No, I mean it. You taught me music, and without that . . ." Nate paused and his dad was looking at him again. "Sometimes I think I couldn't have made it through everything without music."

Shadows swam in his dad's eyes and he pulled Nate into a gruff one-armed hug. The surge of emotion threatened to overwhelm Nate. His dad wasn't usually an affectionate man. Nate couldn't remember the last time he hugged him.

"I love you, son."

"I love you too, Dad."

MONDAY FINALLY ARRIVED and Nate was on cloud nine. Though he would've rather spent the weekend with Camille, he found he enjoyed getting to spend some time with his dad. But now that the school was in view, Nate only had thoughts of Cami. He practically sprinted up the stairs to her locker. Disappointment flooded him when she didn't show up. He checked the time. *There was no way he missed her. He'd gotten to campus extra early just to be sure.*

Nate reluctantly went to class, planning to find Camille after first period. He'd memorized her schedule weeks ago so he could walk her from class to class. But by the time lunch rolled around and Nate still hadn't found Camille, he started to worry. He scanned the lounge, but the sea of students revealed nothing extraordinary. No vibrant colored hair or wild tights brightened the sea of plaid uniforms and blazers, and Nate's heart sank.

One of the Ashleys walked up to Nate. He could never tell them apart. They all had the same blonde hair and wore too much perfume. The unremarkable blonde took Camille's usual seat next to Nate, which made him unreasonably irritated.

"Hey there, handsome," she crooned.

Ugh. It was Ashley Dupree. Her fake syrupy voice gave her away. "Hey," he grumbled.

"Any luck getting Camille to be your prom date?"

"Um . . ." Nate wanted to say it was none of her f-ing business, but was searching for more polite wording.

Ashley took the pause as a no. "You know, I could get her nominated for prom queen. Then she'd have to go. Don't you think that'd be great?"

Something made Nate think Cami wouldn't think so. Prom queen seemed like the last thing a girl who hated the spotlight would want. Nate was about to tell Ashley that but the girl never stopped talking.

"Well, I think it would be just peachy. I know everyone would be happy to do it for poor, sweet Camille. And if she's on the court she has to go, and that means you'll go too, right?"

"Of course, but," Nate said starting to stand, but Ashley grabbed his hand, her long manicured fingernails grazing his skin like talons.

"Tell you what, Nathan. Since you're new to NOAH I'm going to do you a favor and give you your prom ticket." She added, "On the house," in what he guessed Ashley thought was a seductive tone.

"Oh. Um, thanks, Ash, but I sorta need two tickets."

She giggled. "Oh I'm on the prom court silly, I already have my ticket, but I'd love to go as your date.

Nate almost choked on his soda. "No. Uh, I meant for Camille. She's my date."

"Nathan, I said I'll get her on the court. She won't need a ticket. And I feel I should tell you, as a friend whose looking out for your best interest, girls tend to get a little too big for their britches the first time their nominated. And Camille . . . well she's new to this whole world and she already told you no once, sweetie. I just don't want you to get your hopes up."

The balls on this girl! Nate tried to not to glare at Ashley, but she was revolting. *No wonder Camille didn't want anything to do with her crowd.* "Well, I guess it's a good thing Cami already agreed to go with me," he said standing up. "So thanks, but I guess we don't need any favors."

Ashley's face turned five shades of scarlet as Nate walked away.

25

Nate

By Wednesday, Nate was starting to get an uneasy feeling in the pit of his stomach. Camille still wasn't in school. *That was three days in a row. How mad could her parents really be?* She only spent one night in the Bywater. *They wouldn't pull her out of school for that, would they?* It wasn't like she robbed a bank or set fire to an orphanage.

He'd been texting her relentlessly, but every message went unanswered. At lunch, Ashley Dupree came over to Nate's table again. He groaned. He didn't have the patience for her today. She'd been badgering him about prom all week.

"Hey there, handsome."

Nate cut her off before she could get started. "Ash, I'm sorta busy right now."

"You don't look busy," she said staring at his untouched lunch. "Is everything alright, sweetie? You look like you're coming down with something," she said brushing her hand across his forehead.

He shrugged away. "Actually, I had the runs all morning, you might not wanna get too close."

Ashley took a step back and Nate smirked, happy his lie had the desired effect.

"So, I haven't seen you and Camille together lately," Ashley purred. "Trouble in paradise?"

"No. She's just not at school this week."

"Oh, poor thing. I hope she's not sick again."

Nate's breath caught. "Again?"

"Yeah, the cancer sure takes it out of her some days, bless her heart. She's so brave. Gosh, I hope this doesn't mess up your plans for prom."

But Nate had stopped listening after the word *cancer*. Everything started to tunnel around him as the dread he'd been carrying around all week finally latched onto his heart. Pinpricks of ice exploded from his scalp and raced down his spine. *This wasn't real. Ashley couldn't mean Cami. Not his Cami. She didn't have cancer. There was no way. He would know something like that...*

But even as Nate's heart fought against it, his mind started snapping things into place. The wigs, the photos, her bucket list... *fuck!*

Nate barely made it to the trashcan before heaving up his breakfast. He was still shaking as the devastating news slammed into him, releasing new waves of nausea. Clutching his stomach, Nate ran from the lounge. He made it all the way off campus before he crashed to his knees to vomit again.

No, this isn't real. Ashley was messing with him. Nate just needed to see Camille and everything would be okay. He got up and ran. The pounding of his feet on pavement took up the rhythm of his silent prayers. *Please, God. Please, God. Please, God. Not true! Not true! Not true!*

He didn't stop running until he was standing outside Camille's front door, pounding against the wood trying to catch his breath. His lungs heaved, but Nate couldn't get enough air. It was like a weight had been dropped on his chest and seeing Cami was the only way to fix it. Nate slammed his fists into the door over and over. He was screaming her name now, and people on the street were stopping to watch, but he didn't care. He didn't care about anything but seeing Camille's face again. He would climb up the damn Romeo spikes if he had to. He had to see her!

"Cami! Camille! Camille! Please, Camille!"

Finally the door opened and Ray's bewildered eyes met Nate's.

Words sputtered out of Nate faster than ever before. "Is she here? Is it true? Cancer? I need to see her. Cami! I need to see her!"

"Slow down, son."

Nate shrugged Ray's hand from his shoulder and rushed past him, into the house and up the stairs to Camille's room. He stepped inside and his heart dropped two stories when he saw her. She looked so small and foreign lying in her bed. Poo was curled up beside her, his tail thumping against the comforter at Nate's presence. But Nate couldn't move. He only stared at the IV tubes and oxygen mask hiding the girl he loved. *This wasn't Cami. This wasn't her.*

Where was the girl with the big gray-blue eyes and guarded smile? The girl with colorful hair that smelled of lavender and hope? The girl who made Nate feel alive?

The girl in Camille's bed looked half dead, her skin so pale Nate could read every blue vein like a road map. She had fine mousy brown hair, as short as a newborn's and her lashless eyelid fluttered restlessly in sleep.

Ray was suddenly in the room. Poo noticed him first,

lowering his head and flattening his ears with a protective growl. "Nate, would you come downstairs and talk with me?"

But Nate still couldn't move. It was like he was trapped in a dream and couldn't wake up. His eyes were seeing, but his body was frozen, unable and unwilling to process the news.

Ray tried again. "Nathan . . . Cami wouldn't want you to see her like this." This time he put a hand on Nate's shoulder as if to guide him from the room.

Nate sprung to life. "No. I need to see her. I don't understand . . . this . . . when did this happen? I . . ."

"Nate, lets talk downstairs."

"No!" Nate shirked Rays grasp and Poo leapt off Camille's bed barking and snarling at Ray.

A soft, sleepy voice that Nate would know anywhere, slipped through the chaos. "Nate?"

He turned to see Camille's eyes staring back at him. *His Cami's eyes.* And suddenly, it was real.

Nate took a step toward her but had to stop for fear his legs would give out.

"Dad," Cami whispered. "It's okay."

Ray nodded and left the room, closing the door softly behind him.

Camille struggled to sit up and suddenly Nate was at her bedside, his hands gentle on her burning skin, helping her sit up. He carefully placed another pillow behind her head as Poo reclaimed his spot on the bed.

When Camille was sitting comfortable, Nate stood up, backing away. He raked his hands through his hair because they were trembling and he didn't know what else to do with them. Camille's voice stopped his movement, slicing a thousand paper cuts across his heart.

"I'm sorry, Nate."

A muscle twitched in his cheek. "Why didn't you tell me?"

"I-I couldn't."

"You thought it was more fun to lie to me?"

"No! I don't know. I-I just liked that you didn't see me as the cancer girl. That for once, someone just saw me. I just . . . I wanted it to last a little longer."

Nate couldn't look at her, not while the last pieces that held him together were breaking apart. He turned away and focused on the chalk wall covered in Camille's perfect handwriting. A morbid realization washed over him. "This is your goodbye list, isn't it?"

Camille nodded, and Nate's heart shattered into dust. He sunk down, perching on the edge of her bed again and gently touched her hand. "You could've told me, Cami."

Tears welled in her eyes. "Yeah, because you would've been so eager to date the cancer girl."

"You never gave me the chance."

"Please, Nate. Just stop. Okay?"

He stood up again, pacing the length of Camille's bedroom. It suddenly felt very small. He looked back at Camille, trying to see the girl he loved beyond the cancer. He didn't know much about cancer, but his every instinct was screaming that this wasn't the kind you beat. He dreaded the truth, but he asked anyway. "How long do you have?"

"Nate—"

His voice burst forth, in a growl. "How long, Cami?"

"Until graduation."

Her words stole his strength and he sunk down onto her desk chair.

"I'm sorry, Nate. I never meant to let you in."

"Are you sorry you did?"

"No! I'm only sorry that I hurt you. I tried so hard to push you away, but your damn smile was contagious. And when I was with you . . . for a little while you made everything better. Your light took the darkness away."

"And now?"

Cami shook her head. "I'm sorry, Nate. I never should've brought any of this into your life. It was selfish and I'm sorry."

Nate dragged his hands through his hair in frustration. "Stop saying that word!"

"I don't know what else to say," she whispered. "You weren't part of the plan."

"Neither were you, Cami, but in case you haven't noticed, life doesn't go according to plan."

"Mine does."

"Oh really? You planned to have cancer?"

"Not the cancer, just the dying."

"What?"

Camille was silent and Nate knew he should calm down before he said something stupid, but he couldn't. He was back on his feet, pacing, his entire body shaking. He felt like his world was being torn apart all over again and he'd only just managed to piece it back together. His heart was a sledgehammer in his chest. He could barely hear himself think.

Camille's voice broke though the chaos. "Nate. I need to tell you something."

"Something bigger than you having cancer?"

"Actually, yeah."

The serious tone of her voice stopped him in his tracks.

Cami

CAMILLE STARED at Nate's face. The pain in her heart was mirrored in the anguish of his eyes. The brightness she'd come to love had disappeared from his face. It was like someone had turned out the light in his eyes. Camille shuddered, knowing she was the one who'd done that to him. She wished she could just go back and not know him, because the pain of what she had to do was more excruciating than her cancer. But she knew she owed him the truth. And Nate was going to find out soon enough.

She took a deep breath. "I'm going to be eighteen soon and I've elected to stop treatment."

"What does that mean?"

"Please let me get through this, Nate."

He nodded.

"I was diagnosed with non-Hodgkin lymphoma when I was nine. And every day since, I've been fighting it. Last year I found out that I was out of options. I've progressed to stage four. The treatments were just delaying the inevitable. If I stayed with them, I'd have another two years at best. But the treatments make me want to die." Camille laughed softly. "Ironic that they keep me alive. But I don't want to live a half-life of doctor appointments, treatment plans and endless exhaustion. So I made a plan to give myself one good year.

"A few months ago, I started weaning myself off my medications. Last month I stopped going to my oncologist. I'm completely off everything now. And it was supposed to be enough to make it to graduation."

"Then what?" Nate asked, his eyes watering.

"Then I met you." Camille's voice hitched with emotion. "And you screwed everything up. You made me want things that I can't have."

Nate was pulling her closer but she pushed him away.

"No. Nate. I can't. Don't you get it? Nothing can happen between us."

"Camille, I think it's a little late for that. I'm fucking crazy about you. That night we spent together, it meant something to me. And you can't tell me you don't know that."

"It doesn't matter."

"How can it not matter, Cami? The way I feel about you is the only thing that matters."

"Nate. It can't matter."

"Why not?"

"Because you're making this too hard. I promised myself I only had to make it to graduation. And at this rate, I'll barely have the energy for that. I can't be whatever it is you want me to be."

"Cami, you don't have to be anything but what you are. I just want to be here for you. You said it yourself. I make you better. And you make me better, too. I'm good for you, but you gotta let me in . . . all the way. I'll help you fight this."

"No, Nate. That's what you don't understand. I'm done fighting. After graduation . . ." Camille took a deep breath. She'd never said it out loud before. And staring at the last shred of hope in Nate's eyes was making it impossible. "After graduation, I've decided I'm ready to let go."

"Of what?" Nate asked, huffing a laugh. "Life?"

Camille's eyes pleaded for understanding that Nate couldn't give and she watched him pale.

"Are you fucking kidding me? You're going to take your own life?"

Camille couldn't meet his eyes. Hearing him say it made her queasy.

"Do your parents know?"

"No. But they found out that I've stopped treatment. That's what our fight was about."

"And if I didn't show up here today, when was I gonna find out?"

Camille couldn't find the words, and her lack of reply seemed to say enough.

Nate stood up, pacing again. "No. No, I'm not gonna let you do this."

"Nate, it's not up to you. This is my life."

"Exactly, Cami. Life! You're supposed to live it. You can't just give up."

"You just met me, Nate. You have no right to judge my life."

"I'm not. But you only get one life. It's your duty to live it as well as you possibly can. For as long as you can."

"I have! I've been fighting this disease since I was nine years old! You have no idea what that's like."

"No, I don't know what it's like. But I know that you're stronger than you think. I know you made me feel more alive in the few weeks we've spent together than I have in years. I know that I love you. And that has to mean something."

Tears streamed down Camille's cheeks. "Nate, it does. And I hate that it does. I hate that I didn't meet you until now, but I can't change that any more than I can change my cancer."

"But you *can* fight," Nate begged.

She shook her head. "I'm sorry."

"So what am I supposed to do? Just sit by and wait for you to die?"

"I just thought I owed you the truth."

"And what if I don't accept the truth?"

Cami shrugged. "It doesn't matter."

"How can you say that? It all matters, Cami. Every stupid moment matters. What you do matters to me, to your parents, to kids at school, to your friends at work, to everyone. I don't know how you can't see that."

"Maybe it matters for you. But you're gonna get to grow up and have a life and do things. *Real* things. My time is just a filler until I die. So none of it matters."

"It matters, Cami. None of us know how long we get. But it's our job to make the most of it. Make it matter for you, for the people that love you. Your life is right here, right now. You're the one who wants to give up on it."

"I don't want to give up. But what the hell's the point? I'm not going to get better. And I'm just so damn tired of fighting and waiting for the cancer to kill me. Choosing the when and how I die is all I have left."

"It's okay to be afraid, Cami. I'm afraid all the time. But that doesn't stop me from living."

"I'm glad you're living, Nate. I really am. But I can't be a part of your life anymore."

"Cami—"

"Nate, I want you to leave."

26

Nate

Nate didn't remember how he got home or how long it had taken. The ache in his legs told him he must've walked. He was sitting on his dad's front porch in a daze as his emotions flickered between wanting to run away, to wanting to scoop Camille into his arms and never let her go.

He still couldn't believe it was true. This morning, he'd woken up full of excitement and possibility. His biggest worry was what kind of suit he was going to wear when he took Camille to prom. Now, it was more likely he would be wearing it to her funeral.

Nate replayed their conversation over and over as he stared at the ground. Recalling the sound of Cami's voice nearly broke him. He hated seeing her hurt but he was out of his depth. He didn't know how to help her. *What could he offer her that years of medical experts couldn't?* He knew this wasn't her fault, but he was still pissed. Pissed at cancer, pissed at God, pissed at the universe. *Why the hell did everyone he love leave him?*

Nate's world was sliding away from him. He felt as if he were falling toward something dark and unknown. He stared down the barrel of unwanted choices. He could be a selfish prick and beg Camille to fight. Or he could tell her parents her plans. But they'd probably commit her to a hospital and he'd never see her again. Or he could just do what she asked, and let her go.

None of the choices were viable options.

All Nate wanted to do was forget that today ever happened. He wanted to go back to the night in the bayou—dancing in the rain, the feel of Camille's skin against his. He was desperate to go back, to catch hold of that magic again, if only for a moment.

Nate staggered to his feet. He felt broken apart as he fumbled his way into the house. He didn't know what he was searching for, but being in his room only made things worse. Polaroids of him and Cami dotted the wall. He still hadn't changed the sheets since she had stayed the night. He collapsed onto his bed, clutching the pillow where her lavender scent still lingered.

How could this happen? How could he have found happiness only to lose it again?

Rage filled Nate so swiftly that he was desperate for an outlet. His violin case lay open, taunting him. Nate grabbed the fragile instrument by the neck and slammed it into the wall. The violin snapped in half, pieces swinging like a pendulum on a string. He swung it again, screaming as the instrument shattered apart. But Nate couldn't stop. He drove his fists into to the wall, screaming out against everything he feared the most as darkness swallowed him.

Cami

. . .

CAMILLE COULDN'T CATCH her breath after Nate left her room. It wasn't the usual breathlessness he provoked, but an overwhelming tightness in her chest. She tried to draw in shallow breaths, but even her oxygen mask wasn't helping. And every time she closed her eyes Nate's pained face swam before her.

The hurt in his eyes when she'd asked him to leave stabbed fresh pain through her heart. She kept telling herself she'd done the right thing. She'd let things go too far already with Nate. The best thing for him was to push him away. *It hurt like hell. But what did it matter when she was already dying?*

Dark spots danced in the edge of Camille's vision as she tried to reassure herself that everything was going to be okay. Things would go back to normal as soon as she kicked this cold.

She'd been running a fever ever since she spent the night at Nate's. Perhaps dancing in the frigid rain, then having sex in the back seat of a car was pushing her luck as far as her health was concerned. The stress of fighting with her parents hadn't helped either. But even now, as she shivered from the chill that rippled across her feverish skin, Camille didn't regret anything. Her only regret was hurting Nate. But she was sure he'd get over her. He was a gorgeous musician from California with a smile to rival the sun. *Guys like that didn't fall for dying girls.*

Camille's fingers began to tingle. She made fists over and over to try to increase her circulation. Her chest felt heavy. She hoped she wasn't getting pneumonia again. That would keep her out of school for a while. Then again . . . she didn't need to go back to NOAH to graduate. They were accommodating to her situation. Camille had completed most of seventh grade from the hospital. *Perhaps she could finish the last few weeks of school from home?*

That would make the Nate situation easier. He'd forget all

about her in a few weeks. Camille closed her eyes and fought against the fear crawling up her spine. She just needed the strength to stick to her plan. *Only a few more weeks until graduation. She could make it.*

This was just a little cold. Or maybe she was only heartsick. She'd certainly never felt agony like this before. As shivers racked her body, Camille found herself wondering why people even fell in love in the first place if the fall out was this bad. She'd rather go through another round of chemo than the pain she'd caused Nate.

Telling him the truth about her cancer and her plan to end her life was the worst thing Camille had ever gone through. Fear that she'd made a huge mistake took root in her bones. And as much as she tried to reason with herself, fear didn't listen to the truth—*and Cami wasn't even sure what that was anymore.*

Nate

NATE DIDN'T KNOW at what point his dad had come home, or how he'd stopped him from destroying his bedroom. But Nate stood, arms pinned at his side, crushed against his dad's large frame. He smelled like booze, but his grip was steady and his eyes surprisingly clear.

"I got you. I got you, son." His dad repeated the phrase, crushing Nate hard enough to steal his breath.

It was a long time before Nate calmed down. And even longer before he was able to speak. But eventually, he sat on his overturned mattress with his dad and told him everything that happened with Camille.

Nate was crying by the time he was finished, and so was his dad. Nate had only ever seen him cry once, at Tyler's funeral.

And the sight of his tears now, only made Nate realize how hopeless things with Cami really were.

"I don't know what to do, Dad."

His dad sighed and scrubbed his rough hands over his face. "I wish I had an answer for you, Nate. You've been put in a tough spot."

"I mean she's crazy, right? She can't just quit life."

"I don't think anyone who's fought an illness like that for nine years can be called a quitter, son. None of us have any earthly idea what she's been through or how much more she can take. I think we have a responsibility to let her parents know what's going on in her head. But ultimately, I think she's the only one who can make that call."

"But I don't want to lose her, Dad. I can't lose her, not after Ty, and mom, and . . ."

"You haven't lost your mother. Is that how you feel?"

"No. I know I haven't. I'm glad she's getting to follow her dreams, but sometimes I feel like I've lost so much. Everything's so different. And I know we can't go back, but when I think about how much I miss my old life, when we were all together, it's like I can't breathe. But Cami made it better."

"Nate, I wish I could tell you it gets better, but life's a struggle. Sometimes the only choice you have is who you wanna struggle with."

The answer was simple. *Cami. But how the hell could Nate fight for someone who wouldn't fight for herself?*

"I don't know how to get through to her, Dad."

"This isn't gonna be an easy road to go down, Nate. So I want you to ask yourself if you're really prepared for this. Cause it's not something any parent wants to see their eighteen year old kid go through."

"I know, but I love her. And if I don't at least try to help her, I'll regret it for the rest of my life."

His dad nodded slowly. "If you care for her like you say you do, you have to let her choose her own path, and respect that choice, even if it's not the one you want."

Nate swallowed hard.

"Do you think you can do that, son?"

"I don't think I have any other choice. I just want to be with her, for however long that means."

Nate's dad clapped him on the shoulder. "Sleep on it, and if you feel the same in the morning I'll take you over there. I think I should be there when you talk to her parents."

Nate nodded, although he wanted to go back over to Camille's that instant. He'd wanted to go back the moment he'd left her room. But his dad was probably right. Nate's nerves were fried. He needed to get some sleep before talking to Camille's parents. And he knew one night wouldn't change his mind about wanting to be a part of Cami's life—*nothing would.*

27

Nate

NATE KNOCKED on the front door at Camille's house early the next morning. His dad called, thinking it might not be the best idea to show up unannounced with news like this, but no one answered the phone. Nate insisted they go over anyway.

"I don't like you missing school," his dad grumbled glancing at his watch again.

"Dad, some things are more important than school."

"Yeah, I'll let you try explaining that to your mother if the dean calls her."

Nate knocked on the door again. He could hear Poo going ballistic on the other side. There was no way the LaRue's didn't hear him.

Finally the door creaked open and an unfamiliar face peered out. "May I help you?"

Nate smiled politely at the old woman. "Uh, yes. I'm Nathan

Hawthorne and this is my dad, Charles. We were hoping to talk to Camille and her parents. We're sorry to drop by, but it's important."

"Oh I'm so sorry, dear. They're not home."

Dread filled Nate. *Not home?* Camille hadn't looked well enough to be anywhere but in bed when he'd last seen her. "Do you know when they'll be back?"

The woman gave Nate a sympathic look. "No I'm sorry I don't. They just asked me to stop by and check on their dog while they were gone."

"Where did they go?"

"They left for the hospital last night."

NATE'S LEGS bobbed like pistons in the hospital waiting room. He'd been there for two hours and didn't know anything more than Camille was in the ICU. The nurse wouldn't let him back since he wasn't family.

Nate couldn't stop his mind from racing. He was terrified that this was his fault. *What if he'd upset Cami so much that she'd accelerated her timeline? If she'd tried to kill herself and he hadn't done anything to stop her . . .*

He was sick to his stomach at the thought. Nate's chest felt hollow and tight. He vaguely wondered if maybe he was having a heart attack. At least he was in the best place possible, should his anxiety get the best of him.

His dad's heavy hand clamped down on his jittery knee. "Nate, take a breath. Worrying yourself to death isn't doing Camille any favors."

"Do you think you could try talking to the nurse again?" Nate asked. "Maybe we should tell them what Cami said she was going to do."

Nate's dad eyed him sternly. "Nate, if you think she tried to harm herself you need to tell me right now."

"I don't know anymore than I told you, Dad. I just know she was upset when I left her last night."

His dad sighed. "Let me go talk to the nurse again."

Nate checked his phone for lack of something better to do. He kept flipping through photos of him and Camille. She looked so alive. For someone who claimed to be tired of fighting, she certainly hid it well. She'd said he made her feel better. *But could he really have helped Cami that much?*

Nate studied her smile in each photograph as if trying to spot the lie—by the river, at Jackson Square, on his skateboard, eating beignets, watching the sunset, making donuts at Sweet Thang's.

Sweet Thang's! Did Ronnie know?

Nate was dialing the number before he even knew what he was going to say. Of course Ronnie knew. He was a self-proclaimed psychic! And he'd known Camille forever. He was probably her best friend. Nate didn't know if he was more hurt that Ronnie didn't tell him, or grateful for the time he'd allowed them to have together. Because now that Nate knew, there was no going back.

Ronnie picked up after four rings. "Sweet Thang's, this is Ronnie."

"Ronnie? It's Nate."

The phone was silent for a beat. When Ronnie spoke again all the joy had vanished from his voice. "Is it time?"

"I don't know. I'm at the hospital. They won't let me see her."

"They will, sugar."

"Ronnie . . . I have to ask you something."

"I'll save you the trouble, bebe. There's some things even I can't see."

"But you said—"

Ronnie interrupted. "I told you it wouldn't be easy, Nathaniel. But that it'd be worth it. Did I lie?"

Nate took a deep breath. "No."

"Sometimes love means letting go."

"But I'm not ready."

"We never are, sugar. But keep the faith. I think our girl's stronger than even she knows."

"Can you come here?"

"Already on my way."

Nate hung up. It was strange talking to Ronnie on the phone—he somehow knew the questions before Nate got them out of his mouth. It was like he had a cheat sheet into Nate's mind and it unsettled him. He pocketed the phone and looked around for his dad. He was standing near the desk talking to a doctor, who was taking notes on a clipboard. Nate's dad caught his eye and waved him over.

"This is my son, Nathan Hawthorne," his dad said introducing him to Dr. Hamilton.

"Nathan, would you mind having a conversation with me?" Dr. Hamilton asked.

"Sure."

The doctor led Nate and his dad to a private meeting room just beyond the waiting room. When they entered, Camille's father and a police officer were there. Nate stopped short and his dad walked into him.

"Nathan. Mr. Hawthorne. This is Detective Alva. And I trust you know Mr. LaRue."

Nate nodded, his heart pounding in his chest. He felt such a sudden flash of heat that he thought he might pass out. The room went white and his dad steadied him.

"Please," Nate managed to sputter. "Just tell me. Is she dead?"

Detective Alva spoke first. "No, son. Have a seat. We were

hoping you could tell us what Camille LaRue said to you in regards to taking her own life?"

Nathan stilled.

Camille's dad reached across the table and took his hand. "Nate, you're not in any trouble. And Cami's doing as well as we can hope. But anything you could tell us would be helpful."

After Nate finished spilling his guts about anything that might have endangered Camille, which included telling her father about her planned suicide, their swim in the Mississippi, dancing in a frigid rainstorm and having sex in the back seat of her car, Nate was certain that even if Camille did pull through, he'd never be allowed to see her again.

Satisfied with Nate's testimony, the detective finally excused everyone from the room. Nate hadn't thought he could feel much worse, but he couldn't shake the guilt that his reckless behavior had caused Camille's hospitalization. And he still didn't know what exactly was wrong with her. Everyone in the meeting had tossed around medical words that he didn't understand.

Nate rushed to catch up to the doctor as they were leaving the small meeting room. "Dr. Hamilton. Can you tell me . . . was this my fault?"

The doctor gave Nate a sympathetic smile. "While over exertion and stress can exacerbate the condition, her coronary artery spasm was most likely the cause of years of chemotherapy."

"Coronary artery spasm? Like a heart attack?" Again, Nate felt like he was having his own heart attack.

"It sounds much worse than it is. As far as heart issues go, it's minor."

"But she's in the ICU."

"As you know Camille has stage four non-Hodgkin lymphoma. As a result, her immune system is rather compromised. She's in ICU as a precaution."

"So she's okay?"

"We're monitoring things, but her prognosis looks good for now."

"Do you think I can see her?"

"I'm afraid that's up to her parents."

Cami

CAMILLE OPENED her eyes to the subdued glow of the hospital room. Her mother was sitting in a chair next to her bed. Camille tried to sit up, but remembered the leads attached to her chest. She was sore, but her breathing was coming easier.

"Hey, honey. How are you feeling?" her mother asked. "Is there anything I can get you?"

Camille's mother was in full hover-mode. She always got that way when they were in the hospital, never leaving her bedside, smothering her with questions, fluffing perfectly good pillows, repositioning blankets, requesting second and third opinions.

"Can we go home yet?" Camille asked.

"Not yet, honey. They're just making sure you're stable."

"I've been stable since this morning, Mom. I just want to go home." Camille had a suspicion that there was something her mother wasn't telling her. "Did you remember to ask Ronnie to come over to take care of Poo?"

"I asked Rene to stop by instead."

"Mom! You know Poo hates Rene."

Her mother waved her off. "She's our neighbor, it's more convenient."

"Did you at least tell Ronnie I wasn't coming in for my shift today?"

"He knows."

Camille didn't like the way her mother spoke with such finality. Something was definitely up. "Mom?"

"Honey, please stop worrying. All you need to do is rest."

Before Camille could object, her father walked into the room.

"Hey, sweetheart. Are you up for some visitors?"

Her mother shot her father a warning glare.

"Who's here?" Camille asked.

"Ronnie and Nate."

Camille's heart skipped a beat at the mention of Nate's name. It was echoed on the heart monitor by a loud beep.

Her mother stood abruptly. "Ray, we talked about this."

"Josie, can I speak to you in the hall for a moment?"

Camille watched her parents step into the hall. She read her mother's expression through the glass walls. Her arms crossed tightly over her chest, her mouth a firm line. Her father's body language was the opposite, his hand gestures pleading and open.

A few minutes later, her parents walked back in as a united front, pretending Camille hadn't just witnessed their silent argument through the glass hospital walls.

Her father spoke first. "Camille, we have to ask you something."

"Okay . . ."

"Did you try to kill yourself yesterday?"

"What?" The heart monitor spiked again. "Why would you say that?"

"I just had a conversation with Nate and his father."

"And a police officer," her mother added. "Camille this is serious. Why would you tell that boy you were going to kill yourself?"

Camille was speechless. Betrayal roared through her veins like a tidal wave, but it receded just as quickly. *What had she expected? It wasn't fair for her to leave that burden on Nate. He'd have to tell someone eventually.* At least now that it was out in the open Camille could relax. It was taking so much energy to lie to her parents.

"Look, I'm sorry I said that to Nate, but I meant it."

Her mother looked appalled. "Why didn't you tell us you felt this way?"

"Because you never listen to me, Mom. You push and push for all these treatments and I've done everything for you. But we all know this is it. There's nothing else we can do. And all the drugs and chemo make me feel like I'm already dead. I just want to enjoy the last few months I have left. Is that really so bad?"

"Yes! Camille, you do not get to give up. I know this is a tough diagnosis but you can't behave like this. You can't just try to kill yourself because you had a fight with a boy. You—"

"I didn't try to kill myself! I had a heart attack, because my body is tired."

The monitor beeped faster.

"Well you'll have to excuse us if we don't believe you, Camille. You've been lying to us for months about your medication and treatments. And now you invite this boy into your life with all these bad habits."

"Nate is not the problem, Mom! You are. I'm done. I don't know what part of that you don't understand. I'm going to graduate high school and then I'm done. I'm sorry. But I've given you everything I can."

"And what about what we've given, Camille? Doesn't that count for anything?"

"I'm sorry, Mom. But this is my decision."

"We'll see about that."

Camille's mother stormed from the room and her father moved to go after her, but Camille called him back.

"Dad?"

"Yeah, honey."

She felt bad about the exhaustion she saw in her father's eyes. She knew she was putting him in a terrible spot. But she didn't have a lot of time. "Do you think I could talk to Nate?"

He smiled tightly. "I'll do my best, sweetheart."

28

Nate

WHEN NATE GOT BACK to the waiting room, Ronnie was there. He must've come straight from the café because he still had his hot pink apron and colorful hair net on. He stood up as soon as he saw Nate, running over to crush him into a hug that filled the air with a fine dusting of confectionary sugar. Nate almost teared up at the familiar scent of sugar and fried dough that clung to Ronnie. It always reminded him of Sweet Thang's, and Camille.

"Oh Nathaniel, you are a sight for sore eyes. I can't get any info about our girl outta no one 'round here."

"I spoke to her doctor," Nate replied. "She had a heart attack, but apparently it was mild. She's in the ICU as a precaution because of her weak immune system."

"Oh, poor little lamb."

"Ronnie, why didn't you tell me?"

Ronnie locked eyes with Nate. "I love that girl like she's my own. And when you walked in with her that first day, she made me swear not to tell you about the cancer. And Lord if it didn't almost kill me. But if I had to do it over again, I wouldn't change a thing."

Nate scowled. "Thanks."

"You're welcome."

"I was being sarcastic, Ronnie."

"Well, I wasn't. Maybe you can't see it now, but I sure do. You made that girl glow, bebe. I ain't never seen her so happy as when she was with you. And that is something to be thankful for."

Nate's throat tightened. He knew Ronnie was right. Because it was how Nate felt when he was with Camille. Like he was glowing. Like he was alive. "I am thankful, but I just wish I'd known she was sick. I wouldn't have pushed her so hard to do so many crazy things. I feel like an idiot."

"You're not, sugar. But maybe that's why she didn't want you to know. Everyone treats Camille different. I think she liked the fact that you didn't."

Nate closed his eyes trying to hold back the tears. "I just want to make her better."

"I know, bebe." Ronnie hugged Nate again. "Do you remember what you said to me the night I gave you a reading?"

Nate shook his head. He could barely remember which way was up at this point.

"You told me the best things in life are worth fighting for."

"So?"

"So, the fight's not over yet, bebe."

"But she doesn't want to fight anymore."

Ronnie cocked his head. "And that's okay wit you?"

"No, but I can't fight the cancer for her."

"And you can't let the people you love determine how you gonna love them."

Nate shook his head. "I don't know what to do."

"I wish I had all the answers, bebe, I really do. But one thing I *do* know is real love when I see it. And you got it for our girl. Am I wrong?"

"No."

"Well then you gotta prove it to her while you still got time."

"She doesn't want me around, Ronnie."

Ronnie laughed. "That hasn't stopped you yet."

"This is different."

"How?"

"I don't know. It just is."

"Nathaniel, the way I see it, she's gonna need you now more than ever. Just because she's dying, don't mean she don't deserve you showin' her how to live."

RONNIE'S PEP talk was what Nate needed. His dad and Ronnie had headed home for the night, but Nate decided to stay. He knew the chance he'd get to talk to Camille was slim, but slim was better than none. Besides, if he went home, he'd do nothing but wish he were back at the hospital.

Around midnight, Nate spotted Camille's dad at the coffee machine.

"Mr. LaRue?"

Ray turned around, looking a bit disoriented. "Nate. You're still here?"

"Yeah." Nate shrugged. "I don't think I can handle being anywhere else."

Ray nodded, like he knew the feeling.

"How's she doing?" Nate asked.

"She's good."

"Ray, I know I have no right to even ask, but I have to. Do you think it's possible for me to see Cami? I don't even have to talk to her if you don't want, but I just . . . I would really love to see her."

Ray put a hand on Nate's shoulder. "She wants to see you, too."

Nate was waiting for the but, but Ray was smiling. "Come with me, but keep it short. If Josie finds out I let you see Camille I might be the one in the hospital bed."

Cami

CAMILLE THOUGHT she was dreaming when Nate walked into her hospital room. But his pale expression and lack of smile made her realize it was real. Nate stopped a foot from her bed, looking at her with terror in his warm caramel eyes. Camille hated the look of pity people always gave her—like she was already dead. And it was precisely why she hadn't told Nate. She never wanted to see him look at her like he was now.

"Hey," he whispered.

"Hey."

Nate stood there, staring for a moment longer. He looked like he wanted to come closer and she wanted him to. The Nate she knew had no sense of boundaries. He was always sitting too close, holding her hands, smelling her hair. An ache spiked in Camille's chest, realizing he'd never do that again.

"Cancer's not contagious," she said bitterly. "You can come closer."

"I know. I just figured you probably didn't want me to."

"Why?"

Nate rubbed the back of his neck nervously. "I sorta told your parents about everything."

She sighed. "I know."

"You do?"

"Yeah. We had a fun chat about it for the past few hours."

Nate moved closer, pulling up the chair next to her bed. He straddled it backwards in one swift move and picked up Camille's hand. His warmth spread through her and longing bloomed under her skin. She could feel the apology in the gentle squeeze of his fingers.

"Cami, I'm sorry I told them."

"Don't be. It wasn't fair of me to put you in that position."

"So you don't hate me?"

"You're sorta impossible to hate."

"So where does that leave us?"

"Us?"

"Yeah."

"Nate, there is no us."

"Look, Cami, I know I said some stupid things, but—"

"It is sorta your thing," Cami interrupted with a smirk.

Nate huffed a laugh. "Yeah."

"We both said some stupid things, Nate, but I think the best thing for both of us is to just say goodbye now."

"What? No. Camille, I want to be with you."

"Nate, I have cancer. What's the point?"

"The point is that I'm in love with you. I fell for you, Cami, and cancer or no cancer, it doesn't change the way I feel. And yes, I'm pissed you didn't tell me. But I'd still rather be near you than anywhere else. And I don't care if you think I'm stupid, but I'm not ready to give up on us. I want to fight, Cami. Even if you don't."

"Nate . . ." Tears welled in Camille's eyes. "You're not stupid and you're saying all the right things, but I can't give you what you want."

Nate brushed away her tears. "You already have."

"But we can't have a future."

"I don't need one. Camille, you are everything. And I'm trying to tell you that this is all I need. Right now, with you. Every second I spend with you is worth a lifetime with anyone else. You're it for me, Cami. You're all I need. For however long that is. Just please don't push me away."

"Nate, it's just gonna make it harder in the end."

"I know."

"And I'm not going to change my mind about wanting to die."

"I know. It's your life and it's your choice. But I have a choice, too. And I want to be with you, Cami. For whatever time we have left."

Camille's heart hurt worse now than it had when she was having a heart attack. Her heart monitor beeped rapidly.

Nate glanced at the monitor nervously. "Do I need to get a nurse?"

Camille shook her head, afraid to trust her voice, as tears poured down her face. She patted the bed next to her and Nate's worried expression softened. He climbed into her bed carefully, and she wrapped her arms around him. He held her, whispering soothing words while placing soft kisses on her head. She snuggled into him, drinking in his scent. She squeezed her eyes shut fighting her tears.

Nate settled into the hospital bed, leaning back against the pillows so Camille could lie against him. She rested her head on his chest, soaking in the comfort just being near him brought. They stayed like that for a while, Camille, listening to Nate's heart until her own mirrored its steady rhythmic beat.

"Nate?"

"Hmm?"

"You make me feel better."

"Me too," he whispered, kissing the top of her head.

Camille felt him release a deep sigh and her own body involuntarily echoed it, freeing stress and tension. It was getting harder to keep her eyes open. “I don’t know if I can do this to you,” she whispered.

“Do what?”

“Drag you into my messed up life.”

“Too late. I’m all in, Cami. It’s you and me together until the end now.”

29

Nate

IT WAS three days until Nate saw Camille again. She was battling her parents over her rights to refuse treatment, and Ronnie was doing his best to keep Nate updated. In the end, the doctors sided with Cami. Since her birthday was only two weeks away, they said it would do more harm than good to start her back on treatment, only to stop again once she turned eighteen. After the doctors ruling, Camille's mother finally agreed to let her come home.

Nate was practically giddy when he heard the news. And when Camille called him to say he could come over, he was out of the house before he even hung up the phone. He made record time getting to the French Quarter and had to remind himself to take the stairs to Cami's room one at a time.

He opened the door and his heart jumped to his throat

when he saw Camille sitting up in bed with Poo in her lap. Her face brightened when she saw him.

"Hello."

She laughed. "I feel like you're always saying that."

Nate strode across the room and sat on her bed, petting the excited dog who attacked him with affection. Nate leaned over Poo to pull Camille into a hug. "I missed you," he whispered.

"Me too."

Cami

Camille clung to Nate, drinking in his warmth and intoxicating smell. She wished she could bottle it and keep it with her always. Just having him in the same room did wonders for her heart. Nate had an inexplicable way of making Camille feel steady.

"So how are things with your parents?" Nate asked.

"Intense."

"It'll get better," he said squeezing her hand.

"How are things with your parents?" she asked, eager to change the subject.

Camille needed to escape the guilt she felt for disappointing her own parents. Being stuck at the hospital with nothing but their worried faces for the past three days had drained her strength. Plus, she knew things had been tense with Nate's parents since she dragged him into the middle of her cancer drama.

"Pretty good."

"Really?"

"Yeah. I mean my mom was pissed about me skipping school but she's been pretty understanding given the circumstances. And strangely, this whole thing has brought my dad and me closer. I haven't seen him touch a drink since I freaked out."

"Freaked out?"

Nate got that sheepish grin that Cami loved. The one where he scrunched up his face when he realized he'd admitted something he hadn't meant to. "I sorta went home and trashed my room the day I found out you were sick."

"Nate . . ."

"It's fine. We've already repaired the drywall. And it forced my dad and I to spend more time together and talk about things. He's been opening up to me about the divorce and he even says Tyler's name now."

"That's good," Camille said, snuggling in tighter next to Nate.

She loved Nate's big heart and the way he always focused on fixing other people's problems. But it made her feel bad, knowing she was just one more person he had to worry about. And there was no fixing her problem. Camille had agreed to spend the time she had left with Nate, but she was starting to have doubts that it was a good idea.

He kissed the top of her head as if he could sense her worry. "Tell me what you're thinking."

She sighed. "Honestly, I'm thinking I don't know where to go from here."

"What do ya mean?"

"I know we said we were in this together, but I feel like I'm taking advantage of you, Nate."

He sat up and faced her. "Cami, wild horses couldn't drag me out of here. You're gonna have to face the fact that you're not getting rid of me. And I promise, I'm definitely getting something out of this."

"Like what? I mean, this is probably it. We won't be able to do other stuff." Camille trailed off unable to say what she truly meant. *I won't be a normal girlfriend. I won't have the energy to make out with you or go to prom or have sex.*

"Cami, even if all I get to do is lay in bed with you and watch movies all day, I'd be happy."

"Why?"

"Because I love you."

She shook her head, as sadness filled her heart.

Nate propped himself up so he could look at her. "Cami, you have to know you deserve to be loved."

"That's not it."

"Then what is it?"

"I know this sounds bad, but I don't believe you."

"Why?"

"How can I? You fell in love with someone who doesn't exist."

"I'm pretty sure I fell in love with you. You are Camille LaRue, right?" he teased looking wildly around the room. "I mean you don't have a twin do you, or is this like some Freaky Friday bit?"

"Nate. I'm being serious. If you knew I had cancer from the beginning it'd be a different story, but I feel like I tricked you."

"Cami, I don't know how else to explain it to you. You are the same girl I fell in love with."

She shook her head.

"Okay, fine. Then let's start over and this time we can be brutally honest."

"Nate . . ."

"Come on. We started over before and that went pretty well if I recall." Nate winked and Camille's heart fluttered, remembering their date.

"We can't start over."

"You can always start over. You just have to want to."

She rolled her eyes but that didn't stop him. Nate was already lifting her phone from her nightstand. He grabbed his own from his pocket and set them next to each other on his lap.

"You ready?" he asked.

Cami nodded.

"I'll start."

Nate: Hello, my name's Nate. I smile a lot and do crazy things so I feel alive, because my brother died and I'm terrified of wasting my life.
Cami: I'm Cami. I have cancer. And I'm tired of fighting it.
Most days I don't want to live.
Nate: Sounds like we're both pretty messed up.
Cami: Yep.
Nate: Wanna be messed up together?
Cami: I don't know how much time I have left.
Nate: None of us do.
Cami: I don't want to be a waste of time for u.
Nate: The only waste of time is regret. And if I didn't spend time with u, I would regret it. U make me feel happy Cami.
Cami: U make me feel happy too.
Nate: Can we make each other happy for a while longer?
Cami: I'll give u all the time I have left.
Nate: I couldn't ask for anything more.

Camille put her phone down. The air in the room was heavy from their silent conversation, yet her heart felt lighter. Her phone pinged again and she looked down at her text message.

Nate: One more thing.
Cami: What?

Nate: Will u be my girlfriend?
Cami: Ok.
Nate: Good, cause I'm in love with you.

CAMILLE PUT HER PHONE DOWN. The screen was blurry from the tears in her eyes.

Nate pulled her close. "Hey, what's wrong?"

"I was just talking to my boyfriend."

"Yeah? What's he like?"

She laughed. "Kinda perfect."

"I like him already. But why are you crying?"

"Because he scares me."

"Why?"

"Cause I think I love him, too."

"Is that such a bad thing?"

She shook her head. "Nate, can you promise me something?"

"Anything."

"No grand gestures. I just want time with you."

He grinned and kissed her softly. "I'll take it into consideration."

30

Nate

THREE WEEKS WENT by and Nate spent every day with Camille. He went to her house after school, bringing her assignments and working on homework together. Nate loved entertaining Cami. He gave Poo new hairstyles daily just to hear her laugh. He played Ray's guitars and ukuleles, serenading her whenever she asked him for music. He knew she wanted to hear the violin, but he didn't have the heart to tell her he'd smashed his to pieces. Instead, Nate distracted her with flowers and collectable PEZ dispensers.

But weekends were Nate's favorites. They watched old movies and played board games. Camille complained constantly that she was the lamest girlfriend ever, but secretly, Nate loved every minute he spent with her. He had her all to himself and he felt like he was part of a family again.

Camille's mom still wasn't Nate's biggest fan, but her dad had warmed back up to him. He even let Nate help make dinner and pick out the Sunday night movies, which, according to Cami, was a big deal in the LaRue house. She told him Sundays had always been family days. Her mom wouldn't work, they'd cook a big meal together, play Trivial Pursuit and watch a movie. Nate was honored to be a part of it.

On the first Sunday he'd been invited to join, he brought beignets and coffee from Café Beignet, which Camille and Ray decided had to be added to the Sunday tradition. At first Josie had objected, still wanting Camille to focus on a healthy diet. But Ray shoved a piece of beignet into her mouth to silence her. "I think we can all afford to live a little, Josie."

"They are sort of delicious," Josie admitted reaching for her own pastry.

Camille grinned and Nate queued up the movie, snuggling closer to Cami as the black and white images of *Casablanca* filled the screen.

After that night, Josie seemed to take a step back. Things were still tense between her and Camille, but Nate couldn't help noticing that they were both making an effort to be more understanding of each other.

ONE DAY AFTER SCHOOL, Nate was lying on Camille's bed while she sat at her desk taking a make up exam. He was staring at her *Before I Die* wall. The unfinished goals unsettled him. The empty boxes next to *Beach* and *Graduation* glared at him and it gave Nate an idea.

"Hey, Cami, what do you think about starting a new wall?"

She followed his eyes to the unchecked boxes he was staring at. "Nate . . . we've talked about this. At this rate, I'll be lucky to check those two off."

"I was thinking about more of a *While I'm Alive* wall."

She scrunched up her face. "Isn't that the same thing?"

"No. The *Before I Die* wall is all these massive goals and dreams that people come up with and most of the time they're completely unattainable or they're saved until it's too late. But I was thinking we could make a new wall to celebrate all the awesome little things that we can do every day. We can call it your hello wall, since you already have a goodbye wall."

"A hello wall?"

"Yeah. You fill it with things that you're looking forward to each day. Reasons to get up and greet the day."

"Like what?"

"I dunno." Nate glanced around the room spotting Camille's dog curled up at her feet. " Like, play with Poo."

Camille giggled. "And that is exactly why I named him that."

"We can put other little things we want to do on there, too. Like, kiss my girlfriend."

"Oh, how about, make my boyfriend paint my toenails."

Nate jumped up and grabbed a pen, scribbling *Paint Cami's Toenails* on the wall next to her bed. "What else?"

She tapped her chin in thought. "How 'bout, eat beignets."

Nate wrote it down.

"Smile more."

He gave Camille a cheesy grin, then scribbled on he wall. "Give me another one."

"Say I love you."

Nate scribbled it onto the wall and when he turned around, Camille was standing next to the bed. "I love you," she whispered.

Nate scooped her up and pulled her into bed, kissing her all over until she was giggling and Poo jumped up to see what all the commotion was about.

"I love you, too," Nate whispered back.

Cami was lying on her back, smiling up at him, and it made Nate's heart squeeze with sudden fear. He was normally good at holding back the terror that strangled him when he thought about losing Camille. He couldn't let himself think about it, or he'd break his promise to her and drop to his knees, begging her not to leave him. Begging her to fight for every second they could have no matter what drugs or treatment it meant she'd have to endure.

He bent down and kissed her again, closing his eyes to shut out the selfish thoughts that were twisting around his heart. When Nate came up for air, he turned toward the wall scribbling something new on it. *Make all of Cami's dreams come true.*

She stole the pen, drew a box next to it and placed a checkmark inside. Then she wrote her own sentence. *Tell him how I feel.*

Nate pulled Camille close to him again, kissing her though he was shaking. "I know," he whispered.

"I don't think you do," she said running her slender fingers through his hair. It always made Nate shudder with longing for more. "These last few weeks with you have been amazing," she admitted, her shy smile spreading into a real one.

That right there was what made Nate keep coming back for more. He would do anything for that smile—*including tear his own heart to pieces.*

Cami

CAMILLE SPENT the rest of the day in bed with Nate, trading kisses and filling her Hello Wall with silly things they loved to do together. Nate had just written, *Watch scary movies,* on the wall and Camille crossed it off.

"Hey!" Nate objected, pouting in a way that made her want to kiss him.

"I hate scary movies. And since when do you like them?"

"Since we watched The Shining and you held onto me like I was a superhero."

Camille laughed. "You know, there are other ways to get me to hold onto you."

"Really?"

She smirked, letting Nate crawl over her and press his lips gently to hers. They hadn't done more than kiss since she'd been home from the hospital. And at first it was enough, but now that Camille was feeling better, she couldn't help wanting more of Nate. She remembered the feel of his skin against hers all too well, and something deep inside of her itched to get back to that place with him.

Camille slipped her hand under Nate's shirt, tracing the long columns of muscle that ran down his back. He stilled, his breath warm against her neck.

"Cami," he warned.

She ignored him, running her fingers down his sides.

Nate shivered, letting a low groan slip from his mouth. But when she reached for his belt, he sat up. "Cami, we can't."

"Why not?" She sat up, too. "I'm feeling much better."

"I know. But we shouldn't push it."

"Nate, I know my body. I'm not pushing it." Camille reached for him, stroking her fingers down his chest. *She knew he loved when she did that.* She spent the last three weeks with her hands on his chest, trying to memorize the feel of his heartbeat.

Nate's hands caught hers, stopping them over his heart. "Cami. We can't."

Her face flushed red as a terrible realization gripped her. "Do you not want to?"

"No, that's not it at all."

"Then what?"

"Well, for one thing, your parents are downstairs. I'm not trying to lose my Cami privileges."

She sighed but nodded. It made sense, but still didn't completely quiet her nerves that she wasn't as desirable to Nate now that he knew she had cancer. She wanted to connect with him physically again, if only to be reassured that sex with him the first time hadn't been a fluke.

"And, I've sorta been planning something special for you," Nate added. "But it kinda involves waiting."

Camille's interest outweighed her insecurity. "Waiting? You do know I'm sorta on a strict timeline here?"

Nate looked down and Camille instantly felt bad. She knew he hated when she joked about dying. But the alternative was even more depressing. She almost apologized, but Nate hated *I'm sorrys* just as much, so she took his hand instead and laced her fingers with his. "It's just . . . isn't the guy supposed to be the one trying to get in the girl's pants?"

"Cami, believe me. Spending so much time in your bed without doing everything I want to you, has been a master class in self-restraint."

Hearing him say that made her inner goddess glow. "Really?"

He made that low groaning sound in the back of his throat that she loved. "You have no idea. But I want the next time to be special."

"Nate, it was special."

"The back seat of a car?"

She nodded eagerly and Nate laughed.

"Woman, you need to set your standards much higher."

"I don't know what to say, Nate. You chose a girlfriend with extremely low standards and no moral compass." Camille crawled into his lap and wrapped her arms around his neck. "The back of a car is practically paradise to me."

Nate made his sexy groaning sound again. “You’re gonna be the death of me.”

She smiled sadly to herself, burying her face in Nate’s neck. *She hoped it would be the other way around.*

31

Cami

THE FOLLOWING WEEK, Camille was strong enough to return to school. But going back to NOAH, meant going back to the real world, and suddenly she missed her little bubble, where she and Nate belonged together.

Nate had convinced her to stop hiding behind her wigs and so much makeup. She didn't wear them in front of him for the time she'd been recovering at home, and it gave her the confidence to leave the house that way.

Today she'd only drawn on faint eyebrows and used a little bit of shimmery blush to give herself a healthy glow. Her hair had grown back enough to almost pull off the *GI Jane* look, which Nate said she rocked when paired with the combat boots he'd bought her. But honestly, he was her best accessory. Cami felt invincible with Nate by her side.

But as he carried her up the stairs—which he insisted on doing although she could walk just fine—Camille started to second-guess her minimalistic styling choices. The Ashleys were all standing by her locker ready to welcome her back to NOAH along with the rest of the senior class.

"What is this?" Camille murmured in Nate's ear as he set her back down.

"I know you hate this kind of stuff, but just be glad I talked them out of hiring the marching band."

Camille balked. "What?"

"Just roll with it. It'll be over in a minute."

Camille walked up to her locker with Nate holding her hand as classmates she'd hardly ever spoken to greeted her like they were best friends. She got lots of *'welcome backs'* and *'you look greats'* but the thing that stuck with Camille the most was when Ashley Banks stepped forward and hugged her.

The flawless blonde wrapped her arms around Cami and whispered rapidly. "I'm glad your back, Camille. I'm sorry for being a shitty friend all these years. If you ever need anything, I've got your back."

Camille was in shock at the outpouring of attention from her fellow classmates. Most of them even seemed as genuine as Ashley Banks. Once the bell rang, everyone dispersed and Nate walked Cami to her first period class.

"That was weird," she said.

"I know you hate being the center of attention, but they all really wanted to do something nice."

"Who?"

"Everybody. But the Ashleys orchestrated the locker greeting."

"And you knew about this?"

Nate shrugged. "Yeah, it was the least horrible of their ideas."

Camille snorted. "Anything to make them look good."

"They're not that bad."

"The Ashleys? You can't be serious."

"I've been eating lunch with them while you've been home. Ashley C. and Ashley B. are kinda cool. It's mostly the other one that's full of herself."

A pang of jealousy flared in Camille's chest. "So you've been spending a lot of time with them?"

"Cami," Nate warned. "You know it's not like that."

"How's it like, Nate? Did you guys just sit around and talk about poor Cami cancer girl every day?"

"No, but it's not like it's a secret. You know how high school is. Rumors were going around and I was trying to put them out."

Camille stopped walking. She rubbed her temples. "Maybe I wasn't ready to come back."

"Are you feeling alright?" Worry fringed Nate's voice. "Do you want to sit down?"

"I'm not sick, I'm embarrassed. This is why I hate NOAH and I hate the Ashleys. Everyone here thinks they know me, but they don't. And now they just want to pretend to care about me so they can get the gossip about the girl who tried to kill herself."

"Jesus, Camille!" Nate pulled her into an empty classroom. "No one knows about that."

"They don't?"

"Do you really think I'd tell anyone?"

"No but . . . then why was everyone saying *'I'm here for you'* and stuff?"

"Hello! You had a heart attack, Cami. And they know you have cancer."

"That's all?"

"That's all."

Camille let the news sink in. She was bewildered. "I just think it's weird that they're acting like they care. They've barely spoken to me since middle school."

"Cami, I know you're probably not gonna want to hear this, but whose fault is that?"

"Are you kidding me right now?"

"You don't let anyone in. You just keep saying I'm fine, so people think you're fine. It's like putting up a sign that says keep out and wondering why no one drops by."

"Maybe I don't need anyone."

Nate sighed. "Cami, life is better when you have people to share it with."

"I have you," she shot back.

"Yeah, and even though you look pissed at me right now, I know you're glad you let me in."

Camille didn't reply. Mostly because she was furious that Nate was right.

He looped an arm over her shoulder and pulled her into a hug. "I'm just saying maybe you should give some other people a chance, too."

CAMILLE SAT in her first period class in a daze. Nate's words kept replaying in her mind. He was right. At some point, she was to blame for her own isolation. The realization was painful, because it took away her anger. And without it, all she had left was the cancer.

She opened up her day planner, flipping to the calendar in the back to write the date of their next quiz. As she was flipping it closed, she glimpsed the back page where she had her countdown of days left until graduation. She counted. Three weeks. Fifteen school days. She added the minute number to the tally she'd started at the beginning of the year. The heading of the page was *Days 'til Freedom.*

Camille teared up when she read it. *It wasn't really freedom at all, was it? How could it be if she was the one who made her life seem like something she needed to escape?*

She flipped through the previous months. Each one had a list numbered one through three and was titled *Camille's Plan for Dying.* Each month was the same.

#1: Cross all items off bucket list.
#2: Graduate high school.
#3: Stick to the plan.

IT WAS the last line that struck Cami hardest. It was just like Nate said. She might as well have worn a sign that read *Keep Out*. Yet clearly if she was writing down her plans to kill herself for nearly a year, she'd been crying for help and wondering why no one was answering.

Camille kept flipping until she got to March. That was when she'd met Nate. That was when everything changed. She read the list.

Camille's Plan for Dying
#1: Cross all items off bucket list.
#2: Graduate high school.
#3: Absolutely do not fall for his smile.

HER EYES WELLED with tears as she read the last line again and again. It was too late. She'd fallen for Nate. She was in love with him. And she'd wasted so much time trying not to be.

For the first time since Camille was diagnosed, panic gripped her. And not because she was going to die. But because she wanted to live.

32

Nate

THE NEXT TWO weeks flew by and Nate couldn't believe the changes he saw in Camille. She was bright and open, and even chatty with her classmates who stopped by her locker or lunch table to say hello. It was like someone had flipped a switch and Cami was finally letting the rest of the world see the girl he'd always seen—the one that hid behind wigs and makeup and sarcasm. The girl with the beautiful heart.

Camille was so lively that sometimes it was easy for Nate to forget she was still sick. Her strength and energy had returned and her skin had a healthy glow. Her gray-blue eyes sparkled when she laughed and her baby-fine brown hair had grown into an adorable pixie style that he couldn't resist running his fingers through. In fact, he was having trouble resisting her at all lately.

Cami was presently sitting in his lap in the lounge, stealing sips of his hot chocolate. The afternoon sun was streaming in, turning her flawless skin a brilliant gold. She looked up at him, her big eyes almost translucent in the sunlight. A stab of pain slammed into his heart. It was perfect moments like this that took his breath away. Nate could feel Camille with every fiber of his being, yet somehow it was like she was already a ghost. It made his soul ache. He was trying so hard to be strong, but the fact that he was going to lose Camille grew clearer every day.

Balancing his heart was beginning to exhaust Nate. He flickered between joy and misery moment to moment. But he knew he'd much rather be here with Camille than anywhere else. He just prayed for the strength to make the most of the time they had left.

Nate locked his fears away and kissed Camille, savoring the salty taste of hot chocolate still on her lips. "I love you, Cami."

"I love you, too."

"Have you thought anymore about what I said?" he asked.

"Yes, and I still think it's silly."

"But . . ."

"But if you must throw me a birthday party then I'll allow it."

"Really?" Nate felt bad that Cami was too sick to celebrate her birthday while she was recovering from her hospital stay. And now that she was better he wanted to throw her a party.

Camille nodded. "But I want it to just be us, Ronnie and my parents."

"Are you sure? I thought it would be fun to have some kids from class come, too."

"I'm sure. I've been enjoying all this," she said gesturing to the nosey lounge full of NOAH students. "But I think it'll be more special if it's just us. Well, and I was thinking it might be fun if you invite your dad."

"Really?"

"Yeah. I haven't gotten to spend much time with him."

Nate arched an eyebrow. "You want to spend time with my dad?"

"Well, I'm sorta crazy about his son. So, I figured I might like the guy who had a hand in making him."

Nate laughed. "Okay, I'll ask him."

"Good." Camille smirked. "This wouldn't be when I get this surprise you've been planning would it?"

Nate kissed her until she was breathless. "Patience, Camille."

She swatted him. "You're such a tease."

He laughed, but inside Nate was terrified. He'd been planning something big for him and Cami, but first he needed to get her parents on board. Things were going well and perhaps if the birthday celebration went off without a hitch, he'd be able to approach them with the final part of his plan.

33

Cami

CAMILLE CLAPPED like a child when Ronnie carried out a tray full of lemon meringue cupcakes. She was sitting around the copper fire bowl in her parents' courtyard, enjoying her birthday celebration. Ronnie, Nate and his dad had joined them for dinner, and birthday cupcakes.

"These are my favorite," Camille exclaimed. "Ronnie, I can't believe you remembered."

"Like I could forget." Ronnie turned to Nate and his dad. "The first day on the job this girl ate an entire bowl of meringue when she was supposed to be icing a cake."

"I was twelve!" Camille objected. "Besides, you weren't paying me."

"I was paying you with knowledge."

"I say you were paying me with sugar."

Camille's father laughed. "That sounds like my daughter."

"How *did* you end up working at Sweet Thang's?" Nate asked.

Camille watched her parents' faces tighten at Nate's question. Even Ronnie looked a bit saddened. Nate immediately squeezed apologetically at Cami's hand, seeming to sense he'd said something he shouldn't.

She squeezed back. "No, it's okay. Ronnie is proof that cancer can bring good things into your life."

"Thank you, baby cakes," Ronnie replied.

Camille's mother spoke. "We took Camille to Sweet Thang's to pick out her birthday cake every year."

"And every year Ronnie would ask me what my birthday wish was so he could bake it into the cake with the magic sugar he used," Camille added.

Ronnie smiled sadly. "When she was ten, Camille said her wish was for her cancer to go away."

"I still remember what you told me," Camille said. "You said that some wishes required more magic than even sugar possessed. But that anytime I needed a little extra magic to make me feel better I could come down to Sweet Thang's and have a treat on the house."

Ronnie had tears in his eyes as he nodded. "And I'll be damned if this sweet girl didn't start coming to my shop every day."

"She used to run away from home," Camille's father said. "Ronnie would call us and say she was at the café eating him outta house and home."

Camille laughed. "It's not my fault Ronnie puts magic in his cooking. How's a girl supposed to stay away?"

"It's true," Nate said smiling at her.

"After a while he hired me," Camille said. "Although, I'm pretty sure Ronnie lost out on that deal."

Nate smirked. "For real. I need to find a job where they pay me to eat amazing food."

"Yeah, Ronnie. I probably owe you for all the sweets I ate over the years."

Ronnie laughed and waved Camille off. "Nah, I send your parents a bill every month."

Everyone laughed at that, because you didn't even have to know Ronnie that well to know he'd never even entertained the thought. He was a saint disguised in sugar and glitter, and Camille was lucky that cancer had brought him into her life.

"Okay, okay. Let's light these candles before my frosting melts," Ronnie exclaimed, wiping his eyes.

"Wait!" Camille turned to Nate. There was something she'd been wanting to ask him and she hoped she wasn't putting him on the spot. "Nate, I was wondering if it would be okay if we lit a birthday candle for Tyler?"

Nate looked at her, his brow furrowed in pain.

"Only if you're okay with it," she added.

Nate bit his bottom lip and looked at his dad. He nodded and Nate smiled the most painful smile Camille had ever seen. It made her want to pull him into her lap and hold him, not caring that everyone else was intently watching them both.

Nate took Camille's hand, rubbing his thumb across her knuckles. "I'd love that, Cami. Thank you."

She pulled one of the too many candles out of her cupcake and added it to the one on Nate's plate. Ronnie lit the candles and everyone sang happy birthday. Camille held onto Nate's hand the whole time, feeling the tiny trembles rush through him when they sang Tyler's name. She looked at Nate as everyone sang the last verse. He was already staring at her. There was so much love in his eyes, it hurt.

Camille whispered so only Nate could hear her. "Make a wish."

. . .

Nate

NATE CLOSED his eyes and blew out the candle for Tyler. But he didn't make a wish. *What could he even wish for?* He was here with Camille. There wasn't anything else in the world he wanted, except for more time with her. But he was trying his damnedest not to think about that.

Besides, he knew wishing for something like that was foolish. And if Nate had a wish, he was saving it for Camille. Because all he wanted was to make all her dreams come true in the time that they had left together.

After the cupcakes, everyone gave Camille her birthday gifts. She got a blanket from her mom, an old jazz album from her dad and a secret recipe for meringue from Ronnie. Nate had gotten her a giant bag of PEZ candy, since he'd been helping her with her secret stash in her room. He'd also gotten Cami more film for her Polaroid camera.

Camille lit up when she opened his gifts. She stood and gave each person a hug. And when she was done she whispered something to her dad. He ducked back into the house for a moment and came out carrying a large wrapped box that he handed to Nate.

"What's this?" Nate asked in confusion. "I'm not supposed to get presents on your birthday, Cami."

"It's really a present for me," she said, eyes sparkling with mischief. "Open it."

Nate tore off the paper and opened the box to find a thick black case inside. The shape of it was familiar enough to make his heart skip. It was a violin case. He hadn't played his since he smashed it in his rage over a month ago.

He popped open the latches on the case and lifted the lid. A brand new violin gleamed back at him. Tightness tugged at the back of Nate's throat. He looked at Camille. "How did you know?"

He'd been too embarrassed to tell her what he'd done to his violin, and spent the last few weeks making excuses every time she asked him to bring it over and play.

"I talked to your dad," she said, smiling.

Nate looked between them. "I thought you hardly knew him?"

They both laughed.

His dad held up his hands in surrender. "Ray and I worked together putting some of the pieces from your old violin on this one, but it was all Cami's idea."

"We salvaged your old pegs, chinrest and bridge," Ray added.

Camille walked over to Nate and slipped the bow into his hand. "Give it a try."

He held it up, resting the new violin in the crook of his neck. He let the familiar smell of wire and wood wash over him as he settled his chin against the worn rest that both he and Tyler had played on. He closed his eyes fighting tears as his bow pulled a cry from the cords. The sullen sound echoed his despair.

Nate played, pouring himself and all the emotions he'd been fighting, into his music. He played for the unjustness of Camille's life, and for Tyler's, and for himself to be strong enough to keep going, when soon, he would be the only one left.

Her voice was so soft that at first that Nate didn't realize that Cami had joined the whine of his violin. It wasn't until he was on the fourth verse of *'Hallelujah'* that her words reached him. He hadn't even remembered choosing to play *'Hallelujah'*. But now that he heard Camille's voice, lilting softly in time with his music, he didn't want her to stop. Her father was right, Camille had the voice of an angel, and it broke Nate's heart all over again.

He played the sad song again, just so he could hear Camille's voice a bit longer—*even though he knew anything short of forever would never be enough.*

34

Cami

CAMILLE'S BIRTHDAY WAS A SUCCESS. After Nate played for everyone in the courtyard, Cami suggested they move inside to her father's music room. She sensed Nate needed a break, because she'd never seen him so emotional. He didn't leave her side for the rest of the night as her father and Mr. Hawthorne played song after song on the piano and guitar. Even her mother and Ronnie sang along. Ronnie couldn't carry a tune to save his life, but watching him try made Camille laugh so hard her sides hurt.

It was late by the time Ronnie and Nate's dad left. Nate stayed behind to help clean up. Camille's parents insisted he didn't have to stay, but Cami wanted him to. Honestly, she never wanted him to leave. Spending time with Nate was pretty much her top priority. And that's why tonight had been perfect. Her house had been filled with everyone she cared about. Camille wished it could always be like that, right up until the end—*just her, Nate, Ronnie and her family.*

Camille gave both her parents a big hug before going up to bed. "Thank you for tonight," she said. "It really means a lot to me to get to spend time with all of you together."

Her mother kissed both her cheeks. "You're welcome, honey. It means a lot to us, too."

Her father gave her another hug and glanced at Nate, who was waiting for her at the bottom of the steps. "Not too late, you two."

Nate saluted and scooped Camille up, carrying her upstairs in a fit of giggles.

"I don't want you to leave," she whispered once she was snuggled under the covers in her room.

Nate and Poo were both fighting for the remaining mattress space.

"I don't want to leave either," Nate crooned kissing her softly.

"Tonight was perfect, Nate. Thank you for making me do this."

"I should be the one thanking you. I didn't think I'd ever play the violin again."

"Why didn't you tell me you broke it?" she asked.

Nate grinned. "Probably because I knew you'd go and do something spectacular like this and I'd never be able to top it."

Camille let him kiss her again. "But really, Nate. Why didn't you tell me it was broken?"

"Because I was embarrassed."

"About what?"

Nate let out a breath. "I broke it the night we got into our fight."

"Why?"

"I dunno. I was pissed and scared and I felt useless."

"Smashing things made you feel less useless?"

"For a little while."

They were silent for a while. Camille let Nate hold her, and she clung to the steady rise and fall of his chest. "It's okay to be scared," she whispered.

"Are you scared?"

She nodded.

Nate kissed her forehead and held her tighter.

"Nate?"

"Hmm?"

"Do you think you could stay?"

"Cami . . ."

"Just a bit longer?" she pleaded. "Tonight was perfect. I just don't want it to be over yet."

Nate sighed, but kicked off his shoes and slid fully onto the bed. Camille snuggled against him, resting her head on his chest once he was settled. Nate wrapped his arms around her and Poo climbed over Camille, nestling himself in the valley between them.

"This is perfect," she whispered. And it really was.

Nate

Nate waited until Camille was fully asleep before untangling himself from her arms. He hated leaving her, but he didn't want to push things with her parents. They'd been so kind to him, inviting him into their lives because it was important to their daughter. But he knew it couldn't be easy. They wanted to spend time with her, too, and it was probably hard when Nate was always there.

As Nate tiptoed downstairs, he was surprised to see the light still on in Ray's music room. He peeked his head in and Ray looked up.

"Oh, sorry, Mr. LaRue. I didn't mean to stay so long, but Cami fell asleep and I didn't want to wake her so I tried waiting and must've dozed off myself."

Ray smiled. "It's alright, Nate. I've been meaning to talk to you about something anyway. Do you have a moment?"

"Sure." Nate sat down on one of the comfy chairs in Ray's office.

"I know it means a lot to Camille to have you around. I can see you're good for her. You make her smile and open her heart in a way I didn't think I'd see again. I want to thank you for that."

Nate didn't know what to say, so he nodded and kept his mouth shut.

"Josie and I spoke to your father tonight and before we put it to Camille we wanted to ask you how you would feel about staying in the guest house for these next few . . ." Ray trailed off fighting to find the right words to say. "Well, for however much time we have left with Camille."

Nate's heart leapt. "Really? I mean I don't want to be in your way."

"You make Camille happy, Nate. That's all any parent ever wants."

Nate couldn't believe this was happening. Maybe birthday wishes did come true. All he wanted was more time with Camille and this would certainly give him that. He wouldn't have to ride the bus or streetcar back and forth anymore. He could be with Camille everyday.

"So what do you think?" Ray asked.

Nate didn't have words and he was afraid if he opened his mouth he might cry. Instead, he stood up, walked across the room and hugged the man.

~

Nate woke up a bit disoriented. Ray had helped him settle into the guest house last night, saying it was too late to send him home and he might as well get used to his new accommodations.

The high from the news that Nate would be spending everyday with Camille gave him the courage to ask Ray for permission to move forward with his secret plan for Camille. And to Nate's surprise, Ray was pretty agreeable, saying he'd talk to Josie but didn't see a problem with what Nate proposed. Now all that was left was to get Cami to agree to it.

35

Cami

A FEW MONTHS AGO, Camille would've rather have stabbed her eyes out than sit at her lunch table chatting about prom with two of the three Ashleys. But strangely that's exactly what she was doing. And even more surprising—she didn't hate it.

Apparently Nate asked the Ashleys to help with the big surprise he was planning, which she now knew was for prom night. And knowing the Ashleys were involved in the scheme scared her.

Ashley Banks and Ashley Calhoune had switched over to Team Cami, which sort of freaked Camille out because she didn't even know there were teams. But Ashley Dupree was still being her normal bitchy self, which Camille actually appreciated. The world just wouldn't seem right if Ashley Dupree decided to be nice, too.

"So," Camille asked. "Are you guys gonna give me any hints?"

"Absolutely not," Ashley Banks replied.

"It's so worth being surprised," Ashley Calhoune added. "I wish my boyfriend was as sweet as Nate."

Camille laughed, "Yeah, I did sorta win the boyfriend lottery, huh?"

"Yeah. What's your secret?" Ashley Banks asked.

Camille shrugged. "Cancer?"

Both Ashleys paled, their eyes as big as saucers.

Camille winced, forgetting they weren't used to her sarcastic wit. "Kidding."

"Oh, right." Both Ashleys laughed nervously.

And this was why Camille shouldn't be left alone with normal people. It was like she'd been raised in the wild and needed Nate to translate for her. *Where the hell was Nate, anyway?*

They always ate lunch together, but as Camille glanced around the lounge, she didn't spot Nate's lanky frame anywhere. "You wouldn't happen to know where my amazing boyfriend is right now, would you?" she asked.

The blonde girls giggled sharing conspiratorial glances.

"We might," Ashley Banks said, "But you're not getting it out of us."

Camille sighed, fighting the urge to roll her eyes.

Ashley Banks nudged her. "Prom is tomorrow, Cami. And I promise, it'll be worth the wait."

A strange bubble of excitement took hold of Camille and she realized she hoped they were right.

Nate

. . .

NATE MET Cami after her last class, walking her to her car. He'd become her chauffer since she left the hospital. The doctors advised she shouldn't drive in case she had any more heart issues. And Nate certainly didn't mind driving her badass Range Rover around.

"So where were you at lunch today?" she asked.

"Working on some last minute details for the plan."

Cami smirked. "I have to say, you've certainly built up '*the plan*'," she said using air quotes. "Hope it holds up, Hawthorne."

Nate raised his eyebrows. He loved when Cami called him by his last name. It meant she was feeling feisty, which was always a sign that her strength was up. He'd been hoping her good health streak would hold out until prom.

"Don't worry, LaRue. I'm gonna blow your mind."

She giggled. "I don't know, I have pretty high standards."

He playfully looked around. "Have you seen my girlfriend? About yay high." He exaggerated her shortness by a good foot. "No morals, low standards, but really great ass?"

Cami jabbed him in the ribs. "Oh my God, is the plan about sex?"

Nate's face flushed red and he turned away getting into the Range Rover.

She continued to badger him when she got in the car. "It totally is, isn't it?"

"Camille, not everything is about sex," he teased. "You'll find out the plan tomorrow. Just promise me you'll go along with it."

"How can I promise when I have no idea what you're plotting?"

"It's about prom."

"Okaaay," she drawled. "I agreed to go with you *and* let the Ashleys pick out my dress, which I still haven't seen, by the way. What else do you want me to agree to?"

"Just say yes," Nate crooned, repeating the prom theme.

She rolled her eyes. "Worst theme ever."

Nate smiled. "We'll see."

NATE PULLED up in front of Camille's house instead of into the courtyard as usual.

"What are you doing?" she asked.

"Dropping you off."

"You're not coming in?"

"Not tonight. I have some last minute things to prepare." He ran his fingers through her short hair and kissed her until his heart physically hurt. "I'll pick you up tomorrow, okay?" he whispered, his forehead pressed against hers.

"I'm not gonna see you until tomorrow?"

"It's only one night."

"Nate . . ." her voice was desperate. The quiet plea in it saying everything they both knew—*one night could be all she had left.*

Cami

CAMILLE WAS cranky when she got home. She couldn't believe she wasn't going to get to spend the night with Nate. They hadn't been apart since her birthday. He'd moved into the guest house, but Camille was convinced it was basically just a way for their parents to feel like they weren't doing something taboo by letting their teenaged kids sleep together every night. It's not like there was a handbook for how to parent your terminal daughter and her heartbroken boyfriend. Not that Camille and Nate were doing anything wrong. He was respectful beyond reason, refusing to do anything more than sleep next to her—no matter how much she wanted more.

She stomped up the stairs, missing Nate already. He usually carried her upstairs, like saving her the trip would somehow prolong their time together. She always protested, but now that he wasn't there to do it, she had to admit how much she loved the way he spoiled her.

She'd been realizing a lot of new things about herself lately. For one, she actually enjoyed talking to some of the kids at NOAH once she gave them a chance. And it was strangely nice to have girls to talk to. The Ashleys, minus Ashley Dupree, were kind of fun. It was interesting to listen to them talk about their boyfriends, prom, and plans for after graduation. Camille never would've imagined in a million years that they were just as insecure as she was about things.

Camille had always looked at the Ashleys from the outside, thinking they had it all. And to some extent, they did. They were going to graduate and go on to college and hopefully get to live long, healthy lives. But beyond that, they were just girls, with as many worries as Camille.

At some point, during all these realizations, something had changed in Camille. Thanks to Nate, she'd woken up and decided to make the most of the time she had left. And now that it was ticking down, she had perhaps the biggest revelation of all—*she wanted more.*

Camille wanted more everything. More Nate. More friends. More items on her bucket list. More time. Just more . . .

Every time she thought about it, her chest hurt, sending her into mini panic attacks thinking she was having another coronary spasm. She sat down at her desk and rubbed tight circles over her chest to ease the tension. She knew from the moment she met Nate that this would happen. Perhaps that's why she'd resisted so long. She'd known all along that smile of his—full of blinding sunshine and possibilities—would make her want the whole damn world.

Camille sat at her desk for a while, quietly staring at the unchecked boxes on her wall. Nate had moved her desk weeks ago when she told him about the goals she'd hidden behind it. Now, *Kiss, Love, Prom* and *Paris* were clearly visible, along with *Beach* and *Graduation*. Nate had teased her relentlessly about the *Kiss* and *Love* portion on the wall, doodling hearts and kisses all around it and carving C. L. + N. H. on every surface possible. Secretly, she loved that he did that.

Nate brought complete chaos to Camille's orderly life and now she wondered how she'd ever lived without him. She laughed to herself. Perhaps that was the real problem. Camille hadn't really been living. But Nate made her want to. For the first time in over a year, Camille felt strength burn deep in her bones. It rumbled in her ears, whispering the same word with each beat of her tired heart. *Fight. Fight. Fight.*

Camille flipped open her day planner to the back pages. There was only one week of school left. She wrote the number seven under her *Days 'til Freedom* heading. Suddenly, she felt sick. She didn't want freedom, not when to her it had always meant ending her life.

Before, her life had been an endless treadmill of torture. Doctor appointments, trial treatments, medication after medication. No wonder she'd been ready to give up. But now, when she looked at the number seven, panic sliced through her. It was such a small number. She wasn't ready for it to be over.

Camille looked back at her calendar and the fathomless empty dates after graduation. She hadn't penciled anything in. She hadn't planned to be around then. Her fingers trembled as she picked up a pen and drew a shaky question mark on the next Sunday. It was the day after graduation. And Camille unexpectedly had an overwhelming urge to see that day, and the next, and the next. She wondered with cautious hope if maybe there was still time to turn things around. She picked up her phone and dialed the number to her oncologist.

The receptionist picked up. "Hello? Hello?"

Camille almost lost her nerve. But the word *hello* changed her mind. It had been the first thing Nate ever said to her. And that one little word had changed Camille's world. She took a deep breath, hoping it could do the same thing twice.

"Hi, this is Camille LaRue. I was wondering if I could talk about my treatment options?"

AFTER HER CONVERSATION with her doctor, a strange feeling of hopefulness washed over Camille. She penciled in the words *Oncologist 2:15 pm* on the following Wednesday. It was a full four days after graduation. Her heart was pounding with excitement. *Maybe she could find more time after all?*

Camille opened her desk drawer and pulled out her stationary set. She hadn't used it in years. She'd never had anyone to write to before now. The pale gray paper had her initials monogrammed at the top in a flourishing lavender font. Cami put pen to paper and started to write.

She'd always been cautious and orderly, and though hope had taken hold of her, she didn't want to leave anything to chance. She'd been saving this task as long as she could. And even though she'd changed her mind about her future, she still knew her expiration date would be here before she was ready.

She clicked the top of her silver pen and started to write. *Dear Nate . . .*

36

Cami

CAMILLE AWOKE to a knock at her bedroom door.

Her mother poked her head in. "Are you awake, honey?"

"Yeah, mom. I'm up."

"Good. I made your favorite breakfast."

"Banana pancakes?"

"With whipped cream and pecans."

"Thanks Mom! You're the best," Camille said trying to hug her around Poo's growls.

Her mother hugged her tightly for a moment before walking toward the door. "Oh, and there's a delivery waiting for you downstairs."

Camille rubbed the sleep from her eyes. "A delivery? What is it?"

Her mother gave an unconvincing shrug. "Why don't you come see?"

Camille brushed her teeth, pulled her purple bathrobe on and was down the stairs in record time. Waiting on the buffet was a giant white box with the words, *Jenny Packham PARIS,* printed in silver on top.

Goose bumps rushed down Camille's arms. "Oh my God," she whispered.

Jenny Packham was her favorite Paris designer. Once, Camille had found a gorgeous Jenny Packham headband at a vintage boutique on Royal called Bambi DeVille. She'd worn it so much that a few of the beautifully cut crystals were now missing and she'd had to retire it.

Camille's fingers were trembling as she lifted the edge of the hinged box. A single white notecard lay atop a mass of white tissue paper. She opened the card carefully, her heart thumping when she recognized Nate's scribbly handwriting.

Camille,
You deserve the world.
Let's start with Paris.
X – Nate

CAMILLE FOLDED BACK the tissue paper and was greeted with a sea of sequins, beading and tulle. She gasped, carefully lifting out the most beautiful dress she'd ever seen. It had a full-length tulle skirt the color of the midnight sky and a sheer V-neck top that glittered like the stars. A rich, inky velvet sash rested at the drop waist and Camille thought she was going to cry. She'd never dreamed she'd own a Jenny Packham dress, yet somehow Nate had dreamed it for her, and then made it come true.

Ronnie's words echoed in her memory. *"Sugar, that boy is the one. He's gonna give you the sky and all the stars in it."* Camille hugged the dress to her and closed her eyes. Suddenly, she wanted everything Ronnie had ever told her to be true. Because if she believed anything, it was that she and Nate belonged together, and she never wanted to let him go.

Camille heard the click of a camera and opened her eyes. Her parents were standing in the hall beaming at her.

"How?" Camille asked holding up the dress.

Her mother smiled, shaking her head. "I've gotta hand it to him. That boy has great taste."

"But how did he know I love Jenny Packham?" Cami asked.

"You didn't tell him?" her father asked.

Camille shook her head.

Her parents looked at each other, smiling. "Dumb luck, I suppose," her father mused.

Camille's mother, swatted at him. "Like you've ever believed in that."

Camille's father was almost as superstitious as Ronnie. *But if neither of her parents told Nate of her designer crush, how could he have known?*

She was still running the question over in her mind when her mother handed her another envelope. Camille gave her parents a questioning look but they only smiled, and then her father snapped another photo.

Camille glared at him.

"What? I told Nate I'd document this for him."

"Where is he?" she asked.

"Read your note," her mother prompted.

Camille pulled out the notecard and read Nate's message.

Camille,
Everything you need is waiting in your room.

I'll pick you up soon. Be ready.
X – Nate

CAMILLE WALKED UPSTAIRS in a daze after woofing down her breakfast. She was still wondering what in the world Nate meant by, *everything was waiting in her room?* It hadn't looked any different when she'd woken up. She gripped the dress box tighter, feeling like she needed to pinch herself. She wanted to call Nate. She didn't know what he was up to, but it seemed his stay of grand gestures was over.

As Camille walked down the hall she heard the sounds of muffled giggles coming from her room. *What the hell?*

She opened the door to see Ashley Banks laying an assortment of accessories across her bed, while Ashley Calhoune unfolded an army of makeup brushes on her desk. They saw her and immediately rushed toward her in a flurry of squeals, demanding to see the dress.

"You knew about this?" Camille asked in surprise.

"Of course!" Ashley B. replied.

Ashley C. grinned. "Who did you think directed him to Jenny Packham?"

"She truly is a goddess," Ashley B. added.

Camille unboxed the dress and held it up, making both Ashleys swoon.

Ashley C. sighed. "You're going to look like a queen in that dress."

"How did you know I love this designer?" Camille asked, still flabbergasted.

Ashley Banks snorted. "Oh please. You wore that Jenny Packham headband until it fell apart. Anyone with an eye for fashion knew it was something special."

"I was so envious every time you wore it, so I looked it up,"

Ashley C. admitted. "That's when my Jenny Packham love affair began."

"So you guys picked out this dress?" Camille asked.

"Oh no, this was all Nathan. We just told him he couldn't go wrong if he got something from the designer you love."

Ashley C. ran her finger over the delicate fabric. "God you are so lucky, Camille. I can't believe your boyfriend ordered you a couture dress from Paris."

Camille's mouth dropped open. "It's couture?"

Both Ashleys looked at her like she'd said something foul. "Dresses like this are *not* off the rack, Camille."

Camille traced a finger over the plunging neckline. *How did Nate afford something like this?*

"Come on," Ashley B. urged. "We gotta get you ready for the ball, Cinderella."

"What?"

"Nate sent us to help you get ready," Ashley C. replied, going back to her legion of makeup.

"That's right." Ashley B. was beaming. "We're your fairy godmothers for the next two hours. Then we have to go get ready ourselves."

"You guys that's really sweet, but I can get ready myself. I don't wanna make you late for prom."

Ashley B. smiled. "Nate said you'd say that, but he sent us to make sure you're ready in time."

"Yeah. He said you're always late," added Ashley C.

Camille gasped. "Whatever. It's not my fault. I blame the cancer."

The girls laughed. "He said you'd say that, too."

Ashley C. wielded a makeup brush like a sword. "We're on to you, Camille. So quit resisting. This is all part of the plan."

Camille's heart skipped. *The plan.* She'd wanted to know what Nate's big secret plan was for weeks. But now that it was here, she wasn't sure she could handle it. She already loved him so much that sometimes it was hard to breathe when she thought about it. And when Nate did things like this, things that showed he truly knew her, it made her feel so inadequate. *She didn't deserve him, not when she only had so little of herself left to give.*

The overwhelming ache of Camille's love for Nate pressed against the back of her throat. She swallowed hard, giving in to the Ashleys so she wouldn't think about how scared she was to say goodbye to moments like this.

WHEN THE ASHLEYS finished working their magic, Camille hardly recognized herself. She looked like a princess. And it was her own hair and complexion staring back at her—not the false face she'd so often presented, hidden by wigs and copious amounts of careful cosmetics. She was wearing makeup, but somehow, the Ashleys managed to highlight Camille's features, bringing out her true beauty.

When they were done, they each gave her a tight squeeze, wishing her the best night ever.

Ashley Calhoune was packing up the last of her supplies when Ashley Banks approached Camille with another white envelope from Nate. "Here's your next clue."

Camille took the card. "Thank you, Ashley. And not just for today. I've enjoyed hanging out with you these past few weeks."

Ashley surprised Camille by pulling her into another hug. "Me too," she admitted. "I wish I hadn't waited so long to be your friend. You're a really cool person, Camille. I wish I could be more like you."

"What do you mean?"

She shrugged. "Strong, brave, not afraid to be who you are."

Camille wanted to laugh, because she wasn't any of those

things. But she was too stunned by the honesty in Ashley's voice to respond.

"Have a great time tonight, Cami. You deserve it."

"You too."

Ashley squeezed Camille's hands one last time. "See you at prom."

Nate

"How do I look?" Nate asked, coming out of his bedroom in his tux.

He'd been hoping to emulate Humphrey Bogart's character in *Casablanca* by wearing a white tuxedo jacket with black lapels, black pants and a crisp black bowtie.

His dad gave a low whistle, beaming proudly. "You look like a million bucks, boy-o."

Nate hugged his dad, and then let him straighten his bowtie.

He released a nervous sigh. Nate wanted tonight to be amazing for Camille. He'd spent the past few weeks planning every detail of tonight and he was praying it went perfectly. Cami deserved nothing less.

"So, are you ready for this?" his dad asked, patting him on the back.

"More than ready."

"You look nervous," his dad added. "Can I give you a piece of advice?"

"Sure."

"Don't hold back, Nate. Tell her everything that's in your heart. Life is too short for regrets."

Nate hugged his dad again. "Thanks, Dad."

"Nathan, I'm proud of you, son. I'm proud of the man you've become."

"Thanks, Dad. And thank you for helping me with all of this."

His dad smiled. "Thank you for letting me be a part of it."

"Always."

His dad pulled Nate in for one more hug, patting him hard on the back. "Now go show that girl of yours a night she'll never forget."

37

Cami

After the Ashleys left, Camille sat down on her bed. She was feeling overwhelmed by emotions and it was gnawing away at her energy. She leaned back against her pillows and stared at the scribbles she and Nate had added to her Hello Wall over the past few weeks. It was a map of their time together, and as her fingers traced over the words, her heart clenched with regret. *Why now? Why didn't she learn to live until she was dying?*

In truth, Camille had always been dying. At least since she was diagnosed with lymphoma. But it wasn't until she met Nate, that she realized how much of her life she'd wasted acting like she was already dead.

She'd walked around like she was already a ghost, never letting anyone in, keeping her parents at arms length to make saying goodbye easier. It had all been a waste. Because no matter what Camille did, it still hurt. Even if she fought and got a little more time, she knew she couldn't outrun her fate. It was like trying to fight a shadow.

Camille shuddered. She'd wasted so much time trying to shut everyone out to make things easier. But they weren't. She was still terrified of saying goodbye to her life, especially now that she wanted so much more of it.

A soft knock at her door pulled Camille from her thoughts. She sat up, feeling a bit dizzy with grief. Her mother poked her head into the room. She was carrying a tray of food and drinks.

"Camille . . ." Her mother's mouth dropped open when she saw her. "You look . . ." She started to tear up.

"Mom, don't cry or I'm gonna cry and then the Ashleys will have to come back, and there's already enough glitter in the carpet from their makeover to last a lifetime."

Her mother laughed. "Okay, okay. No tears. You just look so beautiful, honey."

"Thanks, Mom."

"I brought you something to eat."

"Oh, thanks Mom, but I think I'm too excited to eat."

Her mother looked at the tray of half eaten sandwiches she'd delivered to Camille and the Ashleys for lunch. Camille could tell her mother wanted to scold her for not eating more. But she didn't. All she said was, "You have a big night ahead of you. Are you excited?"

"Yeah, I really am." Camille paused. "Mom, does love always hurt like this?"

"What do you mean, honey?"

Camille's voice wavered. "I'm terrified of losing Nate, or hurting him. I just love him so much, and it scares me."

Her mother sat next to her on the bed and pulled Camille into a hug. After a while she took Cami's hands. "I know what you're going through isn't something any of us can imagine. But love is love, Camille. It's always a risk. Whether you have cancer or not."

Camille nodded and her mother stroked a hand down her cheek, tilting her chin so she could look into her eyes. Camille always loved that she and her mother had the same eyes—steel blue—like storm clouds over the ocean. It spoke to their strength.

"Honey, all I can tell you is that love isn't easy, but it's always worth it."

"I'm in love with him, Mom."

"I know, honey. And I know he loves you."

Camille squeezed her mother tighter.

"You deserve to be loved, Camille."

"But I'm gonna hurt him in the end."

"Maybe," she whispered. "But not tonight. Let's take things one day at a time."

Camille took a deep breath and nodded.

"Nathan wanted to make tonight special for you. We all did. I know we've had our differences, Camille. But I want you to know I love you more than anything in the world. And I just want you to be happy."

"Nate makes me happy, Mom. And you and Dad make me happy. I love you."

"I know, sweetheart." Her mother kissed her forehead. "I love you, too." She gave Camille another hug and then helped her up from the bed. "Now come on. We have to stay on schedule."

Camille realized she hadn't opened the envelope Ashley gave her. She flipped open the tab and pulled the notecard out.

Camille,
By the end of tonight,
You'll be putting a checkmark,
in each box on your wall.
Tonight we do it all.

X – Nate

"What's he talking about?" Camille asked.

Her mother grinned and shrugged.

"You know, don't you?"

"He ran the master plan by us."

"And?" Cami prodded.

"And you're just going to have to go along for the ride tonight, Camille."

"But—"

"It's okay to let someone else make the plans once in a while, honey."

Camille eyed her mother suspiciously. She was the biggest control freak Camille knew, and most likely who Camille inherited her neurotic obsession for order from.

Her mother laughed. "Yes, I realize it's the pot calling the kettle black."

Camille laughed. "Maybe Nate really *is* a good influence around here."

"Very funny. Now come on, your father isn't letting you out the door without taking a million photos and I still want you to eat something before you leave."

Camille grinned and followed her mother downstairs, leaving the ache and apprehension from earlier far behind.

Nate

Nate's heart was in his throat when he knocked on Camille's front door. It felt strange to be standing there again. For nearly a month he'd been living at the LaRue's sprawling French

Quarter home. And spending the night away had really given him perspective. He'd promised Camille that he would take whatever time she could give him and not pressure her for more. But after spending a night alone, staring at the cracks in his ceiling, he began to feel like they would soon be a reflection of his heart—*cracked and broken.*

Nate was so used to having Camille sleep nestled against his side, that he hadn't been able to sleep at all without her. He hadn't realized how alone he would feel without the touch of her breath at his neck, or the pump of her heart against his. She had become as much a part of Nate as his shadow, and the ache of losing her weighed on his soul.

He had hoped that his plans for today would be enough to drive his dark thoughts away, but as Nate stood at her door waiting for Camille to answer, he could think of nothing else. And when she finally answered, looking like a goddess in her ball gown, he wanted to drop to his knees and beg her to fight for every damn second she could. His heart pounded the same words over and over again, *Don't leave me. Don't leave me.*

"Speechless, huh?" she said, grinning back at him like a porcelain doll.

"You look beautiful, Camille."

She suddenly had her arms around his waist, hugging him tight. "Thank you for the dress and everything. Today has been . . . perfect."

She looked up at him with those big sparkling eyes of hers and Nate's resolve snapped into place like armor. For her, he would hold it together. She deserved one perfect night where all her dreams came true and he was going to do his damnedest to make that happen—*for the both of them.*

"It's just getting started," Nate said, brushing a light kiss against her cheek. "Are you ready?"

"Are you kidding? My dad's not letting us outta here without a kajillion more photos."

Nate laughed, and let Camille lead him into the house, glad for the familiar ease holding her hand brought him.

When they'd been fully paparazzied, Nate led Cami back to the front door, blaming their quick getaway on the strict schedule he'd mapped out. Nate watched Camille glitter as she sashayed a step ahead of him. The dress had been worth every penny. He'd drained his savings account to purchase it and took a loan from his mom to cover the rest. His mom agreed to help pay for Camille's dress only after Nate promised her he'd let his dad take pre-prom photos to send to her. Nate would've agreed to just about anything to make this night perfect for Camille, and so far, it was. And he had to admit it was kind of nice to share it with his dad, too. They'd had a good talk before driving to Camille's.

Nate was thankful for the way Cami had brought his family together. He and his dad had taken big steps in mending their relationship in the past few weeks. They had a better line of communication since the day Nate had broken down in front of him over Cami's cancer news. Nate was grateful to have his dad back in his life. He knew he was going to need his dad's support if there was any chance of surviving what losing Cami would do to him.

Nate said goodbye to his dad and Camille's parents, and then helped Cami into her black velvet wrap. He trained his eyes on her to be sure he wouldn't miss a moment of her reaction when he opened the door. From her gasp, to her shriek of joy, Nate knew every hoop he'd jumped through to hire a horse and carriage to take them to prom had been worth it. Camille was bouncing on her toes.

"Nate! Oh my God! I can't believe you did this!"

"You said you used to love them when you were little, so . . ."

He trailed off, watching her grin from-ear-to-ear as she walked up to the massive white horse.

He snapped a Polaroid of Cami kissing the horse's nose, before helping her into the carriage.

"Is there anything you haven't thought of?" she asked, snuggling in under his arm.

"I hope not." He pulled her closer. He'd missed everything about her in the night they'd spent apart. Nate drank in her light smell of lavender that encapsulated the air around them, letting it wrap around his heart like barbed wire.

"Nate, this is incredible."

Nate stowed his fear and grinned at Camille's glowing face. "You want the moon, just say the word and I'll lasso it, my darling."

She giggled.

"We'll always have Paris, kid."

"You're mixing up all the movie quotes."

"I'm making up my own. That's what tonight is all about. Think of it like the greatest hits of romance. We're doing it all, baby! Starting with riding off into the sunset."

Camille smiled so bright, the tiny dimple in her cheek showed. Bringing that dimple to the surface could be Nate's sole goal in life. He'd die a happy man if he couldn't count the amount of times he'd seen it.

"Isn't the riding into the sunset supposed to come last?"

"Not tonight, mon cheri."

She giggled again. "I think I like Romantic Nate."

"Good, because you're gonna get a whole lot of him tonight."

38

Cami

Camille loved every minute of her sunset horse and carriage ride. Instead of giving a guided tour about the history of New Orleans, the driver played a romantic jazz station as they meandered through the streets, revisiting all the places in New Orleans that were now special to them.

She was astounded to find how many places they could claim as their own. It was funny to have lived somewhere her entire life, but not truly have experienced it. Nate had shown her an entirely different view of New Orleans. And it made her want to see everything through his eyes.

She'd been tired earlier, overwhelmed by her emotions for Nate and the unfair amount of time they'd have left. But now, tucked under his arm, with his warmth coursing through her, she felt strong.

Camille studied the way the setting sun cast a bronze glow

over the sharp planes of Nate's face. His eyes glowed golden and the sun turned the waves of his thick brown hair into art, shifting between hues of copper and honey. Nate was making up words to the love song the driver was playing and Camille couldn't get enough of the way his voice sounded as it echoed through him into her chest. His face was all smiles and teeth, and she'd never seen anything more beautiful in her life.

Shamefully, Camille wondered how she hadn't seen it the day they'd met—his savage beauty, and the fact that they'd been made for each other. Nate had changed her—swept away all her broken pieces until she was bare and exposed. At first she'd hated the feeling of vulnerability, but in letting go, she'd found the courage to live, and she didn't want to let go.

Camille reached up taking Nate's face between her hands. "I love you," she whispered against his lips.

"I love you, too."

She buried herself in his kiss as the urge to fight for him swelled in her chest.

CAMILLE WALKED into The Paris Room at Café Soule and it was as if she'd been transported to France. The ballroom sparkled with a massive Eiffel Tower lighting up the vaulted powder blue walls. Chandeliers glittered above the sea of dancing students as the sultry sound of the live jazz band wafted toward her. Everywhere she looked there were clusters of long white feathers and bouquets of white peonies on white linen tablecloths. The elegant bistro tables for two dotted the banquet room. And a buffet of pastel-colored sweets took up nearly one entire wall. Camille recognized the hot pink logo of Sweet Thang's adorning the table.

"Oh my God," she whispered. "Is Ronnie catering prom?"

"Just the desserts."

Camille heard a familiar booming voice behind her. "Like I would miss this for the world."

She turned to see Ronnie smiling at her. He was wearing a purple and gold paisley tuxedo jacket and jade green pants. A gold shimmer highlighted his cat-like green eyes and Cami had never seen him look more fabulous.

"Ronnie!" She exhaled his name and ran into his arms.

He wrapped her into a hug. "No tears yet. You have pictures and dinner and dancing to get through, baby cakes."

"I'm so glad you're here."

"Me too. Have I mentioned you look radiant, Camille?" Ronnie turned to Nate and gave him a fist bump. "Excellent choice on the dress, Nathaniel. But then I always knew you had great taste."

Camille laughed. "Did everyone know about the dress but me?"

"That's kinda how surprises work, Cami," Nate teased.

"Well I don't wanna keep you two," Ronnie said, giving Camille a kiss on each cheek. "But save me a dance, sugar."

"I will," she said, relishing in the smell of burnt sugar that followed Ronnie everywhere.

"I was talking to Nathaniel," he teased, coyly blowing him a kiss as he sauntered away.

"So . . . what happened to the *'Just Say Yes'* theme?" Camille asked.

"Turns out the Ashleys weren't very attached to it."

"Yeah right. What aren't you telling me?"

"Okay I sorta had to sell my kidney to Ashley Dupree, but it's not a big deal, I have two."

"Nate . . . I'm serious."

"I am too. I just asked if we could make it a Paris theme because it would really help me do something special for you."

"That's all?"

"Yes. I know you still don't believe it, but a lot of kids at

NOAH care about you, Cami. People are good, in general. You just gotta give them a chance."

Camille bit her lip, nodding as the Ashleys spotted her and Nate, waving them over. *It wasn't that Cami didn't believe Nate, it was that she'd waited too long to realize he was right.*

Nate

The Ashleys had outdone themselves. They'd barely had a month to make the changes to the prom theme, but they'd completely pulled it off. The hardest thing had been getting the venue changed to The Paris Room. But Ashley Dupree had put her persuasive charm to good use for once. And besides renting the light up Eiffel Tower and backdrop for the photos, all the other silver and white decorations worked seamlessly.

Nate *did* have to promise Ashley Dupree a dance, but he had a back up plan for that, too. He'd called her boyfriend, Xavier Hale. Xavier went to Tulane, and Nate asked if he would come to prom to surprise Ashley D. Nate figured if Xavier was there, then it would keep Ashley off his back, and Cami's.

Plus, from all the time he'd spent with the Ashleys while Cami was recovering, he'd found out that most of Ashley Dupree's bitchiness was all a front. She was really just worried that her boyfriend of forever was moving on without her. So getting Xavier to come to prom was as much to make Ashley Dupree's night special, too. It was the least Nate could do to say thank you for helping him give Camille a night in Paris.

Nate wanted to do something to repay the other Ashleys for helping him with the dress and giving Cami a pre-prom makeover. But they'd insisted that the only thing they wanted was to see Camille happy. They really were sweet girls. And Nate was glad that Camille had let them in. Cami was currently posing with Ashley Banks and Ashley Calhoune in front of a Parisian backdrop. They giggled while making silly faces much to the photographer's dismay.

"Nate! You're next," Ashley Banks called.

He joined the girls and their dates for a few group photos but then interrupted to make sure he got a photo of just him and Camille. "You all look beautiful, but if you don't mind, I want one with just my girl."

The Ashleys swooned, but exited with their dates.

"How you holding up?" Nate asked, running his fingers down Camille's rosy cheeks. He knew she got tired quickly and didn't want her to over do it. They still had a lot of night ahead of them.

"I'm fine."

He kissed her forehead. "Yeah?"

"You don't have to check my temperature."

"I'm not."

Camille gave him that look. The one that said, *I know you.* The one that was like a knife to the heart.

"Okay, busted." Nate thought he was subtle, but he should've known Camille was on to him. She didn't miss much and he was surprised he'd managed to keep this much of the night a surprise so far. "I just want to make sure you don't get too tired for what I have planned later."

"There's more?" she asked looking surprised.

"I told you I'd knock your socks off," he teased pulling her into a kiss.

Camille lifted the hem of her skirt, showing off her combat boots. "I'm waiting."

Nate snorted. "Only you could pull off military boots with couture."

"Well, I think that's the nicest thing you've ever said to me, Nathan Hawthorne," she joked.

"Come here." Nate scooped Camille into his arms.

He heard the photographer snapping away as Cami shrieked with laughter while he spun her in his arms. He was glad that he'd have photos to capture this moment because he never wanted it to end. He wanted to live here, in the fake Paris skyline, with Camille in his arms and her laughter filling his heart.

39

Cami

CAMILLE ENJOYED every aspect of prom. The food, the photos, the music, dancing with Nate, admiring everyone in their dresses and tuxedos. Xavier Hale even showed up to surprise Ashley Dupree. After a dramatic scene where she screamed and leapt into his arms, she was crowned prom queen and the Ashleys were each awarded tiaras in her court. Everything was as it should be.

"Still sure you didn't want to be up there?" Nate asked as they watched the prom queen and princesses waving like royalty.

"Absolutely. You know I hate the spotlight. Besides, I want to spend every second of tonight in your arms."

"I like the way you think," Nate said, pulling her back onto the dance floor.

They swayed to the slow jazz tune until one song bled into

the next. Camille was in heaven, her head nestled against Nate's broad chest as they swayed back and forth. He'd taken his tux jacket off and she liked it better that way. There was only a thin white shirt between her and Nate's skin, and she was drunk on his smell of sunshine and possibilities.

At some point, Ronnie tapped her on the shoulder. "How 'bout a dance, baby cakes?"

Nate bowed as he passed her off to Ronnie. Camille watched him walk over to the Ashleys and shake Xavier's hand after getting a big hug from Ashley Dupree.

"That boy sure is something," Ronnie crooned as if reading Camille's thoughts.

She smiled. "He makes me feel like anything's possible."

"It is, bebe. There's a lot of magic in this world. And that boy is full of it."

"I love him so much it hurts, Ronnie."

"Well that's how you know it's real, sugar."

"You think?"

"I know."

"I feel like it's not fair to him."

"Love's not supposed to be fair, baby cakes. It's real and all consuming. It lights your heart on fire and sometimes all you can do is hang on. And I'm pretty sure he couldn't ask you for anything more."

"I want more time," Camille whispered. She'd kept her sadness at bay all night, but now in Ronnie's arm, it was seeping back. He always had a way of making it easy for her to speak her greatest fears.

"We all do, bebe. But sometimes that's not up to us."

"What do I do?"

"Live in the moment. And stop worrying about the things you can't control. Life doesn't come with a road map. All you can do is live with no regrets."

Camille smiled up at Ronnie. "So, live like you're dying?"

"Exactly, bebe. What you two got, you ain't never gonna get enough of. Whether it's one month, one year or one hundred. But I promise you, it'll last a lifetime. Don't be afraid to tell him what's in your heart."

Cami wrapped her arms around Ronnie, hugging him tight. "I love you, Ronnie."

"I know, baby cakes. I love you, too."

Camille looked up at the tears sparkling in his eyes. "You said no crying."

"You don't have to be clairvoyant to know I'd be a blubbering fool by the end of this night. My girl's all grown up."

Camille kissed him on the cheek. "Thank you, Ronnie. For everything. I don't think I would've made it here without you in my life. "

"Oh, Lord, child. Go back to that boy a yours before my mascara starts running. I'm still on the clock here."

She laughed. "Okay. I'll see ya, Ronnie."

"Yes, you will, bebe. Now go make some memories."

Camille flounced back over to Nate. She waved to Ronnie, who was still staring after her like a proud papa who'd just given his daughter away. She blew him a kiss and let Nate pull her onto the dance floor. *'As Time Goes By'* started playing and Nate scooped her into his arms. "Here's looking at you, kid."

Camille kissed him. "Thank you for this, Nate. Now we'll always have Paris."

40

Nate

NATE GLANCED AT CAMILLE, barely able to contain his excitement. "No peeking," he ordered.

"Nate! You are ridiculous. Are you going to keep me blindfolded the whole time?"

"Just a little bit longer."

Nate eased his dad's pickup truck off the road. He'd stolen Cami away from prom early to make sure she didn't wear herself out on the dance floor. His dad had dropped off the truck with the prom valet service and packed the things Nate asked for in the back.

Nate was sure the smell of salt air would alert Camille to his plans, even though he'd blindfolded her after they'd crossed Lake Pontchartrain. He didn't want her to get any ideas where they were headed.

"I promise it'll be worth it," Nate said.

Camille made what she probably thought was a growl, but it pretty much sounded like an angry kitten—*basically, it was adorable.*

"Come on, is it that bad?" he asked. "They say taking away a sense heightens all the others."

"So."

"So enjoy your heightened senses."

"Are you trying to tell me that my surprise is your voice sounding extra sexy?"

Nate grinned. "You think I have a sexy voice?" he asked, in a low growl.

"Nate!"

"Okay, I couldn't resist," he said not even trying to hide his amusement. "I'll give you a hint."

Nate rolled down the window as they left the road, creeping along the abandoned stretch of sand he'd scoped out a few days ago. The salt air must've surprised Camille, because she inhaled sharply as the wind ruffled the short fringe of her baby-fine hair. The moonlight washed everything silver and Nate had the strange feeling that he was staring at an angel again as he drank in Camille's ethereal glow.

He shivered at the goose bumps that assaulted his skin. The sound of the ocean was unmistakable to him, and he had the sensation of being home as he listened to the push and pull of the sea. He missed that sound—the breathing of the ocean. It had been the soundtrack of his life in California, and he couldn't wait to share it with Camille.

He reached over to take her hand and she jumped. Her skin was cool and stippled with goose bumps. She was trembling. "You okay?" he asked.

She turned toward him, her blindfold still secured. "Are we at the beach?" she whispered her voice as fragile as glass.

"Take your blindfold off."

With shaking hands she removed the blindfold. He saw

tears instantly fill her eyes as she gasped at the scenery. Nate had parked the truck on the moonlit beach facing the ocean. Camille gazed around in wonder, her large eyes reflecting the shimmer of the water like a mirror. The look of pure awe on her face slammed into Nate's heart. He wanted to remember it forever.

Cami

"NATE . . ." Camille exhaled his name like it held magic. She couldn't tear her eyes from the water, but she reached for his hand, squeezing it with trembling strength.

He slid across the bench seat so he could be closer to her. "Do you like it?"

"It's more beautiful than I ever could've imagined." She sucked in a breath. "I can't believe I waited so long to come to the beach."

"Me either," he said kissing the top of her head. "Come on."

"Where are we going?"

"We're not here to just look at it. The beach is meant to be experienced."

Camille let Nate unlace her boots and lift her out of the truck, his steady hands firm at her waist. The coolness of the sand on her feet surprised her and she let out a tiny yelp.

It made Nate grin wide enough to rival the moon for brightest light source on the beach. "God this was so worth it to see your face. You'd think I brought you to the moon."

"It sorta feels like you did," she admitted. "Where are we anyway?"

"Biloxi."

"I had no idea there was something this beautiful an hour and a half away."

"This is nothing," Nate teased. "I wanted to take you to Florida or to an island, where all you can see for miles is white sand and crystal blue water. But I was trying to tick all your bucket list boxes, so I'm hoping Biloxi will do."

"It's perfect."

Nate laughed. "I don't think anyone's ever said that about Biloxi before."

"I'm serious, Nate. Tonight has been like a dream."

"Good," he whispered against her lips. "Because that's all I want to do, Cami. I want to make your every dream come true."

She looped her arms around his neck and kissed him. "You already have."

It took everything in Camille's power to let Nate stop kissing her, but he was inching them toward the water. "Wait. What about my dress?"

"What about it?"

"I don't want to get it all sandy."

Nate raised his eyebrows and gave her a crooked smile. "Take it off."

"What?"

"Last one in the water's a rotten egg."

"Are you crazy?"

"Crazy 'bout you," he said nipping her lips with a kiss before pulling off his shirt.

"We're gonna freeze to death!" she exclaimed.

But Nate was already kicking off his shoes and unbuttoning his pants. "Cami, trust me. I've got you covered."

She blushed when Nate shimmied down to his boxers. "Are we really doing this?"

"Says the girl who made me swim in the Mississippi?"

"Oh, I *so* did not make you do that."

"All I know is you're about to be a rotten egg," Nate taunted jogging backward toward the water.

"Not fair!" Camille cried. "I can't get this off by myself." It was a total lie, but she didn't want to lose.

"Camille LaRue, are you asking me to take your dress off?"

"Why yes I am. I have no morals and low standards. You know this about me."

Nate laughed coming back to her. His breath was warm on her neck as he slowly unzipped her dress, peppering kisses down her spine. "That's precisely what I love about you, Miss LaRue."

Camille couldn't help but shiver. The warmth of Nate's lips against her wind-chilled skin was like ice crackling in fire. Her whole body came alive under his touch, and suddenly, she didn't want to beat him to the water. She didn't want to be anywhere but in his arms.

Nate unfastened the last clasp on her dress. Only her hands held it up. She turned slowly to face him. The moonlight made him glow. He was all shadows and bone. And in that moment Nate looked more like a statue carved from marble than the boy she knew and loved. He was so staggeringly beautiful it took her breath away. She let go of her dress, feeling the rich fabric pool at her feet. She stepped out of the dress toward Nate, nearly naked.

Camille had never felt more exposed, but Nate made her feel secure. The last time she and Nate had been together like this had been such a frenzy. It was a rush of emotion and passion, over almost before she realized it'd started. But this time would be different. She could tell from the smoldering gaze with which Nate regarded her.

Tension pulled every muscle taught across his chest and abdomen. He was holding himself back. Camille shivered as she pulled off the last of her undergarments. She stood completely bare in front of Nate. The muscle in his jaw twitched as she took a step toward him. Then another. Then another. Until there was no space between them and finally

Nate gave in, his arms circling around her, pulling her closer and closer, as if they could dissolve into each other.

Nate hoisted her up and Camille wrapped her legs around him. Her fingers twisted in his hair and across the muscles of his back as he kissed her, carrying her into the water. She gasped when it first reached her toes, clinging tighter to Nate, until the water was lapping at her waist. They moved deeper still, until the water took her weight and they floated together, kissing and bobbing with the gentle roll of the waves.

The water was warmer than the air and Camille relaxed into it, focusing only on Nate. His lips were soft and cool and tasted like salt. She clung to him as he traced feather-light kisses across her throat. She felt her pulse throbbing beneath her skin as Nate captured her mouth with his. She couldn't get enough of him. She was broken and he was the only thing that could fix her.

"Is this okay?" Nate asked when their passion started to progress.

"Yes," she panted between kisses.

"You're sure?"

"Nate, I've been sure since the moment I met you. I'm just sorry it took me so long to figure it out."

"Cami . . ."

"Nate, I don't want to talk. I want this. I want us."

It was all the coaxing he needed and Camille lost herself in him.

Nate kissed her as wave after wave of bliss crashed over. Her arms shook as she tried to contain the joy erupting inside her. It was like a million stars exploding under her skin at once, and she was sure even the heavens could see her glow.

41

Nate

NATE LAY in the bed of the pickup truck staring up at the clouds. Camille was curled against him. Her breath warm on his neck was enough to make his heart turn over in his chest. It was a soft reassurance that soothed him like nothing else. The rise and fall of her breath matched the ocean, creating a euphoric lullaby that made him close his eyes.

He held her tightly, willing himself to stay in the moment. He just wanted to hold onto the happiness. Making love to Camille had broken him apart and put him back together again. He laced his fingers with hers, trying not to think about how fragile she was. He could truly feel it now, with nothing between them.

Camille was putting up a good front, but it was hard not to notice how much thinner she was. Rage ignited inside of him. Nate wanted to burn the world apart for being so unjust to someone like Camille. Nate shoved his anger aside. He'd become an expert at locking it away. He knew there would be time for it later. But right now, he just wanted to be present with Cami.

He kissed the top of her head and she snuggled closer. She sighed into him. He tried to remain focused on the good. Like the warmth of her body and the strength with which she clung to him when they made love. Her resilience amazed him. Every day he watched and waited, knowing each moment brought them a step closer to goodbye. But she was still here. The girl he loved was still with him. And he was desperate to make himself believe that was enough.

He took it as a good sign that she hadn't had a relapse since the hospital. There was a time when she'd first come home when her parents had wanted to call in hospice. Nate didn't know what that meant at the time, and since Camille hated talking about anything cancer related, he'd decided to Google lymphoma and hospice. It had been a mistake. One horrible webpage led to the next and before he knew it, Nate was being swallowed by the black hole of cancer and the stages of dying. He'd promptly thrown up his dinner and spent the next forty minutes hiding his tears in the shower until the water ran cold.

Nate had abstained from morbid online research ever since. But still, he knew Camille was dying. No matter how tangible and warm she was, he was losing her little by little each day. It was excruciating to watch someone you loved disappear before your very eyes. Nate felt like he was constantly trying to hold water in the palm of his hand, but no matter what, it kept slipping through the cracks.

He felt guilty thinking like this when he was with Camille. Each moment with her was so exquisite that he didn't want to waste it not being completely present. But it still didn't stop him from being angry. He was mad at everything. Mad at cancer and the doctors for not being able to fix it. Mad at Cami for not wanting to give them more time. Mad at God or maybe the universe, because sometimes Nate didn't know what he believed in anymore. The world seemed upside-down. *Because in what universe was it okay for someone as wonderful as Cami to be taken away? And why did it have to hurt so bad?*

Nate had never experienced pain like this. He thought losing Tyler was the worst thing he'd ever have to go through in his life. And it *was* awful. But Nate had survived. He'd fought through the grief and suffocating depression of losing his only brother. And he'd come out the other side. Nate was stronger for it. He'd learned to grab life by the balls and soak up every opportunity to live. This wasn't supposed to happen. He wasn't supposed to get knocked down again. Not like this. It wasn't fair.

With Ty it had been different. Not better or worse. Just different. Ty was there one minute, gone the next—just wiped away. There was nothing for Nate to do. But with Cami, it was a constant tilt-a-whirl of torture. And it was killing him. Nate wanted to scream and cry and shake her, begging for her to fight.

He'd promised her he wouldn't ask her to change her mind, but it still didn't stop the wave of despair that pulled him under. It was worse in the quiet hours of night, when Nate held Camille in his arms, just trying to hold on—to stay in place. It was becoming impossible to do without imagining what it soon would be like without her there beside him. *How could he not try to memorize her, when he knew she was going to be taken away?*

Nate knew he had no right to ask her for anything more. Not after all she'd already given. Everyone asked for more. Her parents, the doctors, teachers, students—but Nate couldn't be one of them. No matter how much the voice inside him was screaming—*Stay! Stay with me. I'm nothing without you. Don't leave me.*

He needed to be strong for her. He needed to be what she

needed. Nate pushed his thoughts down deeper, shutting them away as he studied the sliver map of scars that disrupted Camille's perfect skin. They shimmered in the moonlight as he traced his fingers across them. It'd taken months for Nate to be able to skim his fingers down Camille's back without her flinching. He knew she hated her scars, no matter what he told her. He saw beauty and strength, but he could see it in her eyes . . . she only saw the surgeries and biopsies. And that was why he couldn't ask her to give anymore of herself. *She'd already given too much.*

Nate was lucky to just be in her presence. He held her tight praying for a tenth of her strength, so he might be strong enough to keep going, when she could not.

Cami

Camille reveled in the warmth Nate spread through her. She could still feel the echoes of fireworks beneath her skin. Making love to Nate in the ocean had been a form of magic she didn't know existed. She was currently lying next to him, reliving every moment of their night together.

As if the night wasn't already everything she'd ever hoped for and more, Nate had surprised Camille further by carrying her from the ocean to the truck where the entire bed of the pickup was full of blankets, cushions and pillows. Nate had dried her off, wrapped her in a blanket and climbed into the bed of the truck with her. And Camille had never felt more at peace, as she lay there, wrapped in Nate's arms gazing up at the stars.

It was a rare cloudless night, and the sky glittered with winking starlight. It reminded Camille of the dress Nate bought her for prom. He was the most thoughtful person she'd ever met. The way he constantly surprised her was mind-boggling. And as she looked at him, his face turned up to stare at the heavens, she wondered how she'd ever managed without him.

Thinking of herself without Nate was like listening to a song missing a chord. The thought struck Camille and her heart faltered. Nate turned to look at her, as if he somehow sensed her sorrow. The grief she witnessed in the shine of his eyes was impossible to bear. She knew she was breaking his heart, because she too was shattering apart and Nate was the only thing holding her together.

This wasn't part of the plan. She was never supposed to fall in love. Love made everything impossible. And for the first time, Camille could name her fear. She realized that she wasn't afraid to die, but to die afraid. If she let go now, she would always regret it. She owed it to Nate to fight. She owed it to herself.

Nate's hand brushed her cheek, catching the tears she hadn't realized she'd shed. "Cami?"

She grabbed his hand and pulled it to her lips, kissing his knuckles. "I love you, Nate."

"I love you, too." His eyes searched hers. "Are you okay? Do you want to go inside?"

"Not yet." She sat up and so did he.

"What's wrong?"

"I need to tell you something."

"Okay."

Nate took her hands, warmth and patience present in every touch.

Camille didn't know how to start. She closed her eyes. "I never planned for this. I never planned to fall in love with you. But now . . ." She took a shuddering breath and let the rest of the words tumble out in a rush. "But now all my plans are ruined. I'm ruined. But I'm grateful for it. Because you showed up with your ridiculous smile and your chaos and you showed me what it's like to be alive. You make me want to forget my plans, Nate. You make me want to live."

Camille watched her words register on Nate's face. Even with the moonlight washing the world pale, she could see the color drain from his cheeks.

"Cami . . . what are you saying?"

"I want to fight, Nate. I don't know how much more time it will give us, but I want to fight for every second."

His voice was so soft that she barely heard him over the crash of the waves. "You want to fight?"

She nodded. "I want to fight."

Nate threw his arms around her and pulled her into a trembling embrace. "Oh thank God," he whispered, tears streaking down his face.

In that moment Camille knew it had never really been a choice. She couldn't leave Nate of her own free will. He was her heart, and it wouldn't beat without him.

42

Cami

CAMILLE WOKE up to Nate drawing open the blinds of their hotel room. The floor-to-ceiling windows overlooked the ocean and he scrambled back over to watch the sunrise with her from their bed. She drank in his familiar warmth as he settled under the covers, pulling her into his arms.

"This is perfect," he whispered, kissing her behind her ear.

Camille's toes curled whenever Nate did that. Last night after she'd told him she wanted to fight for them, he'd carried her up to their hotel room and made love to her again. In the night they'd spent together, he'd perhaps kissed every inch of her body, but the delicate skin behind her ear was strangely her favorite.

"*You* are perfect," she said, pulling him closer. She turned to face him, snuggling into his chest.

"How are you feeling?" he asked for about the tenth time.

"Perfect."

Nate peeled himself away so Camille had to look into his eyes. They glowed like honey, crinkling as he grinned. He hadn't stopped smiling since she told him she'd changed her mind and wanted to fight her cancer.

"You're sure?" he asked.

"Yes."

"And you're still sure about everything you said last night?"

"More sure than ever."

Nate was practically giddy. "So, what do we do first?"

"Well, I guess we go home and tell my parents. Then I go back to my oncologist to see where I'm at and what my options are."

"Do you want to call now?" Nate asked excitedly.

Camille blushed. "I sorta already did."

"What do you mean?"

"I made an appointment the day before prom."

Nate stared at her, blinking in shock.

"I'm sorry. I should've told you right away. But it wasn't something I wanted to say over the phone and you were running around making all of this happen," she said gesturing to the hotel room. "Plus, I don't want to get your hopes up."

"Too late," he said pulling her into his arms. "And don't be sorry. I don't care how or when you told me, only that the ticking time bomb has stopped."

"Paused," she corrected. "I'm not going to get better, Nate. This is about fighting to hold on for as long as I can."

The sentence was sobering and Nate sat up, pulling Camille into his lap. "Cami, I only want you to do this if it's what you want."

"It is, Nate. More than anything. I just don't want to give you unrealistic expectations."

"Cami, you gave me hope. And that's enough."

. . .

Nate

THE DRIVE HOME to New Orleans was exhilarating. A huge weight had been lifted off Nate's chest. He held Camille's hand with renewed life. He couldn't believe she'd changed her mind. When they'd talked earlier that morning, a tiny kernel of doubt that maybe she'd change her mind again had crept up, but he'd slammed it down easily. It was nothing compared to the demons he'd been battling over the past few months. Now he felt free and he couldn't rein in his excitement.

"We can do anything we want. We can even go to Paris for real now."

Camille giggled.

"Don't laugh. I'm serious. We need to make outrageous plans. We need something to look forward to."

"How about spending more time with my amazing boyfriend?"

"No, think bigger!" Nate yelled over the sound of the road rushing by.

"Well, Paris *is* pretty big."

"That's the spirit. Let's do it. Let's go to Paris. It'll be our graduation present to each other."

"Nate. Be real. We can't just go to Paris."

"Why not? Cami, there's a great big world out there and I want to see it with you. We have time now. And we can't waste it. I want to fill every wall in your room, hell every wall in your house, with all the things we want to do together."

Camille frowned.

"What's wrong?"

"I was just thinking, do you think you'll still be allowed to stay in my guest house?"

"Cami, I'm pretty sure you have a get-out-of-jail-free cancer card for the rest of your life. Your parents are going to be so happy you decided to fight for more time they're not gonna care about anything else."

"Huh." She looked thoughtful for a moment. Then a bright grin slid across her face. "Maybe we really *can* go to Paris."

Cami

NATE WAS RIGHT. Camille's parents would let her get away with just about anything at this point. They'd been in tears when she and Nate came home and she told them she'd decided to go back to her doctor to work on a treatment plan that would give her as much time as possible. They didn't even shoot down Nate's crazy suggestion that they could go to Paris for real now.

Guilt gnawed at Camille as she heard the relief and joy in her parents' voice. She hadn't realized how much her decision was hurting them. It made her chest ache. Of course she knew they didn't want to lose her. They were her parents—no parent ever wanted to lose a child. But despite Camille's change of heart, she knew her parents would still outlive her. And when that time came, she'd hoped they would feel relief. That when she was gone a burden would be lifted from them.

But now, as she let her parents hold her, sobbing with joy, she realized how wrong she'd been. She may have bought more time, but she couldn't go back and fix her past mistakes. And no matter how many days she cheated from her disease, she would never be ready to say goodbye.

43

Nate

THE LAST WEEK of school flew by in a flurry of excitement, and not just because of Camille's renewed determination to fight for her life, but because they'd made it. They were graduating—him and Cami. They'd finished their last class today and had the rest of the week off before the ceremony on Saturday. Nate's mom was flying in for the celebration and he couldn't wait to introduce her to Camille.

Her parents were planning a graduation party at their house after the ceremony and invited Nate's parents to attend. Nate made himself useful by helping prepare for the party. That is, when he could tear himself away from Cami. She'd seemed tired lately and he was worried she was overdoing it.

Camille blamed her exhaustion on the excitement of graduation and all their future plans. She'd applied to Tulane and the dean at NOAH pulled a few strings to get her accepted. *Nate and Camille were going to college together!*

He couldn't believe how much his life had changed in just a few days. They were currently pouring over the course catalog at Café Beignet while Nate polished off a plate of sugary pastries.

"So when do we have to finalize our classes?" Camille asked.

"We have a little time," Nate said. "But, I was thinking, if we're gonna go to Paris, we should probably submit our class selections as soon as possible."

"Nate . . ."

"What? My parents said they'd buy me a ticket for graduation. And you know your parents would buy you a ticket to the moon if you asked for it."

"I know."

"So what's stopping us?"

"Honestly? I don't know. It's just surreal. For so long I didn't think I'd even make it to graduation. And now, it's almost dizzying to have all these possibilities."

Nate scooted his chair closer until Camille's knees were between his. He gave them a squeeze. "Anything's possible, Cami. You taught me that."

"You really think we can do it? Paris? College?"

Nate kissed her. "And more."

She sighed. "Okay. But I hope you know you've created a monster. Because I want it all, Nate. I want you and Paris and this every single day," she said kissing him again.

He pulled her onto his lap and kissed her passionately, not caring about their borderline scandalous display of public affection. Camille LaRue was Nate's world, and he wanted everyone to know it. She'd chosen him and they'd survived against all odds. If that wasn't something to be celebrated, nothing was.

"Okay, it's settled," Nate said after he came up for air. "You know what that means?"

"What?"

"It's time to make a plan," he teased.

"You joke, but you'll be thanking me when all our classes match up and we earn sightseeing badges on Tripadvisor for seeing more of Paris than most Parisians."

Nate laughed. "Nothing would make me happier than to watch you plan your little heart out."

"Good. Then it's settled. We'll meet here tomorrow to finish picking classes and start our Paris plan."

"It's a date." Nate looked at his watch. "I better go. My mom's flight gets in soon and I told her I'd bring her one of Ronnie's famous donuts. Are you sure you don't want to come with me?"

"I would, but I told my parents I'd try on my cap and gown so they can take photos. They want to have one framed at the party for everyone to sign."

"That's a great idea." Nate smirked. "Maybe I'll stop by later and take some of my own." He gave her a wink. "More cap, less gown."

Cami rolled her eyes.

Nate pulled her into a hug. "Okay, gotta go. Until our next hello."

Cami

"DAD, I'm pretty sure you've captured the perfect photo," Camille whined.

She'd been posed in just about every room of her house. With her cap, without it. With Poo, with each of her parents and even some of all of them with the help of his tripod and timer.

Secretly, Camille was having fun. It reminded her of when she was little and her father would try to take a family photo for the annual Christmas card. The photos that ended up getting scrapped were always her favorite. Ones where Poo was barking or her father was a blurry image running into the scene. And then there were the ones that captured them laughing or folding a collar or tucking back a piece of hair. She loved the little moments that captured their love best.

At some point during her teenage years, Camille realized the reason her father took so many photos. He wanted a way to remember her—to preserve his memory of all their moments as a family. She couldn't fault him for it, but it made each photo session melancholy. But Camille had continued the charade of pretending the photos were a bother. She knew her father looked forward to fussing over lighting and laughing at the silly faces she made. If she smiled and went along with him, it would steal half the fun.

Camille was trying to get Poo to wear her graduation cap, much to his irritation. He was growling as she posed next to him making kissy faces. Her father snapped away while her mother tried to contain her laughter.

"That's animal abuse," a voice called through the courtyard.

Camille turned to see Nate striding toward them dressed in a red cap and gown that matched hers.

"Nate! What are you doing here?" she exclaimed, running into his arms while her father continued to take photos.

"My mom's flight got delayed. She's not getting in until late tonight. So, I decided to crash the photo shoot, if that's okay?" Nate asked looking over her head toward her parents.

"Of course!" her father said, greeting Nate with a handshake.

Her mother gave Nate a hug. "You look so handsome, Nathan. Can we get a few photos of you and Camille together?"

"Of course," he replied.

"Mom, can you take some with my Polaroid, too?"

"Sure, honey."

Camille, Nate and her family spent the last of the afternoon light snapping photos and making silly faces. One of Camille's favorite photos turned out to be of Nate chasing Poo after he'd started to carry off his graduation cap. Her father had joined in the chase and Camille and her mother laughed until they had tears in their eyes.

After the photo session they all sat down to have dinner together in the courtyard. The weather was starting to warm up and Camille lounged under the strings of white lights, holding her stomach. Her father made his famous crawfish crepes and she'd eaten herself silly.

Nate was eating what she'd left on her plate. "Ray, these are phenomenal."

"Thanks, Nate. Cooking is just like making music. Both fill your soul."

"Well said, honey," her mother said, leaning over to kiss her father.

Camille groaned. "You guys are so cheesy."

"If by cheesy you mean in love, then yes," her father teased. "But speaking of love and music, can I convince you two to play us a little something tonight?"

"Oh, Dad . . ."

The protests of everyone at the table made Camille laugh. She knew a losing battle when she saw one.

"We really should play our song," Nate said.

"We have a song?"

Nate faked shock, putting his hand over his heart in horror.

Of course, Camille knew exactly what song he was speaking of, but watching Nate's over the top antics was worth it. He stood up, holding out his hand and she laughed, taking it so he could lead her into the music room.

For the first time that Camille could ever remember, her

parents left the table a mess and followed them into the house. In no time they were all settled in the music room around the instruments.

Camille sat at the piano with her father while he played. Nate stood nearby, weaving magic on his violin, while her mother recorded the whole thing. They played '*As Time Goes By*' and Camille filled the room with her voice, loving the freedom she felt as she sang.

44

Nate

NATE LAY in Camille's bed, much longer than he should. If he didn't leave soon he'd be late to pick up his mom. But he couldn't seem to detach himself from Camille. She had a peaceful glow about her tonight that made his heart ache with joy. It was strange loving someone to the point of pain. But that's how it was when Nate was with Cami—*excruciating pleasure.*

"Thank you for tonight," she whispered.

"It was fun," he murmured kissing her. "Can you believe there's only one more day until graduation?"

Camille grinned. "We made it."

"This is just the beginning, Cami."

"I know." She looped her arms sleepily around his neck and pressed her lips to his.

He groaned. “I’m just gonna tell my mom to take a cab. She’ll understand.”

She giggled. “Nate. You can’t.”

“I don’t want to leave you.”

“I’ll see you tomorrow morning.”

“Café Beignet?”

“Yes. We have lots to plan.”

“Hell yes we do,” he said kissing her again. “I love you, Cami.”

“I love you, too.”

Nate stared into her beautiful gray-blue eyes. He could get lost in them and die a happy man.

“You better go,” she said, still grinning.

“Okay, okay.” Nate managed to untangle himself from Camille and her bed. “But you’re killing me, beautiful. I’m gonna have to take a cold shower tonight.”

“Dream of me,” she said blowing him a kiss.

“Always.” Nate bent down and kissed her one more time. “Till our next hello.”

Camille smiled. “That word is growing on me.”

“Duh. It’s way better than goodbye.”

“Way better.”

“Love you, babe.”

“I love you, too.”

Cami

CAMILLE WATCHED Nate’s silhouette as he left the room. He turned around twice to blow her kisses. It made her heart squeeze with joy until she was almost breathless. She closed her eyes to catch her breath and she could still picture his face. The way his lips curved into a perfect bow. How the right side of his smile always started first. The amber glow of his eyes that danced every time the light hit it. The calm beauty that washed over him when he played the violin.

The melody of '*As Time Goes By*' was stuck in her head. It would always make her think of their perfect prom night together. Dancing and moonlight. The ocean at night. Affection rushed into Camille's heart as she thought about Nate and how deeply she loved him.

She'd never imagined she could feel this way about someone. It was overwhelming. She'd found herself wondering how different her life might have been if Nate hadn't said hello to her that day. *Would she even still be here?*

Emotion made her throat tight and she hugged her pillow against her. Camille's heart threatened to burst as she recalled all the joy Nate had brought her in the few months they'd known each other. She was so grateful for the way he'd shaped her life. He'd taught her not to be afraid to hope for so much more in life. And now that she was, she couldn't stop.

She'd never expected to meet the man she wanted to spend the rest of her life with at eighteen. But now that she had, her future was wide open. She knew it wouldn't be easy, but it would be worth it. Cami wanted to fight for every moment—for graduation, for Paris, for college and beyond. She wanted to fight for Nate and the endless possibilities his smile evoked. She knew her time wasn't guaranteed, but she was grateful for however much she had left.

Camille closed her eyes, letting visions of Nate carry her off to sleep. She felt her lips curve into a smile as her heart squeezed. His face was so lovely, even in her dreams. His voice, his smile, his music—her favorite images of Nate flickered through her mind like a film reel. Nate and Cami dancing in the rain. Nate and Cami in the ocean. Nate and Cami in Paris. Nate and Cami. Nate . . . Nate . . .

. . .

Nate

Nate was chattering nonstop to his mom on the ride home from the airport. She was staying at the swanky Hotel Monteleone, in the French Quarter and had gotten Nate a room, too. They talked nearly every day over the past week, but nothing beat seeing his mom in the flesh. She'd nearly smothered him at the airport. And now she was teetering between tears and laughter as they drove back toward the city.

"I wish it wasn't so late," Nate said. "I can't wait for you to meet Cami."

"Me too. But strangely I'm not that tired. I'll probably crash tomorrow, but for now, I'm wide awake."

"Are you hungry?" Nate asked.

"Always."

He grinned. He'd inherited his sweet tooth from his mother. "Then I know just the place."

"Oh yeah?"

Nate nodded. "How about you check into the hotel and I'll run across the street and grab us some coffee and donuts."

"That sounds like heaven, Nate."

Nate walked into Sweet Thang's and Ronnie popped his head up from behind the counter to greet him, cheerful as ever.

"What are you doing here?" Nate asked, surprised to find Ronnie working the graveyard shift.

"I knew you'd be stopping by and I have something for ya."

Nate grinned, shaking off the goose bumps. "I'll never get used to your all-knowingness."

"I'm not all-knowing, sugar. Just blessed with a deeper vision and impeccable style."

"Obviously," Nate said taking in Ronnie's ensemble.

Tonight he looked more subdued than usual. He wore black tuxedo pants, a royal blue short-sleeved dress shirt and a yellow-plaid bowtie. His hot pink apron and vibrant hairnet took the outfit to a whole new level of colorful.

"So, since you knew I was coming, I'm guessing you know I'm here for donuts and coffee?"

"One doesn't need to be clairvoyant to know that, Nathaniel."

Nate laughed. "Guess not. I just picked my mom up from the airport and I wanted to treat her to the best donuts in town while we catch up."

"What happened to the ones you picked up earlier?"

Nate blushed. "Yeah. I sorta ate those while I was waiting for her flight."

Ronnie laughed, already boxing up Nate's favorites. "How's my Camille doing?"

"Amazing. I swear, I didn't know it was possible to love someone like this. She just makes me smile."

"Don't I know it, bebe?"

Nate stuffed his hands in his pockets, his cheeks heating. "And I'm gushing like a school girl."

"Ain't nuthin to apologize for."

"It's just so good to see her excited about the future."

Ronnie tied the white baking twine around the pink box and handed it to Nate with a smile. "That it is, bebe."

"How much do I owe ya?"

"On the house, sugar."

"Thanks, Ronnie."

"And I have something for you and Camille. It's a bit of a graduation gift, but something's telling me to give it to ya a bit early." Ronnie slid a white envelope across the counter. Nate reached for it, but Ronnie held tight. "You're a good man, Nathaniel. What you've done for Camille . . . you made that girl glow and that's a gift I want you to hold in your heart."

Nate nodded past the lump in his throat and Ronnie released the envelope. The intensity of the moment passed and Ronnie was smiling again. "Open it."

"Don't you want me to wait for Cami?"

Ronnie waved him off. "I'd rather see your face."

Nate opened the envelope and pulled out two flight vouchers.

"They're non-refundable so don't even think about arguing."

"Ronnie . . ." Nate was in awe. He didn't know what to say. They hadn't told anyone they'd officially decided to go to Paris. But of course Ronnie knew. Nate ran around the counter and threw his arms around Ronnie. "Thank you," he whispered.

"No, thank you, bebe."

45

Nate

NATE GOT to Café Beignet early. The airline vouchers from Ronnie were practically burning a hole in his pocket. He couldn't wait to tell Camille about them. He ordered two café au laits and beignets before settling in at their usual table. He set the tickets next to the coffee and pastries and snapped a photo. He thought about texting it to Cami, but decided he didn't want to miss the soft smile spread across her face when she realized they were going to Paris for real.

He'd brought the Tulane course catalog in his backpack, but was too excited about Paris to even worry about picking college classes. Nate sipped his coffee as he browsed Paris sightseeing options. By the time he looked down, there was only one beignet left. Nate glanced at his phone. Camille was late—*as usual.* He grinned thinking of her lame excuses. He'd been about to send her a text when her number flashed on his phone.

He answered, a smile in his voice. "Speak of the devil."

The other end of the phone was silent.

"Cami?"

"Nate?"

But it wasn't Camille's voice. It was Ray's, and Nate's stomach dropped to the floor.

NATE WAS ON HIS FEET, running before Ray finished speaking. He didn't want to hear the words. He couldn't even if he wanted to. His heart was pounding so loud he couldn't hear or think. All he could do was run. Nate ran all the way to Camille's house. He flew in the front door and nearly knocked Ray over.

"Nate . . ."

"No!" Nate screamed.

Ray tried to put a hand on his shoulder, but Nate wouldn't let him. He couldn't stop moving. He had to get to Cami. Nate shoved past Ray and raced upstairs, stumbling into Camille's bedroom, breathless and shaking. Josie was there, sitting at Cami's bedside, quietly holding her hand as tears slid down her cheeks.

Nate felt the world tilt. He staggered forward. "Camille? Cami . . ."

Josie stood up, not meeting his eyes. She put a hand on his shoulder, squeezing before she stepped aside, giving Nate a view of Camille's bed.

She was lying there, right where he left her last night. Tucked beneath her covers, her head resting on a mountain of pillows. She looked so small and peaceful and Nate's heart slammed into his ribs. *She's asleep. She's only asleep.*

Nate sat down on the bed and touched Camille's hand. Her skin was like ice and it bit into his heart. He couldn't breathe.

"Cami?" His breath was a strangled sob as he pleaded with every ounce of his being. *Wake up. Wake up. Wake up!* His pulse throbbed in his ears making it impossible to think. *This wasn't real. This wasn't happening.* Now Nate's voice was roaring at *him* to wake up. This was a nightmare, not reality. *Wake up. Wake up. Wake the hell up, Nate!*

He pulled Camille into his arms, sobbing at the strange weightlessness of her still body against his chest. She couldn't just be gone. Cami had been the brighter half of him. Nate rocked her back and forth crying out as the world turned dark. He clutched her tighter in his arms, kissing her forehead. If he could just hold her tight enough, he could keep her there with him. He had to keep her there. There was no light in the world without her in it. This couldn't be real. Camille couldn't be gone. But she was. And Nate knew it the moment he'd picked up the phone.

EPILOGUE

MOONLIGHT SPARKED off the Seine River and Nate drank in the smell of lavender drifting across the water. Paris even smelled like Camille. He'd never been anywhere else that he felt her so deeply. It made him smile, because maybe she was already here —lost among the glittering light and delicate beauty.

Nate was enraptured with Paris. And he knew beyond a shadow of a doubt that Camille would've loved it there. The city of light captured so much of her essence—its pale fragrance, gentle music and vibrant art. Each time Nate walked down a new street, he saw Camille. She was in the pattern of a bright dress. The hue of a flower garden. The soft laugh of young lovers.

Being in Paris without her was breaking Nate apart, but at the same time he felt a renewed strength. Like maybe he was doing something for Camille by coming here. He'd started small, carrying out tasks he'd copied from her Hello Wall. And with each task, he fit a piece of himself back where it belonged. It was a long road, and there were still things he couldn't bring himself to do. College was one.

He'd tried to attend Tulane in the fall, but his heart wasn't in it. In fact it wasn't in New Orleans. It was lost somewhere with Camille. Perhaps it had stopped beating when hers did. It was one of the things Nate found comfort in. Camille had died of a heart attack. She had another coronary spasm in her sleep.

The doctors said she hadn't felt a thing. Of course Nate had to look it up for himself. But strangely, he took comfort it what he found. The symptoms of Camille's type of heart failure was often described by patients as a tightness of the chest, where the heart seems to swell too large.

Nate knew he was romanticizing it, but those were the same words he would use to describe what it felt like to be in love. When he thought back to the moments he was with Camille, he remembered distinctly thinking his heart was too big for his chest. Cami had always made him feel that way, filling him with her light and love that she'd chosen to share with him.

He felt it even now, as he sat alone at a café table with a stunning view of the Eiffel Tower. It was lit up, twinkling in the night sky, its glow blinding even the stars. Nate pulled the large envelope from his pocket. Camille's parents had given it to him after her funeral, but he hadn't the strength to open it until now.

Now seemed as good a time as any. Nate had put it off long enough. He'd dropped out of Tulane for the semester after his parents convinced the school to let him defer for a year. And Nate had spent that year living. It was impossible and wonderful all at once. Just like Camille had been. And that seemed to make his adventures that much more fitting.

There were days when he wanted to give up and cry, and sometimes he did. But then he would think of Camille and her quiet strength. And how everyday, she put one foot in front of the other. And that made him fight. It made him live. He owed that to her.

So Nate had spent that last six months living, for Camille. Seeing all the places he knew she would've wanted to see. Doing all the things she would've wanted to do. He was living for both of them, and somehow, it was making things easier.

Every time he felt weak or sad, he pictured her face. And in every memory, she wore a smile that touched his heart. *How could he be sad when he'd had the privilege of knowing her? How could he be weak when she had been strong?*

At some point, Nate turned his sadness into fire. Letting the sorrow take hold would've been a disservice to Camille. She had brought him so much joy and life. She was too bright to last, and perhaps that's what had drawn him to her in the first place.

Camille had it all wrong. She'd always said Nate was her sunshine. But Camille had been Nate's. Her light filled the unquenchable void that Tyler left. And though she was gone, her light would remain—left behind to inspire Nate, and everyone else whose life she'd touched.

Nate took a deep breath and finally opened the large envelope Camille had addressed to him. Inside were four smaller gray envelopes. Each had a handwritten note on the outside, penned in Camille's looping handwriting. They read:

Open first.
Open when you feel sad.
Open when you feel happy.
Open when you need to hold my hand.

Nate gently opened the first envelope with shaking hands. His eyes misted as he read her words.

You must remember this
A kiss is still a kiss
A sigh is still just a sigh
The fundamental things apply
As time goes by

And when two lovers woo
They still say: I love you
On that you can rely
No matter what the future brings
As time goes by.

Moonlight and love songs, never out of date
Hearts full of passion, jealousy and hate
Woman needs man, and man must have his mate
That no one can deny

It's still the same old story
A fight for love and glory
A case of do or die
The world will always welcome lovers
As time goes by.

She'd written out the lyrics to *'As Time Goes By'—their song.* And beneath it, she'd written him a note.

Nate,
I love you. Like moonlight and love songs. Like the oceans and rivers.

Like dancing in the rain. I will never stop loving you. And I am forever grateful that you gave me so much more than time. You gave me life and chaos and adventure. And I have no right to ask for anything more. But I need you to promise me one thing. Promise me that you'll stay the boy I fell in love with. The boy who says hello and isn't afraid to go after everything he wants. Because there is so much life left for that boy. And I want you to use every second of it to be happy. You are good, Nathan Hawthorne. You make me happy. Be happy, too. It's time to live for yourself now.
I'll love you 'til the end of time.
Until our next hello,
XO – Your Cami

THE SHIMMERING LIGHTS of the Eiffel Towel blurred in the distance as Nate's tears spattered the letter. He was trembling as her read her words over and over. He needed more. He tore into the letters titled *when you are happy* and *when you are sad*. Because Nate had never felt both so equally in all his life. Camille's words breathed life into him. And for a moment, it was like she was there beside him and the happiness overwhelmed him. But it faded quickly, ripping the remains of his heart out along with it.

His eyes poured over the letters. They both said the same thing.

Nate,
I love you. Thank you for saying hello.
Cami

He tore into the last letter. The one that read *Open when you need to hold my hand.* Inside was a pattern she'd traced around her hand. In the palm she'd written a note.

Nate,
The greatest thing I ever held in my hand, is yours. Don't be afraid to let someone else hold it.
Cami

Nate sat alone for a long while. He read and reread the letters until every word had cemented itself in his heart. He felt a weight lift as he tucked the letters back into his breast pocket, above his heart. He had one thing left to do. He picked up Camille's Polaroid camera and took a photo of the Eiffel Tower. He watched the shimmering image of light come to life on the film. When it shone back at him in all its glory, he wrote two words on it before tucking it into his pocket.

Hello Paris

Nate stayed for a while longer, holding onto the peace of this moment. He'd saved Paris for last. It was the final item on the Hello Wall he and Cami had created together. He thought he'd feel sadness, like he'd lost his connection to her. Yet, it was the opposite. Nate felt the static energy of life flowing around him. He finally realized by coming to Paris he was letting go in a sense. But that was okay. Because sometimes, love meant letting go.

As Nate stood to leave, someone bumped into him. Her purse fell to the ground, spilling its contents onto the street. Nate scrambled to help collect the items, but his breath caught as his fingers met a pink and white Hello Kitty PEZ dispenser. He picked it up, half expecting to see Camille standing there grinning at him. Instead, a petite French girl greeted him with a smile.

"Merci, merci!" She exclaimed thanking Nate for his help. She righted her purse and extended her hand. "Bonjour. I'm Zoë."

Nate's chest swelled, and slowly he reached for her hand. "Hello."

ACKNOWLEDGMENTS

In June, 2013, I lost my son to a terminal illness. This story was strongly influenced by the love and loss I struggle with every day. For a time, I let depression and darkness control my life. I felt completely lost, and sometimes I still do. I am a work in progress and that is okay. Because I am still here. I am still fighting. I have surrounded myself with faith, an amazingly supportive group of family and friends, and I've found the courage to allow the loss in my life to change me for the better.

It took the devastating loss of my son to wake me up to the fact that life is short. My hope for this book is that it teaches that lesson without the heartache. Dream big, follow your heart, pursue happiness, love fully, forgive easily, don't live with regret, know what's important.

Mostly, I hope this book helps readers know they are not alone. So many of us experience loss and suffering. To those of you, I say, let it change you for the better. Hold on to the memories, let go of the hurt, remember the laughter, cherish the love, and carve a place in your future to recapture hope, that one day you'll be ready to say 'Hello' again. Until then, put one foot in front of the other and remember the best things in life are the ones worth fighting for.

Thank you to my husband, my ray of sunshine. Your smile is everything. You are my heart. You inspire possibility and you always make me want to say 'Hello'.

Thank you to my family and friends whose generosity is immeasurable. And thank you to the counselors and physicians who dedicate their lives to giving us as much time as possible. Lastly, thank you to Dalton. You make me happy. You make me brave. You make me everything I never dreamt I could be. The sunrise will never be the same. I love you for always. Until our next hello.

AUTHOR'S NOTE

1.2 million new cancer cases are diagnosed in the US each year. Cancer claims the life of 1,500 people per day in the US. That means everyday at least 1,500 people lose someone they love to illness. 1 in 10 suicides are linked to terminal illness Coping with cancer, terminal illness and loss is devastating for all those affected by it, including those left behind. This level of tragedy can leave those dealing with it feeling desperate and alone. You are not alone.

The number of people suffering in silence is staggering. In the US alone, 20% of the population suffers from mental illness; that's over 42 million people. Of that number, 1 in 5 of them are teens. Suicide is the 3rd leading cause of death for those between the ages of 15-24. Depression is the leading cause for suicide in the US, where over 15 million people suffer.

I share these numbers so you can see that you are not alone. If you feel like giving up, don't. You have a voice and it is one of many. Please use it to ask for help. Don't allow the stigma that goes along with any kind of illness make you suffer in silence. Put one foot in front of the other and get help.

If you or someone you know is struggling with loss, illness, mental or emotional issues, depression, suicidal thoughts, bullying, or abuse, you are not alone. Numerous resources are available.

National Suicide Prevention Lifeline is available 24/7. It's free, confidential support available to help those in distress. They have resources for you and your loved ones. Call if you need help.

The American Cancer Society has tremendous resources dedicated to finding support and programs in your area. The National Cancer Information Center is a hotline available 24/7 providing information, answers and hope to those fighting cancer every day. Call if you need to talk.

To my readers,

I want to personally thank you for taking the time to seek out this great little indie book. Writing is truly my passion. I believe each of us can find a small part of ourselves in every book we read, and carry it with us, shaping our world, our adventures and our dreams.

Following my dream to write frees my soul but knowing others find joy in my writing is indescribable. So thank you for your support and I hope your enjoyed your brief escape into the magic of these pages.

If you enjoyed this story, don't worry, there's plenty more currently rattling around in my rambunctious imagination. Let me and others know your thoughts by sharing a review of this book. Reviews help shape my next writing projects. So if you want more books like this one be sure to shout it from the rooftops (or social media.) ;-)

- Christina Benjamin

PLEASE LEAVE A REVIEW HERE

THE HOLIDAY BOYFRIEND

Book 4
Chapters 1-5

PROLOGUE

A Haute Chic's Holiday Survival Guide

1. *Family drama is much easier to face with fierce lips.*
2. *Manolos are as last season as mistletoe.*
3. . . .

Emma Rhodes stared at the blinking cursor on her laptop. She needed a third bullet point for her fashion blog, *Fifth Ave Fab – A Haute Chic's Guide to Life,* but nothing was coming to her. She popped another wintermint Tic Tac into her mouth, crushing it in frustration. She looked at the empty candy container. *Damn.* She'd gone through a whole pack already.

Sighing, Emma turned back to her laptop. She needed to wrap up her latest entry. She'd promised her guidance counselor she'd have it ready to add to her portfolio by the time she returned from winter break.

Emma was perhaps the last high school senior at Stanton Prep to not submit her college applications. It's not that she didn't know what she wanted to do. She'd known she was going to go to school for fashion since she was old enough to spell Versace. And until last year, Emma would've said she was only applying to her dream school, Parsons, in New York City.

But twelve months ago, Emma found herself fleeing to Boston with her mother after divorce and deception had rocked her perfect Manhattan existence. And now, with only one term of high school looming between Emma and her future, she had a big decision to make.

Boston or New York? Her mother or her father? Boston University or Parsons School of Design? Flee for a fresh start or face old wounds?

Emma stared at her laptop, the cursor taunting her. Writing witty commentary on her blog had been her outlet since she left New York, and it normally came easy to her. But as her train chugged steadily toward Manhattan, she couldn't concentrate. Perhaps she was more nervous about her first trip home than she'd thought. After all, she'd left the city for a reason—*a tall, dark and handsome reason.*

Emma sighed, trying to expel her jitters. She'd been looking forward to going home for the holidays for months. This would be the first Christmas she got to spend with her father since the divorce, and she wasn't going to let anyone keep her from enjoying it. Especially not a particularly gorgeous blue-eyed boy with a devastating smile. For all Emma cared, Will Taylor's chestnuts could be roasting on an open fire. She was going to explore her collegiate options and enjoy her holiday homecoming. Besides, nobody did Christmas like Manhattan.

1

Emma

Emma knocked on the door again, louder this time. But still there was no answer. "Great. Just great," she muttered. One Christmas in Boston and her father had forgotten about her. Emma heard the bitter words of her mother echoed in her subconscious. *'He's replaced us.'* Emma shuddered against the classic divorce cliché. She knew marriages fell apart, but parents didn't replace their kids. Surely Emma's father hadn't replaced her. She'd always been his princess—a daddy's girl to the core.

She knocked one more time before slumping to the floor. Leaning against the door, Emma released a frustrated breath. *Where the hell was her father?* They were supposed to spend Christmas break together, and Emma had been looking forward to it for months. Her last Christmas was awful. Her mother hadn't even let the ink dry on her divorce settlement before hauling Emma to Boston, where they spent the holiday eating Chinese food in a cold, empty brownstone.

Emma hated everything about Boston. She got that her mother needed a fresh start, and if she were being honest, Emma had wanted one too. But trading Manhattan for Boston was a like going from couture to off-the-rack—depressing.

Emma's parents were well known in the elite Manhattan social circles and their divorce had been a very public and nasty one when word of her father's mistress got out. Even the students at Emma's prep school, the prestigious St. James Academy, were whispering about her father's affair with some gold-digging model from South Carolina. But that's not why Emma had been eager to flee. She was running from a broken heart of her own, caused by her ex-best friend and debilitating crush, Will Taylor.

Emma was grateful when the ding of the elevator distracted her from her spiraling thoughts of Christmas past. She looked down the hall of the posh high-rise apartment sure she'd see her father rushing toward her, an apology gift in hand for his tardiness. But it was only a well-dressed elderly couple. Emma sighed, sinking further into her spot on the floor. She shrugged off her red Burberry peacoat and pulled her iPhone from her Louis Vuitton hoping for a Christmas miracle, but it was still dead, just like it had been thirty minutes ago. She'd been watching movies on the train from Boston and killed the battery. And of course, she'd forgotten to pack a charger.

Tapping her foot restlessly, Emma racked her brain trying to remember if she knew anyone that lived in this building. Her father had sold their palatial penthouse apartment right after he divorced her mother, claiming he could no longer afford it after, "the God damned settlement your mother clawed out of me." Emma knew that wasn't true. Her father was a Wall Street legend. He owned a rather prestigious investment firm and according to the press, was doing just fine. She figured the change of scenery was because he'd wanted a fresh start too. Emma wished he could have just admitted that. It would've made losing her childhood home a bit easier.

Emma used to be close to her father, but since the divorce they'd grown apart. This would be the first time she saw his new place. She'd wanted to come back over spring break, but her father said he was in the middle of moving. Then over summer break, his excuse was he'd just started dating someone and thought it was, "too soon," to introduce her to Emma. *Although, is there ever a good time to meet the woman wearing your mother's Louboutins?*

Emma hated thinking about her father's new girlfriend, but the mystery woman seemed to keep finding a way into her thoughts. Especially now that Emma was back in New York. She was used to being the center of her father's attention—learning to share the spotlight might be more difficult than she'd imagined. Particularly because Emma couldn't help wondering if the other woman was the reason why her father was currently standing her up. *Was he out wining and dining his new girlfriend somewhere? Or worse, were they in the middle of some romantic liaison?*

Emma pressed her palms into her eyelids until she saw spots. She did *not* want to think about her father and some other woman. *Gross!* Old people romance gave Emma the creeps. Her father was fifty-seven. He was supposed to be collecting expensive cars, not notches on his bedpost.

The elevator dinged again. Emma didn't bother looking up this time. It was probably just another stuffy old Manhattan couple. She closed her eyes and pretended to be sleeping to spare herself the pity from whoever walked by. Because no matter how fabulous Emma was dressed, there was no way to make looking abandoned before the holidays seem in style.

"Well, well. Looks like Christmas came early this year."

Emma's eyes flew open. She'd know that voice anywhere. And when she looked up, her heart stopped. There he was, staring at her with that irresistible smile and looking as alarmingly good-looking as she'd remembered—Will Taylor.

2

ill

Will practically stumbled when he saw Emma Rhodes sitting in the hall of his luxury apartment building. He pushed his thick dark hair back from his eyes, blinking twice to make sure he wasn't hallucinating. But there she was, as gorgeous as ever in Gucci and lip gloss. It was all very ghost of Christmas past, and Will shuddered at the painful longing she evoked. *How many times had he dreamt of this moment in the past year?* Too many.

Thankfully, Emma's eyes were closed, giving Will a minute to collect himself. Although, as usual, he hadn't really used the time to his advantage. He'd wanted to say, "You're back. I've missed you. How are you? What are you doing here?" Any number of those things would've been better than what came out of his mouth. "Well, well. Looks like Christmas came early this year."

Emma's vivid green eyes snapped open at the sound of his voice. Will watched shock flare across her features, before it simmered into something like resentment. Will knew it was petty but he didn't care. Emma had hurt him like no other girl had, and apparently his heart wasn't ready to forgive her—regardless of it being the holiday season.

"Will?" she asked, staring at him like she'd seen a ghost. And sort of like she'd rather be anywhere else in the world right now. *Good*. Emma should feel bad. She stood him up at the winter formal last year. Will had stood outside the Plaza holding her stupid corsage for an hour waiting for her to show up. He'd looked like a total loser. He ended up going in with Liz Vanderveer and getting drunk on peppermint schnapps.

"What are you doing here?" Emma asked scrambling to her feet.

Will's scorned heart hijacked his brain and snark poured out of his mouth before he could stop himself. "Not that I owe you an explanation, but I live here."

Emma crossed her arms. "Since when?"

"Since when do you care?" he countered.

She blew out a breath. "I guess I don't. I'm just here to spend Christmas with my father."

Will stuffed his hands in his pockets, giving Emma a snide smile. "Looks like a fun reunion."

Ever since Theodore Rhodes moved into the apartment next door to Will's, he'd been waiting for Emma to come visit. But now that she was here, he was tongue-tied by the dormant hurt that smoldered in his heart.

"Are you sure you were expected?" he asked nodding to the nest of designer accessories and luggage on the floor. "You do have a reputation for not showing."

Emma glared at him. "He's just running a bit late."

Will scoffed. "Ya know, that's what I told myself at the formal last year."

"Excuse me?" Emma asked arching her pale eyebrows.

"Whatever," Will mumbled starting to walk away. He didn't feel like dredging up old wounds in a hallway for anyone to overhear, but Emma called after him.

"Will, wait."

He turned around and the pleading look on Emma's face hit him like a punch to the gut. *Shit. Why couldn't he get over her?*

"About last year . . ." she started. But something kept her from saying more, and suddenly Will didn't think he could handle hearing more.

"Forget it," he mumbled. "And don't worry about your father. He probably just took Hodor for a walk. I'm sure they'll be back soon."

"Hodor?" Emma asked, confusion pinching her delicate features.

"Yeah. Colin's dog."

"Who's Colin?"

"Tara's son."

Emma's pretty face paled and her mouth hung open in a perfect O. That was not the face of someone who knew her father was living with his mistress and her son. *Nice work, Will.*

Emma took a step toward him, her familiar scent of vanilla sugar cookies invading his space. Emma's vibrant green eyes sparkled furiously like slivers of cut emerald. "Tara? As in the Tara that broke up my parents' marriage?" she asked blinking rapidly. "Does that sheet serpent live here?"

"Uh . . ." Will's mind went blank. Being so close to Emma made it impossible to speak. She was stunning. Her long ash-blonde hair hung in soft waves over her shoulders as she moved toward Will. And despite her fury, all Will could presently think of doing was running his hands through it. He stared at Emma's lips. They were perfectly glossed in pale pink. She pursed them in annoyance and he was instantly reminded of the pale pink rose buds in the corsage he'd bought her last year. His heart twisted and he took a step back. "I don't know, Em. I'm not his secretary."

Emma looked crestfallen. She bit her lip, crossing her arms. "That's great. Just freaking great! I can't believe this." She turned away from Will and started pacing in front of her father's door, muttering to herself. "My first time home . . . He doesn't even have the decency to show up . . . He's probably with *her!* He never let *me* get a dog! I guess I'm doomed to have terrible holidays from now on."

Will watched Emma's mini-meltdown in silent fascination until she started to gather her things. "Where are you going?"

"Home," she muttered.

Will caught her arm as she tried to push past him. "You are home."

"I meant Boston."

"New York is home, Em."

"Yeah, well it certainly doesn't feel like it."

"Look, why don't you come to my place to wait for your father? My parents aren't home and—"

Emma interrupted him with a shrill laugh. "I'm sorry. Are you seriously hitting on me right now?"

"What? No!"

"Oh really? The whole, my parents aren't home routine? Good to see not everything has changed. You're still the same old Will."

"What's that supposed to mean?"

The elevator dinged and they both turned to see Emma's father step out, one arm around a gorgeous brunette, the other holding the mittened hand of a rosy-cheeked little boy. Will's hand was still on Emma's arm and he felt her go rigid.

"Emma!" her father greeted. "What are you doing here?"

3

Emma

If Emma were made of glass she would've shattered right there on the spot. Seeing the picturesque family scene unfolding in the elevator had stolen her breath. But when her father looked at her with a mixture of confusion and surprise, her heart broke. He'd truly forgotten about her—and she could see why. He was attached at the hip to a woman who looked like she could be Cindy Crawford's younger sister. *Much, much younger sister.*

The woman who'd stolen her father certainly wasn't the old maid Emma had been imagining. She probably wasn't even thirty. And the apple-cheeked little boy getting sloppy dog kisses from the regal-looking golden retriever only added to the perfect family portrait—one that Emma was definitely no longer a part of.

The little boy looked at Emma as soon as her father called

her by name. His blue eyes brightened and he pushed his pale, snow-covered hair from his eyes. "You're Emma? You're gonna be my sister!"

The super model spoke, corralling the little boy and his dog before he could make his way toward Emma. "Honey, remember what we said about grown up talk? Let's let Teddy speak to Emma first."

Teddy? Did that woman just call her father, Teddy? As in a cute, cuddly stuffed bear? Emma's father was Theodore Rhodes, world-renowned Wall Street mogul. No one called him Teddy.

"Emma, I'm glad you're here," her father announced.

"I've been here, Dad. For like an hour. Did you forget about me?"

"No . . . " He glanced at the super model. They exchanged secret smiles. "It's been a bit exciting around here lately. I just lost track of time. But come inside, we have a lot to talk about."

"Clearly," Emma muttered under her breath.

"I guess I'll see you later?" Will called, startling Emma.

She'd forgotten he was still standing there. She watched him walk away, leaving her to follow her father and his strange replacement family into the apartment. Emma took a deep breath, grabbing her things. She stared up and down the empty hallway of the posh Manhattan apartment building, wondering when New York had changed so much.

4

ill

ONCE INSIDE HIS APARTMENT, Will leaned against the door. He couldn't believe Emma was actually here. Her soft vanilla fragrance still invaded his senses as he replayed their conversation over and over in his mind. *Why did he have to come off so arrogant and sleazy when he was nervous?*

He hadn't meant to hit on her. At least he didn't think he had. But he couldn't deny he still had some sort of feelings for her. Call it unrequited love, but there was unfinished business between them, and Will wouldn't be able to get Emma out of his head until he got to the bottom of it.

He needed to figure out a way to see her again. He thought for a minute and pulled out his phone, selecting a contact under favorites and banging out a text.

Will: Hey Cran, feel like throwing a party?
Cranston: What's the occasion?
Will: When have you ever needed one?
Cranston: Touché

WILL CRACKED A SMILE, practically able to hear Cranston's preppy drawl.

Will: Tomorrow night. The hotel.
Cranston: Done. Guest list? The usual suspects?
Will: Actually, I need you to invite our whole class.
Cranston: This just got interesting. Do tell, William.

WILL COULD PICTURE Cranston's look of amusement. He didn't normally mingle with the '*little people,*' as he called them. But then again when your father owned one of the biggest hotels in Manhattan, everyone was the '*little people*.' But Cranston liked to think of himself as the Gatsby of St. James, so slumming it sometimes appealed to the philanthropist in him.

Will: I'll explain later.
Cranston: You bet your ass you will, but my priorities are on the ladies. Any special requests?
Will: Nah. I got my date covered.

OR HE WOULD RATHER, if Emma accepted.

Cranston: Nice. I'm feeling a martinis and mistletoe vibe. You down?
Will: Sure, whatever you want. Just send out the blast.
Cranston: On it.

WILL SLIPPED his phone into his pocket and let the utter silence of his empty apartment wash over him. He looked around the massive space with disgust, still bitter his parents had uprooted him to move to the giant flat six months ago. In Will's opinion it was a total waste. The Upper East Side was all the same to him. Who cared that they moved two buildings closer to Central Park and had a few more square feet? They certainly didn't need the extra space.

It was just Will and his parents who lived there. Although, *lived*, was quite a loose term considering his parents were away more than they were home. Will was closer to the full-time staff that cared for the palatial apartment than he was to his parents these days.

He was the youngest of five boys, with a six-year gap between his closest brother, Gabe. Once Gabe graduated and shipped off to college, Will's parents started traveling. Each year the trips grew longer. This year, they'd hardly been home at all. He knew they didn't need to. Will's mother didn't work and his father owned an international software company that allowed him to work from anywhere. But Will couldn't help feeling slighted. It's not that he needed looking after, but it was his last year of high school. It would've been nice if his parents at least pretended to care, like they had with his brothers.

Will sighed, wagering whether his parents would make it home for Christmas. Just the other day, Sharon, his favorite housekeeper, had asked him if he wanted a Christmas tree delivered in case his parents were held up. Sharon had been with Will's family since before he was born. She was like a sudo-mom to him. And although he knew Sharon was only looking out for him, Will had stubbornly declined her Christmas tree offer.

Picking out their holiday tree was the one tradition his family had. Every year, they drove to a little tree farm upstate and picked out the perfect Christmas tree. They cut it down and everything. He knew he shouldn't hold his breath, but Will wasn't quite ready to let go of the last of his childhood just yet.

5

Emma

EMMA'S JAW dropped when she walked into her father's new apartment. Everything was white and silver, polished to a near blinding glare. The style was so modern it made the Museum of Modern Art look outdated. Emma was afraid to touch anything. Her heart ached for their old home. It had been cozy and warm, full of buttery leather sofas, crackling fireplaces and thick rugs you could curl up on. This place was cold, and the white marble floor reflected the feeling.

The other thing that struck her as odd was the size of the apartment. It's not that it was small. The living room, kitchen and dining room were more than spacious, and the floor-to-ceiling windows gave an impressive view of the Upper East Side. But their old apartment had been larger. Eight bedrooms larger—as if her parents had had plans to one day fill the empty rooms with brothers and sisters for Emma. Instead, they'd filled the space with enough betrayal and resentment to cost her a lifetime of therapy.

"Emma!" The cherub-cheeked little boy tugged on her sleeve. "Do you wanna see my room?"

"Your room?" *Did he live here?*

"Colin, honey, why don't we take Hodor to your room and let Emma settle in."

The dog's name finally registered with Emma. Hodor . . . as in *'Game of Thrones.' Did that mean the pint-sized progeny watched the violent HBO saga?* He couldn't be more than seven or eight. If that were the case, Tara wouldn't be winning Mother of the Year anytime soon. She should probably start saving for therapy now.

Emma watched as Tara guided Colin and presumably, Hodor, away, leaving Emma alone with her father at last. She did a quick scan of the apartment. Only three doors led off the hallway. She assumed one was a bathroom, and that meant . . .

"Darling," her father called from the wet bar where he was mixing a fru-fru looking vodka drink. *Since when did he drink vodka?* Her father drank scotch, neat. Maybe it was for Tara. It looked like something a wannabe super model would drink.

"I have some exciting news," her father said, startling Emma back to reality—*if that's what this was.*

"More exciting than your new love of the absence of color?" she asked gesturing to the blank apartment walls as she plugged in her phone to charge.

He chuckled like she was joking, then took a sip of the pink drink. *So not for the mistress, then?*

Emma watched as he sighed and rubbed his forehead. "This isn't how I'd hoped to break the news to you."

"What news?"

"Tara and I are getting married."

"What?" Emma's voice was barely a whisper, but her father held up a hand.

"And we're expecting."

"Expecting what?" *A lobotomy, an alien invasion, the apocalypse?*

Aside from those reasons, why the hell would Emma's father be marrying his mistress? The woman who ruined their lives!

"Expecting a child," he clarified with finality.

Emma blinked rapidly, trying to wake from the nightmare she was trapped in. It was an effort to stay on her feet.

"I hope I can count on you to be mature about this, Emma. It's a joyous occasion and I'd like you to be a part of it."

"A joyous occasion? Are you joking?"

"Not at all. I've always wanted more children."

"And what, Mom couldn't give them to you so you traded her in for a hot pair of birthing hips?"

"Emma—"

"What? It's the truth, isn't it?"

"That's enough," her father bellowed. "I expect you to be respectful of Tara and her son. They're part of our family now."

"What family?" Emma hissed.

"Em . . ." Her father took a step toward her but she backed away.

"Just tell me one thing, Dad. Do I still have a room here with our *new family*?"

His tired sigh was all the confirmation she needed.

"That's what I thought." She grabbed her coat and stormed out of the apartment. *So much for coming back to New York!*

ALSO BY CHRISTINA BENJAMIN

YOUNG ADULT CONTEMPORARY ROMANCE

(All Boyfriend Books are Stand-Alone Novels and can be read in Any Order)

The Practice Boyfriend (Book 1)

The Almost Boyfriend (Book 2)

The Goodbye Boyfriend (Book 3)

The Holiday Boyfriend (Book 4)

The Stand-In Boyfriend (Book 5)

The Maybe Boyfriend (Book 6)

The Accidental Boyfriend (Book 7)

The Summer Boyfriend (Book 8)

The Wedding Boyfriend (Book 9)

The Winter Boyfriend (Book 10)

To my readers,

I want to personally thank you for taking the time to seek out this great little indie book. Writing is truly my passion. I believe each of us can find a small part of ourselves in every book we read, and carry it with us, shaping our world, our adventures and our dreams.

Following my dream to write frees my soul but knowing others find joy in my writing is indescribable. So thank you for your support and I hope your enjoyed your brief escape into the magic of these pages.

If you enjoyed this story, don't worry, there's plenty more currently rattling around in my rambunctious imagination. Let me and others know your thoughts by sharing a review of this book. Reviews help shape my next writing projects. So if you want more books like this one be sure to shout it from the rooftops (or social media) ;-)

C. Brin

ABOUT THE AUTHOR

Award-Winning author, Christina Benjamin, lives in Florida with her husband, and character inspiring pets, where she spends her free time working on her books and enjoying a macaron with a glass of wine.

Christina is best known for her bestselling Young Adult romance novels, The Boyfriend series. The Boyfriend series proves that book boyfriends are like Chocolate… you can never have enough. Check out the Boyfriend series for fast, fun, YA romance reads. These stand alone novels let you fall in love with new characters every time.

Want to talk books with Christina? Join her super secret Facebook group Words & Wine with Christina Benjamin, where she'll answer questions and discuss upcoming novels with her readers.

To learn about new books and more fun stuff, follow her at:

FACEBOOK
@ChristinaBenjaminAuthor

TWITTER
@authorcbenjamin

INSTAGRAM
@authorcbenjamin

PINTEREST
@authorcbenjamin

WEBSITE
www.christinabenjaminauthor.com

www.ingramcontent.com/pod-product-compliance
Lightning Source LLC
Chambersburg PA
CBHW030525310726
48979CB00010B/1799/J

* 9 7 8 1 7 3 2 6 1 2 3 4 1 *